CENTRAL SAANICH

THE GOLDSMITH'S DAUGHTER

THE GOLDSMITH'S DAUGHTER

Kate Sedley

This first world edition published in Great Britain 2001 by
SEVERN HOUSE PUBLISHERS LTD of
9–15 High Street, Sutton, Surrey SM1 1DF.
This first world edition published in the USA 2001 by
SEVERN HOUSE PUBLISHERS INC of
595 Madison Avenue, New York, NY 10022.

British Library Cataloguing in Publication Data

Sedley, Kate
  The goldsmith's daughter. – (A Roger the Chapman mediaeval mystery)
  1. Roger the Chapman (Fictitious character) – Fiction
  2. Monks – Fiction
  3. Detective and mystery stories
  I. Title
  823.9'14 [F]

ISBN 0–7278–5732–0

Typeset by Palimpsest Book Production Limited,
Polmont, Stirlingshire, Scotland.
Printed and bound in Great Britain by
MPG Books Ltd, Bodmin, Cornwall.

One

In a long life, it has seemed to me that there are two things which excite the popular imagination above all others. The first is a royal wedding, the second, a royal scandal; and just before Christmas of the year of Our Lord, 1477, information reached us in Bristol that the country was shortly to be edified by both.

With my wife, Adela, and our two small children, Elizabeth and Nicholas, I was paying a Sabbath visit to the Redcliffe home of my erstwhile mother-in-law, Margaret Walker, when I first heard the news. We were all returning to her cottage from the nearby church of Saint Thomas, where we had stood, crowded cheek by jowl, with the rest of the weaving community for morning Mass, when we were overtaken by Jack Nym.

By trade, Jack was a carter and had, until six months earlier, worked mainly for the late Alderman Weaver, bringing bales of raw wool from the Cotswold pastures to the Redcliffe weaving sheds, or carting the finished cloth to its various destinations. But now that the alderman was dead, his looms and house sold, his wealth passed into the hands of his younger brother who lived in London, Jack Nym took work wherever he could find it, and had, he was pleased to inform us, but recently returned from delivering a cartload of merchandise to the capital.

'Yes,' he said, puffing out his skinny chest with pride, 'it was a very important order. Thirty ells of our special red Bristol cloth to be shared amongst the aldermen and guildsmen of London, so that they can replace the shabbiest of their gowns before the royal wedding.'

'What royal wedding?' Adela and Margaret demanded almost in one breath. 'Come inside, Jack, and take a cup of ale before you go home,' Margaret went on eagerly, unlocking her

1

cottage door and holding it wide. 'And while you're refreshing yourself, you can tell us all about it.'

'Yes, please do,' urged Adela. Glancing round, she caught my mocking glance and had the grace to blush before tilting her chin and adding defiantly, 'We shall be most interested to hear your news.'

As she shepherded the children before her, I reflected that these first six months of my second marriage had been the happiest of my life. And I reflected, too, on how lucky we were that my three-year-old daughter and Adela's three-year-old son (Nicholas was the elder by just one month) were so fond of one another; were such good playmates in spite of their frequent disagreements. And fortune had also favoured us insofar as my wife was cousin to Margaret Walker, who had planned and worked for the match from the moment she knew that Adela had been widowed. Margaret, therefore, had experienced no difficulty in accepting Nicholas as her grandson, for neither woman had any other kinsfolk worthy of the name, and for that reason alone the blood-tie, though tenuous, was strong.

Once inside the cottage, Jack Nym sniffed the air, his nose twitching appreciatively at the rich smells of rabbit and herbs and newly baked bread. His goodwife, I seem to remember, was something of an invalid and not favourably disposed towards the cooking pot, so Jack was always hungry and accepted sustenance whenever and wherever it was offered. And once safely perched on the stool nearest the fire, he was happy to sample a plate of Margaret's honey cakes as an accompaniment to his mazer of ale.

'Now,' said the former, seating herself at one end of the long bench and taking Elizabeth on her lap, 'let's hear this news of yours, Jack. A royal wedding, eh? But who in God's name is to be married? I thought all members of the royal family were safely leg-shackled years ago.'

'It's the Duke of York. He's to be wed to the Lady Anne Mowbray, the late Duke of Norfolk's daughter,' Jack informed us thickly, through a mouthful of cake.

Margaret let out a screech that made Elizabeth jump like a startled hare. 'Little Prince Richard? But he's only a child,' she protested. 'He can't be more than four years old now, surely? Five, at the most. I remember distinctly that he was born the same year as the Duke of Gloucester's son, Prince Edward. I recollect saying to Goody Watkins at the time that the two brothers must be very close for each to name his son after the other.'

Jack Nym cleared his mouth with an effort. 'Ay, you're right,' he agreed. 'I overheard someone say that the Duke was only four years of age. And she – Lady Anne, that is – is six. Of course,' he continued knowledgeably, as befitted a man who visited the capital at regular intervals, and who was on more than a mere nodding acquaintance with London ways, 'they won't be living together for a long while yet. Not for years and years and years.'

'Then what's the point of marrying the poor little souls?' Margaret demanded indignantly. 'It could blight their lives if they should happen to grow up and fall in love with two other people.'

Jack Nym shrugged. 'It's the nobility's manner of doing things,' he answered vaguely. 'It's not for us to question why.'

'The late Duke of Norfolk was a very rich man,' I cut in, 'and I believe this girl is sole heiress to his fortune. The King would naturally be anxious to harness all that wealth to the Crown. Hence this marriage.'

'Well, I still think it's a wicked thing to do,' Margaret said severely, glancing down at Elizabeth, who was for once sitting quietly, docilely sucking her thumb. 'Imagine forcing this baby into marrying anyone!'

'When is the wedding to take place?' Adela asked from her seat on the opposite side of the table. 'Or don't you know, Jack?'

I looked round at her with narrowed eyes. There was a purposefulness in her tone that roused my suspicions.

'The fifteenth day of next month,' the carter answered promptly, anxious to dismiss any suggestion of ignorance on his part. He added for good measure, 'In Saint Stephen's Chapel at Westminster. Two days after the feast of Saint Hilary and the day before the Duke of Clarence is brought to trial in Westminster Hall.'

'Brought to trial!' I exclaimed, almost dropping my mazer of ale in astonishment. 'Duke George is being brought to trial?'

3

Jack nodded, pleased by my reaction to his news. To have captured my interest was, he plainly felt, a feather in his cap. 'That's right,' he said.

I leaned forward, compelling his attention. 'You're sure of this?' I urged.

'Of c-course I'm sure!' he spluttered. 'There's not much else being talked about in the London alehouses and taverns, I can tell you. Even the Duke of York's wedding, and the tournament that's to be held the following week, have taken second place – and a poor second place at that – to news of the trial. It seems that until recently no one thought that it would happen. Ever since last June, when the Duke was arrested and sent to the Tower, most people have been expecting to hear of his release.'

I nodded. 'I have, myself. The King has forgiven his brother so often in the past that there seems no reason why he shouldn't do so this time. I thought that imprisoning him in the Tower was just meant to frighten him.'

'Perhaps,' Adela suggested, 'the Duke will be acquitted. Or, if not, maybe King Edward will pardon him afterwards. This is to be a lesson not lightly forgotten.'

Jack Nym shrugged and finished his ale, wiping his mouth on the back of his hand.

'That's not the current opinion of the Londoners. The feeling now is that the rift between the brothers is more serious than was realised; that the Woodvilles are baying for Clarence's blood, and refuse to be appeased this time.'

Margaret slid Elizabeth off her knees and rose to her feet. Taking her big ladle, she stirred the contents of the iron pot that hung above the fire, and the cottage was once more filled with the savoury smell of rabbit stew.

'Why would the King want to bring his brother to trial the day after his son's wedding?' she asked curiously. 'It's bound to throw a damper over the jollifications.'

'Probably,' I suggested, 'because most of the nobles will be in London for the wedding. It's the sensible thing to do, if you think about it carefully. It will save them all another journey later on.'

Margaret sat down again, looking around for Elizabeth, but my daughter had seized the opportunity to slither away to play

4

with Nicholas. 'A strange business,' she remarked thoughtfully after a moment's silence. 'But the King wouldn't dare put his own brother to death, surely? Imagine the scandal! And what would be his mother's feelings, poor lady? You met her once, Roger. What is she like?'

I tried to conjure up a picture of that redoubtable dame, the Dowager Duchess of York, as I had seen her six years ago in a room at Baynard's Castle, but the essence of her eluded me.

'I'd say that she's a very strong-minded woman,' I answered slowly, 'who has known a great deal of tragedy in her life. My guess would be that whatever happens, now or in the future, she will cope with her grief.'

Jack Nym was regarding me with sudden respect. 'I didn't know you'd ever met the Duchess Cicely, Chapman.'

'Oh yes! And the Duke of Clarence,' Margaret told him proudly, before I could prevent her. 'While the Duke of Gloucester is very nearly a bosom friend.'

'Mother,' I interrupted swiftly, 'you know that's not true. I've had the honour to do a service or two for Duke Richard in my time, but I assure you, Master Nym, there's nothing more to it than that.'

Adela, noting my discomfort, came to my rescue as she so often did. 'How I wish I could see this wedding,' she sighed. 'I've never been to London, and everyone who's been there says it's a wonderful place. I should love to go.'

Jack Nym turned to me. 'Why don't you take her, Chapman? I'm going that way again on the sixth day of January. I'm carting a load of soap to the Leadenhall for Master Avenel, and I'll gladly take you both along.'

Adela looked at me, her eyes alight with excitement, and I answered hastily, 'That would be impossible, I'm afraid. We have two young children to care for.'

'If that's all that's bothering you,' Margaret said at once, 'shut up your cottage and leave Elizabeth and Nicholas here with me. I shall be thankful for their company. It gets very lonely in the dead of winter, even though I do see you and Adela almost every day. And by your own admission, Roger, you've had a profitable season so far. Spend a little of your hard-earned money, my lad. Don't be miserly. You're only young once.'

5

'Mother,' I protested irritably, 'you've just said yourself that it's the dead of winter, with all the bad weather still to come. Do you think I'm so irresponsible that I'll allow my wife to go junketing about the countryside in . . .' I caught Adela's eye and pulled myself up short. 'In January?' I finished lamely.

For once in her life, Margaret Walker allowed her own needs to overrule her better judgement. So fond was she of the two children, and so desirous of some human company during the long dark evenings ahead, that she made light of a journey that she would normally have condemned as foolhardy, if not downright insane.

'Adela's a strong woman. Make sure you're both wrapped up warmly and you'll come to no harm. After all,' she added with a conclusive gesture, 'you both walked from Hereford to Bristol at this same time last year, and carrying Nicholas as well.'

And that had also been her doing, I reflected. Margaret was quite ruthless when it came to getting her own way, as had been Lillis, her daughter, my first wife and Elizabeth's mother. And as was Adela, Margaret's cousin.

My wife smiled triumphantly at me as she began to make plans with Margaret and Jack Nym. I said nothing then, for I had given my promise to keep our secret until Adela should give me leave to speak; but that evening, in the privacy of our own cottage in Lewin's Mead, and as soon as the two children were in bed and fast asleep, I remonstrated with her.

'Adela, this idea of going to London is utterly foolish, and you know it. You're three months pregnant.'

She laughed and, rising briefly from her chair, kissed me lightly on the forehead.

'Who should know that better than I? But my early morning sickness has passed, and I feel as well as I have ever done in my life. Margaret's right, I'm strong in body. I always have been.'

'But the journey will be tiring,' I protested, 'even if we go all the way in Jack Nym's cart.'

She rested one elbow on the table between us, cupping her chin in her hand and regarding me with that faintly mocking stare that never failed to unnerve me.

'My dearest,' she said, 'while you are out peddling your

wares each day, I clean the cottage, make the bed, cook the food, chop the kindling, fetch water from the well, go to the market. Above all, I deal with the tempers and tantrums, bickering and squabbling of two small children who constantly vie with one another for my attention. Have you never considered that all that might be much more tiring than a journey to London?'

I had to admit that such a thought had never occurred to me. Baking, sweeping, looking after home and children was the normal business of women; what God intended them for in His earthly scheme of things. I must have looked puzzled, for she laughed again – that deep, full-throated laugh that was so peculiarly hers – and came round the table to sit on my lap, entwining her arms about my neck.

'Master Nym has assured me that we shall travel at a steady pace, taking frequent rests. He knows all the religious houses along the route and says that we can take our pick of where to rest up. Roger, with *three* small children to look after in the future, this may well be my last chance to see London for many years to come.'

'But what about the return journey?' I asked, still determined to make difficulties if I could. 'And where shall we stay?'

'At a decent inn,' she answered with some asperity. 'I'm sure there are many such in London. Indeed, you've told me yourself that there are. What Margaret said is true. You've worked hard since you came back from Devon in the autumn. You've been out on the road every day from dawn to dusk, rain or shine, at a time of year when most pedlars use any excuse to remain under cover. We have a little savings in the hiding place under the floor, so we can afford to put up at an inn. And Jack Nym will bring us home again, he said so. I can see the wedding – and you can see the Duke of Clarence's trial.'

The witch had found my weak spot. She had known, of course, from the moment that the trial was mentioned, that I must be longing to attend. I knew both Clarence and the Duke of Gloucester, had spoken to them face to face, had served each of them to the best of my ability, the latter on more than one occasion. I had even been offered a position in his household.

My devotion to Richard of Gloucester, a young man with

whom, according to my mother – God rest her soul! – I shared my birth day, the second day of October, 1452, was as great as that of any of those who served him personally. But I had never wanted to give up my freedom and independence of will, and so I had declined his proposal. Nevertheless, knowing his fierce loyalty to both his surviving brothers – *Loyauté me lie* was, appropriately, his motto – and his equally fierce hatred of the Woodvilles, I could only guess at what his feelings must be now that the long struggle for power between the King's family and the Queen's was nearing its climax. I suspected that, at what must be the bitterest moment of his life so far, he would need the prayers of all those friends who wished him well. (Was it presumptuous of me to consider myself his friend? I did not think so; nor did I believe that he would, either.)

'Well?' Adela asked, kissing me again. 'Are we to go or not? If you don't wish to stay at an inn, there are those friends you've mentioned so often, Philip and Jeanne Lamprey. Perhaps we could lodge with them.'

This time I was able to speak with decision. 'No, for unless fortune has favoured them since we last met, their cottage is too small to accommodate even one extra person, let alone two. We shall certainly call upon them, for they would never forgive me if I didn't take you to see them, but there is no question of being their guests.'

Adela pulled away from me a little, her dark eyes glowing with excitement.

'Does this mean that we are to go to London? That you have agreed?'

I realised that I was now as eager to make the journey as she was, but I made one last, desperate stand on the side of common sense.

'Suppose the weather turns bad? We might be snowed in for weeks on the road.'

'Master Nym assures me that that isn't likely to happen,' my wife said, getting up and going to pour me some ale. 'I was questioning him while you were drawing water for Margaret, and he's adamant that it's as mild a winter as he can remember, and thinks it almost certain that it will remain that way. All the signs point to it, he says.' She put the overflowing beaker down on the table beside me and went to fetch a cloth to mop up the overspill. This done, she knelt down by my stool. 'Roger, my love, just this once let's take the risk. The children will be well cared for by Margaret. You know as well I do that we need have no fears for them. And when we're old and grey, I'd like to have something to look back on. When you're deaf and doddering around with a stick, when I'm bent double, when the children are grown up and beginning to treat us as though we're not safe to be out alone on the streets, we'll be able to laugh and say to each other, "Do you remember when we were young enough and mad enough to travel to London in the depths of winter with Jack Nym and his cartload of soap? Do you remember the wedding of the little Duke of York and the Lady Anne Mowbray? Do you remember the trial of the Duke of Clarence?"'

I knew I had lost the argument. I knew that, stupid and hare-brained as the adventure appeared, I was suddenly as committed to it as was Adela. I sighed and pulled her back on my lap.

'And when does Jack Nym think of returning?' I asked.

'He's hoping to stay long enough to see the wedding tournament on January the twenty-second. In the meantime, he intends to tout around for someone who needs a load transported back to Bristol.'

This, I calculated, meant at least a week in the capital, and I could not help wondering if our meagre savings were sufficient to support us for such a length of time. Then I reflected that if I took my pack with me, I could earn money by selling my goods. I had done it before in London on more than one occasion. I could do it again.

I smiled at Adela, putting up a hand to smooth her cheek. 'Don't look so worried. We'll go.'

The twelve days of Christmas were over, and still the weather held, crisp and dry and bright.

Adela and I shut and locked our cottage in Lewin's Mead, warned our neighbours and the Brothers at Saint James's Priory that it would be standing empty for some weeks, took what few valuables we possessed, such as pots and pans and bedlinen, to Margaret Walker's for safety, saw the children happily ensconced in her tiny house and, on the sixth of January, not without some lingering misgivings on my part, set out for London, sitting up beside Jack Nym on the front board of his cart. Behind us, locked in by the tailboard, the crates of grey Bristol soap rattled and clattered and bumped.

I suppose I ought to have guessed what lay ahead, but for once I was lulled into a sense of false security. I presumed that God, if not sleeping, had forgotten me. He had, after all, a lot at present to keep Him busy elsewhere. It never occurred to me that He might have another job for me to do.

Two

S ometime around midday on the fourteenth of January, Jack Nym brought his cart to rest before the strange, wedge-shaped building of the Leadenhall, announcing with relief, 'Here we are at last.' Inside were innumerable market stalls, a granary, a wool store, a chapel in which Mass was celebrated every morning for the stallholders, and the great King's Beam, where goods were weighed and sealed by the customs men.

I knew from past experience that every sort of commodity was on offer within, from iron to cloth, lead to soap, food to second-hand clothing. And it was this last reflection, as well as a sense of obligation, that made me offer to assist Jack Nym to haul his crates of soap indoors.

Our nine-day journey had been uneventful, confounding all my prophecies of doom. The weather had stayed mainly fair with only two or three scattered showers of rain; and after Adela had taken Jack into her confidence regarding her condition, he had behaved with the greatest concern, making sure that at all the places where we found shelter along the route, she was treated with the highest degree of care and attention. Now, however, having reached our destination, we were to part – Jack, once he had made his delivery, retreating to a kinsman's alehouse in that insalubrious, riverside quarter of the city known as Petty Wales, whilst Adela and I had to seek out a cheap, but clean and comfortable inn.

This was partly the reason why I accompanied Jack into the Leadenhall, in the hope that it might be one of Philip Lamprey's days for serving behind his old-clothes stall in the market; for he, if anyone, could advise me where best to look. Adela had borne up remarkably well under the rigours of the journey, but I noticed that since passing through the

11

Lud Gate, some half an hour earlier, she had begun to look pale and strained. No doubt she had thought herself fully accustomed to the noises, smells and heaving masses of a large city. But London had three or four times the number of people crowded within its walls than did Bristol. Furthermore, unless you knew what to expect, the continuous clamour of the bells, the constant, full-throated cries of the street traders and the deafening clatter of iron-rimmed wheels over cobbles could come as an unpleasant shock to the first-time visitor.

Added to all that, the stench of the gutters seemed to assault the nostrils far more pungently than it did at home. We were fortunate that, by the time of our arrival, the rakers had already done their early morning rounds, carting away the previous day's refuse either to the pits outside the various city gates or to the river, where boats were moored, waiting to ferry it out to sea. But the filth was already piling up again, and by nightfall the mounds of stinking rubbish would be just as high as they had ever been. Keeping the London streets clean, then as now, was a never ending struggle.

Inside the Leadenhall it was a little quieter than without, but not much. I seated Adela on an empty, upturned wooden box while I helped Jack to locate his buyers, two soap merchants who sold not only tablets of Bristol grey, but also both the expensive white Castilian sort and the cheap black liquid kind. Then, with Jack's instructions ringing in my ears – 'We meet again here, the day after the tournament, the twenty-third of January, around midday' – I went in search of Philip Lamprey.

I was lucky enough to find him almost immediately, haggling loudly with an elderly woman over a pair of tattered, particoloured hose which I should not have considered worth even the carrying home; or which, if I had, Adela would most certainly have consigned to the dust heap.

'Philip, you old rogue,' I said, putting an arm about his shoulders, 'surely you're not going to charge this poor soul for that disgusting old garment?'

He whipped round, a martial light in his eyes, but this faded as soon as he saw who it was that had addressed him.

'Roger, you great lump!' He threw his arms around me. 'What are you doing in London? But whatever the cause,

I'm delighted to see you. And Jeanne will be as pleased as I am.' He turned to his customer. 'All right, mother, you can have 'em for nothing. Go on, put 'em away before I change my mind.'

He looked the same as ever, small and wiry with the thinning grey hair that made him appear older than his forty-four years. His voice still retained that rasping quality, which reminded me of iron filings being rubbed one against the other, and his weather-beaten skin was as heavily pock-marked as I remembered it. And when he moved, he still walked with the military gait he had acquired as a young man while soldiering in the Low Countries.

As soon as I had made him free of the reason for my being in the capital, and as soon as he understood that I had married again, nothing could stem the tide of his enthusiasm. He immediately shut up his stall, ignoring the line of waiting customers, and piled his unsold clothes into a basket to take back to his shop.

'Where is this wife of yours, then?' he demanded. 'Come along! Lead me to her and then you're both going home with me.' As I started to jib about his loss of trade, he slapped me on the back. 'Don't talk such blethering nonsense, man! Jeanne would never forgive me if I didn't bring you to see her right away.'

Jeanne Lamprey was indeed as pleased to see us as Philip had promised, and even more excited than her husband, if that were possible, at the news of my marriage. In the one room daub-and-wattle cottage behind their shop in the western approaches to Cornhill, she embraced us both fervently and plied us with meat, bread and ale, despite our assurances that we had eaten a good dinner at ten o'clock.

I could see that Adela, in spite of being forewarned by me what to expect, was at first somewhat taken aback by our hostess's youth and vitality. This little, bustling body, with the bright brown eyes and mop of unruly black curls, was, at that time, not yet twenty-one years of age and a most unlikely wife for someone like Philip. But she loved him deeply, ruled him with a rod of iron, had curbed his excessive drinking habits and pulled him up from penury and

13

the gutter to be a respectable trader with a shop and a stall of his own.

Her unreserved pleasure at meeting me again I found touching, considering that the last time we had met, a year ago, I had placed Philip in danger of his life. But Jeanne Lamprey was not one to bear a grudge, and one of her many qualities was her loyalty to friends. She was also extremely observant, and within quarter of an hour of being introduced to Adela, had wormed her secret out of her.

'Well, I think you're very brave to journey all this way in your condition in winter,' she said, kissing my wife's cheek. 'But,' she added accusingly, turning on me, 'I can't understand Roger allowing you to do it.'

'You mustn't blame him. He was given no choice,' Adela answered quietly. 'I was determined to come. I'd never been to London and I badly wanted to see it. And I also wanted to see the little Duke of York's wedding.'

Philip expressed surprise that this news had reached us in Bristol as long ago as Christmas. 'But in that case,' he continued, 'you must also have heard that Clarence is about to be brought to trial. With one event following immediately after the other, it's difficult not to speak of both in the same breath.'

I acknowledged that we had heard, and for the next ten minutes or so he and I were engrossed in the inevitable speculation as to why King Edward had at last decided to take action against his troublesome brother – when he had forgiven him on so many former occasions.

'It's all very well people saying that he's just lost patience with the Duke,' Philip remarked, thoughtfully rubbing his chin, 'but it's my opinion that there's something more to it than that, although I doubt we'll ever get to the bottom of what that something is. However, I did hear one titbit of gossip that might have some bearing on the mystery. Yesterday, when I was over by the Moor Gate . . . Which reminds me, Jeanne! Don't, as you value your purse, go anywhere in that direction. They're rebuilding and repairing stretches of the wall on either side of the gate, and the locals are out rattling their money boxes, waylaying anyone and everyone for contributions. But as the Common Council's already decided that each household has to pay fivepence a week towards the cost, I told 'em straight that I'd be damned if they got anything extra out of me, or out of any of my friends.'

He seemed inclined to brood darkly on this enormity until his attention was gently recalled by his wife.

'You were telling us what you heard yesterday, Philip, about the Duke of Clarence.'

'Oh . . . Yes! Although it wasn't exactly to do with him.' Philip cleared his throat impressively. 'I was told that the Bishop of Bath and Wells had been arrested and imprisoned round about the same time as the Duke, but was released after paying a heavy fine. This man – the man I was talking to – seems to think that the two events might have some connection, although I honestly can't see why they should. But I was wondering if you'd heard anything in your part of the world, Roger?'

I shook my head. 'Not a whisper. It must have been a very brief imprisonment. But then, I reckon Robert Stillington's a man who'd buy his way out of trouble as quickly as possible. All the same,' I added slowly, 'your informant could have grounds for thinking there was a link between the two arrests.' And I told Philip of the meeting I had witnessed some eighteen months earlier between the Bishop and George of Clarence at Farleigh Castle.

We were all sitting around the Lampreys' table, and out of the corner of my right eye I saw Jeanne shift uneasily on her stool. Philip must have noticed it, too, because he laughed and said, 'You've always known too much for your own good, Roger, ever since we first met, which is almost seven years ago now. You're a dangerous person to be around, as I've found out to my cost. So, if you're up to anything on this visit to London, we'd rather not be told.'

'He isn't, I promise you both,' Adela quickly reassured them. 'Our sole purpose is for me to see London, especially the Duke of York's wedding procession. And Roger would like to attend the Duke of Clarence's trial.'

'We'll all go to see the wedding,' Jeanne announced, clapping her hands together like a child suddenly proffered a treat. 'We'll shut up shop tomorrow and make it a holiday. But in the meantime, we must find somewhere for you to stay.' She

15

glanced around at the cramped conditions of the tiny cottage before turning an apologetic face towards Adela and me. 'I only wish we could offer you a lodging here, but you can see how very little room we have.'

'We wouldn't dream of imposing on you,' my wife answered firmly. 'But we should be very grateful if you could suggest a decent inn that won't cost too much.'

'The Voyager!' Philip exclaimed suddenly, snapping his fingers. 'Its proper name is Saint Brendan the Voyager, and you'll find it not far from here, in a street called Bucklersbury. The landlord's name is Reynold Makepeace, and he has the reputation for fair dealing and for not overcharging his guests. Go to the Great Conduit, where The Poultry runs into West Cheap, and Bucklersbury is on your left, running down to the Walbrook. The Voyager's about halfway along, crammed in between all the grocers' and apothecaries' shops. Its sign is the saint in his coracle, perched on top of a huge sea snake.'

We thanked him and prepared to take our leave, not without protests from both our hosts. But I felt that the sooner we were settled, the happier I should be, so without more ado I picked up the big linen satchel in which we had brought a change of clothing and slung it over one shoulder. (I had not, after all, brought my pack, having been dared to do so on pain of my wife's deepest displeasure. And an unexpected gift of money from Margaret Walker had made it easier for me to comply with Adela's wishes.)

We left matters that if the Lampreys heard no more from us before nightfall, they could safely assume that we had been successful in finding lodgings at the Voyager, and that they would call for us there the following morning. Adela and I would spend the remainder of the short January day exploring the delights of West Cheap.

January the fifteenth dawned cold and grey, with a dank mist rising slowly from the river. But the weather in no way dampened the spirits of the crowds gathered in the vicinity of the Chapel of Saint Stephen at Westminster.

My wife and I had been successful in finding lodgings at the Voyager in Bucklersbury, and had taken an immediate liking to the landlord. Reynold Makepeace was a short, stocky man

16

of some fifty summers, with a large paunch, sparse brown hair, bright hazel eyes and surprisingly good teeth, who exuded warmth and friendliness; and he had offered us a small but cheap and clean room, opening off an outside gallery that ringed three sides of the inn's inner courtyard. The bed, which took up most of the space, had a goosefeather mattress and big, down-filled pillows, with the result that we had slept like logs and risen that morning refreshed both in body and spirit.

Mind you, we had been very tired, having spent the rest of yesterday's daylight hours as we had intended, exploring the delights of West Cheap. Adela had drunk at the Great Conduit, rebuilt and enlarged during King Edward's reign, its crystal-clear water piped in from the spring whose source is to be found in the fields around Paddington. Then we had given thanks for our safe arrival at the Church of Saint Mary-le-Bow, so called because of its underpinning of stone arches. And, finally, as we approached Saint Paul's, visible at the top of Lud Gate hill, its steeple crowned with a copper-gilt weathercock, we had feasted our eyes on the magnificent display of wares in the windows of the goldsmiths' shops.

I've heard it said that there are more goldsmiths' shops crowded together in West Cheap, and spilling over into neighbouring Gudrun and Foster Lanes, than there are in the whole of Milan, Rome and Venice put together. Whether this claim is justified or not I have no means of knowing, never having visited any of those three cities; but I do know that even on a dull January afternoon, our eyes were positively dazzled by the gleam of gold and silver, of precious and semi-precious gems. Rings, necklaces and brooches, ewers, mazers and plates, ornately decorated salt-cellars, chalices and candlesticks all glittered in the fading light.

Outside each shop had stood the apprentices, touting their masters' wares, but secretly, I suspected, longing for curfew and the chance to remove themselves and the merchandise indoors. One undersized lad with a shock of wavy brown hair, who seemed to have no companion, had given up even the pretence of attracting custom, and was leaning against the door jamb, idly watching the passers-by and yawning behind his hand. Adela, smiling sympathetically, had drawn my attention to him, and even as I followed her pointing

17

finger, an elderly man, spectacles perched on the bridge of his nose, had leaned from an overhanging upstairs window and severely reprimanded the boy.

After that, we had had just time enough to walk along Paternoster Row, where the rosary makers have their shops, and where there are also one or two fine private houses, before the bells had rung for Vespers, and we had made part of the mass of people crowding into Saint Paul's. Even the lawyers, who daily conduct their business in the cloisters, had stopped advising or haranguing their clients in order to join in the service; although as soon as it was over, they returned eagerly to the business in hand. (Time, I have often heard it said, is money where the legal fraternity is concerned.)

Now, with a good night's rest behind us, and a breakfast of bacon collops and oatmeal cakes to warm our stomachs, we were outside Saint Stephen's Chapel awaiting the arrival of the bride and groom. True to their word, Philip and Jeanne Lamprey had called for us at the Voyager, and during our walk to Westminster, Adela had had her first good look at the Strand with its splendid dwellings, their gardens running down to the water's edge, and at the beautiful, if crumbling, Chère Reine Cross, that monument to the power of true love.

We had, fortunately, arrived early enough to position ourselves close to the main entrance to the chapel, and so had a clear view of the interior, ablaze with candles, the walls glowing with the rich reds and greens, purples and blues of tapestries. Jeanne, with womanly forethought, had brought a cushion, so that Adela, whenever she grew tired of standing, was able to sit down on the steps.

Jeanne could also enlighten us as to the identity of some of the guests and members of the royal family. The little Prince of Wales, she said, was not present, being, presumably, hard at work at his lessons in distant Ludlow Castle; but the magnificent gentleman just entering the chapel door was his guardian and uncle, Earl Rivers, the Queen's eldest brother. And behind him were the Queen's two sons by her first marriage, the Marquess of Dorset and *his* younger brother, Lord Richard Grey. And here were the four princesses, sisters of the groom. The eldest, Elizabeth, some eleven or twelve years old, was clutching the hand of the baby, Anne, and turning every now and then to frown at the other two – 'Mary and Cicely,' Jeanne hissed in Adela's ear – who showed a deplorable tendency to shuffle their feet and cough and admire one another's dresses in high-pitched, penetrating whispers, much to the amusement of the crowd.

There were many more guests, some of whom I remember clearly, and some of whom I cannot recollect at all. Amongst those I do recall are the little bride's mother, the Dowager Duchess of Norfolk, resplendent in violet cloth-of-gold, and the King's sister, Elizabeth, talking animatedly to her husband, the Duke of Suffolk. His heavy, surly features unexpectedly creased into a grin before they disappeared inside the chapel, the Earl of Lincoln, their eldest son, hard on their heels. The Duke of Buckingham was eye-catchingly attired in silver and green, and arrived in the company of Lord John Howard, a cousin of the Mowbrays (or so someone behind conveniently informed us). They were followed by a plump, but very pretty woman, in a gown and veil of pale blue sarcenet that defied the January cold, and which seemed to sparkle as she moved. At her appearance, a low murmur of disapproval rippled through the crowd.

'Who's that?' asked Adela.

'The King's chief mistress, Jane Shore,' was the prompt reply. 'The people don't care for her because she isn't noble. She was plain Jane Lambert, daughter of a London mercer, before she married a goldsmith by the name of William Shore. They say she first caught the King's eye on his return from France, two and a half years ago. And I've heard it rumoured,' Jeanne continued, warming to her theme, 'that the Marquess of Dorset and Lord Hastings – that was Lord Hastings who went in earlier, in the scarlet and black – are both extremely enamoured of her and are hoping that the King gets tired of her very soon.'

My wife's smiling face told me that she was enjoying her visit to London even more than she had expected to do. These intriguing glimpses into the lives of the royal family and the court made her feel part of a wider, less parochial world than the one she normally inhabited.

Next came a procession of guildsmen in all their fur-trimmed finery, followed by the Lord Mayor and his aldermen in their glory of scarlet hoods and gowns. And then a great fanfare of trumpets heralded the approach of the bride.

She walked, a small, upright figure between the Duke and Duchess of Gloucester, glancing coldly to right and left, seemingly finding it difficult to move, so weighed down was she by her gown of cloth-of-gold and a multitude of jewels. All I can remember of her expression was the look of blighting indifference she cast at the crowds. Not so the Duke and Duchess, who smiled and nodded and occasionally offered a hand to be kissed. But their greetings were mechanical, and I thought how haggard they both looked. Prince Richard's face, in particular, was pinched and lined with worry, its pallor accentuated by the rich crimson and purple of his wedding robes. Today, he must appear happy and joyful; but tomorrow, his brother would be brought to trial on a charge of high treason.

As the royal party drew nearer, I withdrew suddenly into the shadow of the chapel doorway, wishing that we had not placed ourselves to such advantage. I had no wish to be noticed by the Duke, previous encounters between us having invariably resulted in my undertaking some commission for him – commissions that had led me into personal danger. I therefore breathed a sigh of relief as he, together with the Duchess and the bride, passed into Saint Stephen's Chapel without seeing me.

And now here at last was the little bridegroom, flanked by the King and Queen, and looking every bit as indifferent as his future wife. Boredom was written large on a face that had not yet lost the dimpled curves of infancy, and as we all watched, he gave a tremendous yawn, not bothering to conceal it behind his hand. His mother said something to him sharply, and his face puckered as if he were about to cry. Only the sudden weight of the King's hand on his shoulder seemed to deter him, and he fought back the tears. I recollected Margaret's strictures on the marriage of two such young children, and my heart went out to them.

Mine, it appeared, was not the only one; for while we waited outside in the cold for the Nuptial Mass to be celebrated, the general buzz of conversation was of the iniquity of such a wedding. But then, as Jack Nym had argued, it was the nobility's way, and who were we to say it was wrong, so long as it had the sanction of the Church?

Suddenly the chapel doors were flung open, once more revealing the great cavern of warmth and light and colour, spilling out its radiance into the grey January morning. The bride and groom emerged, followed by the King and Queen and the Duke and Duchess of Gloucester. Two attendants advanced, carrying bowls of coins into which King and Duke dipped their hands, tossing a shower of gold to the waiting people.

Everyone was trying to catch as many coins as possible, and I, momentarily throwing caution to the wind, reached up with the rest. Because of my height, I towered over my neighbours and might have caught more than I did but for the fact that, glancing round, I found myself looking straight into the eyes of the Duke of Gloucester.

Three

I don't know what I expected from this exchange of glances; that Timothy Plummer would suddenly materialise at my elbow, perhaps, with orders that his master wished to see me without delay? Of course, no such thing happened: my lord of Gloucester's Spymaster General was nowhere to be seen.

Nevertheless, I could not shake off a feeling of uneasiness. The Duke's smile had been accompanied by a long, hard stare, and, in consequence, I was unable to enter into Adela and Jeanne's excitement at this sign of royal recognition. It was a source of congratulation, and of some self-importance, to the two women for quite a while after the newly-wed couple and their guests had vanished into Westminster Hall for the wedding feast. But I could see that Philip was unimpressed and shared my worry.

'You want to make yourself scarce, my lad,' he growled in my ear, as we made our way towards the cook shops, all of us hungry from the cold and ready for our dinner. 'The Duke of Gloucester's nothing but a source of trouble where you're concerned.'

I nodded. 'The same idea has already occurred to me. But, on reflection, I believe we're both being over-cautious. He has too much on his mind at this present to think up any commissions for me to do. Tomorrow's trial of the Duke of Clarence must be weighing heavily on his mind. There can be no room in his thoughts for anything else.'

'You won't go to the trial, though, as you originally planned? You wouldn't be so foolish as to tempt fate in that way, now would you?' Philip urged.

'Oh . . . I'll make sure I'm not noticed,' I answered evasively, loath to forgo my purpose.

Philip sighed heavily. 'In that case, I wash my hands of you,' he said.

We exchanged no further words on the subject, but my old friend's disapproval was plain.

We caught up with our wives at one of the many stalls selling hot meat pies and steaming ribs of beef, and Adela, now that we had a little extra money on account of the two gold coins I had managed to catch, wanted to try a dish of baked porpoise tongues, a delicacy that had not before come in her way. I dissuaded her, however.

'They may not agree with the child,' I suggested, patting her stomach.

Reluctantly, she agreed, and settled for a meat pie instead. But then, against my advice – or, maybe, because of it – she insisted on drinking a cup of hot, spiced ale to warm her. I thought it a mistake, but was wise enough to make no further protest. Adela was too independent a woman to be driven in any direction she did not wish to go, and must be allowed to learn her lessons in her own way. I did venture to mention that the Westminster alemongers put a liberal sprinkling of pepper in their beer, but my comment was ignored.

It was no great surprise to me, therefore, as the day wore on, and as we pushed and fought our way from stall to stall through the jostling holiday crowds, to note that Adela's face was contorted every now and then in spasms of discomfort. Eventually, it became obvious that she had lost all interest in the hats and ribbons, laces, shoes and petticoats, and in the hundred and one other goods being offered for sale, wanting nothing so much as to lie down and be quiet.

'I'm sorry,' she confessed at last, 'but I've the most terrible burning pain in my breast. It's the child, of course. You were right, Roger. I should have listened to you and not touched that ale.'

Jeanne Lamprey was immediately all concern, and she and Philip insisted on accompanying us nearly all the way to the Voyager in spite of our urging them to stay where they were.

'There's no good reason why we should spoil your holiday,' Adela protested.

But they would have none of it, persuading us, with, I believe, some truth, that they were tired and would be glad to return home.

'There are too many thieves and pickpockets about on these

occasions,' Philip grumbled. 'A man's hard-earned money isn't safe.'

They went with us as far as the Great Conduit, where we parted company with mutual promises of seeing one another again within the next few days.

'And take my advice,' Philip whispered to me at parting. 'Don't go to Westminster Hall tomorrow.'

I went to bed worried about Adela, and with the idea of following his advice. But when, the next day, my wife declared herself so much better, and only wishful of a morning in bed in order to recover fully from yesterday's exertions, I found myself with time on my hands. The consequence was well-nigh inevitable.

Westminster Hall was crammed to suffocation, and there was not a seat to be had anywhere. Outside, the bitter January wind was whipping through the streets, making the assembled crowds blow on their red, chapped hands and stamp their feet in an effort to combat the cold. But, by arriving early, I had just managed to squeeze through the doors, and now stood at the back of the hall in company with two dozen or so equally determined curiosity seekers. I could already feel the prickle of sweat under my arms and down my spine.

Others were also suffering from the heat generated by this press of bodies. The Duke of Buckingham, appointed Lord High Steward for the occasion, was wiping his neck with a silken handkerchief, while the Duke of Suffolk's fleshy face was suffused with blood, looking like nothing so much as a piece of raw meat. But it was not simply the warmth that was making us sweat. There was another emotion abroad, ugly and dark; the expectation, the anticipation of death.

On some countenances, like that of the Duke of Gloucester, it took the semblance of fear; fear for the death of a loved one. On others, it reflected the shame that two brothers, one of them the King, should be about to rend each other in public. And on still others, as on the face of John Morton, Master of the Rolls, it had twisted itself into a look of greed for the skill and thrill of the chase and the final destruction of the quarry.

The sound of muted cheering heralded the arrival of King Edward; and as soon as he had taken his place on the central dais, the Duke of Clarence, who had earlier been brought by water to Westminster from the Tower, was led to the bar. I was shocked to see how thin and pale he had grown, but at the sight of his old arrogant, contemptuous smile, I guessed that however much his appearance might have altered, no real inward change had taken place.

The King gestured for the proceedings to begin, and the Chancellor, Thomas Rotheram, Archbishop of York, rose ponderously to his feet to deliver a sermon on – if my memory serves me aright – the subject of fidelity towards one's sovereign. When he had finished, he sat down again, drawing his episcopal robes about him, rather like a bird folding its wings after flight, and King Edward indicated that the Bill of Attainder should be read.

The Duke of Buckingham, whose task this was, was noticeably nervous, his breath catching in his throat on more than one occasion, and twice faltering almost to a stop. Finally, he had done, and a profound silence settled over the hall, broken only by the occasional cough or a shuffling of feet. The King waited, his steely gaze resting on first one face and then another, but nobody moved: everyone sat as though carved out of stone. At last, when it became apparent that no one was willing to continue the proceedings, he stood up himself, with a suddenness that made his neighbours jump.

Brother faced brother across the hall.

It began quietly, the King reproaching the Duke for his constant treachery and reminding him of his own constant forgiveness. The Duke answered, in a tone equally subdued, that a divided family had naturally resulted in divided loyalties; and as he spoke, he glanced towards the serried ranks of Woodvilles. There, said his look, was the real cause of the division between himself and his elder brother.

The King hesitated, then shifted his ground. Had he not always loved George and treated him well? Had he not given him more money and lands than any King of England had ever before bestowed upon a brother? Had he not made him one of the two richest men in the kingdom after himself? And how had the ungrateful George repaid him?

'By depriving me of my crown and driving me out of the country! Me! Your own flesh and blood!'

Clarence laughed at that, and I saw the Duke of Gloucester flinch from the sound. I could guess what he was thinking; that the Duke's last hope of throwing himself on the King's mercy had gone. And so it proved. The polite, civilised masks were torn off and cast away. It was no longer brother and brother, no longer subject and overlord. It wasn't even man and man, but two animals, fanged and clawed.

'You are malicious, unnatural and loathsome!' shouted the King.

'And you are a bastard!' yelled the Duke. 'Hasn't our own mother more than once offered to prove you so?'

'Leave our mother's name out of this! Did you not unlawfully order the execution of the Widow Ankaret Twynyho?'

'And did you not retaliate by hanging Thomas Burdet, an innocent man?'

'He was not innocent! On your orders, he maligned the Queen and members of her family!'

Clarence's features were suddenly contorted into a barely recognisable mask of hatred. 'No one could malign that Devil's brood,' he all but screamed. 'Everyone knows that they indulge in the most extreme forms of all the black arts!'

The people in the hall were now avoiding one another's eyes, but glancing furtively every now and then at the Duke of Gloucester, where he sat staring at the ground and biting his underlip. Only the foreign envoys and ambassadors looked on with interest at the unedifying spectacle before them, storing up all the details for their royal masters in their next dispatches.

There was a momentary lull in this exchange of insults, while the two protagonists paused to draw breath. Then, in a torrent of foam-flecked words, the King began reciting all Clarence's many sins: his desertion to Warwick; his marriage to Warwick's elder daughter, Isabel Neville, without his brother's consent; his invocation of the statute of 1470 in order to lay claim to the throne; his attempt to marry Mary of Burgundy (a lady now safely the wife of Maximilian of Austria) until finally . . .

'I could have forgiven you all this,' the King roared, 'but for your last, malicious, more dastardly treason!'

An air of expectancy hung over Westminster Hall. This, surely, must be the moment we had all been waiting for; the moment when we should at last learn the truth; the real reason for the Duke of Clarence's indictment and trial. The charges which had been adduced so far were old tales: they did not account for the King's sudden decision to rid himself of his brother. A few of those present might believe that Edward had genuinely reached the end of his tether, but not very many. Most of us felt that some new and so far undisclosed treachery, something that struck at the very heart of his right to the throne, would now be revealed.

But then, suddenly, it was all over: I never quite fathomed how. A flurry of half-sentences on the part of the King; a bewildered Duke of Buckingham pronouncing a verdict of 'Guilty'; warders closing in on their prisoner, leading him away from the bar, and it was finished.

Abruptly, the Duke of Gloucester was on his feet, shouting his brother's name. For a brief moment Clarence turned, looked steadily at him across the intervening space, raised one hand in farewell and then was lost to view amongst his guards. Prince Richard, his naturally pale face now the colour of parchment and seamed with sweat, sank back into his chair, sightlessly scanning the crowds at the back of the hall. But then his eyes suddenly focused themselves, and he half rose again from his seat. It was with a sinking heart that I realised he was looking directly at me.

'So,' exclaimed Philip Lamprey, 'Brother George was found guilty, but is not yet sentenced. There's time enough still for a reprieve.'

I shook my head. 'Somehow I don't think so. Not on this occasion. Unless you were there, you can't begin to comprehend the animosity – no, more than that, the sheer, unadulterated hatred – that flowed between those two. I can only liken it to a festering sore that one day bursts, letting out all the poison and pus that has been accumulating inside.'

'As bad as that, eh?' said Philip ruminatively, scratching his head. He had come that afternoon to seek me out at the Voyager to enquire on Jeanne's behalf after Adela's state of health, and to satisfy his own curiosity as to the outcome of the trial. 'For I knew that against all my good advice you'd be bound to go and see for yourself,' he had chided me. He added now, 'I trust you kept yourself well hidden and did nothing to attract my Lord of Gloucester's attention?'

'Nothing at all,' I answered truthfully, but being less than candid. 'And both the wedding and the trial now being safely over, Adela and I can spend our remaining days in London in a more leisurely fashion, and go where the fancy takes us. She has a desire to visit Leadenhall market again this afternoon, not having seen much of it the day before yesterday.'

'Then you must promise to have supper with us afterwards,' Philip insisted. When I demurred, knowing that hospitality did not come cheap, he said impatiently, 'Jeanne will be only too delighted to see you, and any information you can give her about the trial will be ample reward for such victuals as we can offer you.'

It was impossible to withstand such an invitation; and so, after browsing amongst the stalls and shops of the Leadenhall, and after the purchase of a whip and top for Nicholas and a doll for Elizabeth, Adela and I walked up Bishop's Gate Street, eventually turning in amongst the narrow alleyways of Cornhill to the cottage behind the Lampreys' shop. There, we were afforded such a warm welcome that it was late into the evening, some hours after curfew and the closing of the city gates, before we returned to Bucklersbury.

We were met on the threshold of the Voyager by a perturbed Reynold Makepeace, who at once took my arm, drawing me to one side.

'There's a man here who says he must speak to you urgently,' he said in a low voice, trying to prevent his words from reaching Adela's straining ears. 'The man,' he added impressively, 'wears the Duke of Gloucester's livery.' Reynold's bright hazel eyes were round with curiosity and also with fear.

'Timothy Plummer!' I exclaimed disgustedly. 'What in Heaven does he want?'

'Did I hear my name mentioned?' asked a well-remembered voice, and, a second later, Timothy emerged from the land-lord's private parlour, just to the right of the inn's front door.

'So it is you,' I sighed. 'For one blessed moment, I was praying I might be wrong.'

'That's not a very friendly greeting,' he reproached me. 'And you've been particularly hard to find. I was asking for a lone chapman. I didn't expect you to be in company with your wife.' His smile faded. 'And the cursed annoying thing is that you've been almost on the Duke's doorstep all along.'

'What do you mean by that?' I demanded irritably. 'We're a long way from Baynard's Castle.'

'We're not at Baynard's Castle,' Timothy snapped back, reverting, as he so often did when pomposity got the better of him, to lumping himself together with the Duke. 'We're staying at Crosby Place, in Bishop's Gate Street.'

As he spoke, I recalled the splendid house and garden Adela and I had passed earlier in the evening, on our way to the Lampreys' cottage. I had mentioned it, in the course of our conversation, to Philip, who had told me that it belonged to Sir John Crosby, an extremely rich wool merchant, who rented out the place to visiting dignitaries. Foreign ambassadors often resided there for a season. Both the French and Danish envoys had certainly done so. And now it appeared that the Duke of Gloucester had hired Crosby Place for the duration of his present unhappy stay in London. I had no idea whether or not Duchess Cicely was in the city; but if she were, I guessed that Duke Richard might feel he had enough sorrow to bear, without having to cope daily with his mother's grief as well.

'Am I to assume that His Grace the Duke of Gloucester wishes to see me?' I asked sarcastically, and incurred Timothy's immediate ill-will.

'I'm not out scouring London on a bitterly cold, windy, sleety January night for my own pleasure,' he rasped. 'Of course His Grace wants to see you.'

'What for? Did he say?'

'No, of course he didn't say! Nor did I ask him. It's not my place. You just come along with me and you'll find out soon enough.'

I put my arm around Adela. 'And what about my wife?'

Timothy raised his eyes to heaven. 'She'll have to stay here until you return. She's surely capable of doing so! She looks like a sensible woman. Which reminds me.' His eyes lit with a malicious pleasure. 'I rather fancied, when I saw you in Keyford last year, that you were after a different quarry.'

'A mistake on my part,' I answered serenely, thanking my lucky stars that I had told Adela all about Rowena Honeyman, and that I therefore had nothing to hide. 'But how did you know? I'm ready to swear I didn't say a word about the lady.'

'It's my job to know everything about everyone,' Timothy replied curtly, disappointed that his barb had missed its mark.

This uncharacteristic spitefulness indicated to me something of his perturbed state of mind, and probably denoted the general anxiety and misery of the Duke's entire household. If the master were deeply unhappy, his servants would be, too.

I kissed Adela. 'I must go, sweetheart,' I said. 'I have no choice. Go to bed and get some rest. Are you all right, now? No more heartburn?'

She shook her head and kissed me back. 'Don't worry about me, Roger. I'm perfectly well, only a little tired.' She smiled up at me, but I could see the worry in her eyes. Lowering her voice, she added, 'Don't undertake anything dangerous. Promise me.'

I didn't feel that I could make any promises that I might be called upon to break, so I just kissed her again without making answer. Then, handing her over to the care of Reynold Makepeace and his wife, and roundly cursing my foolhardiness in going to Westminster Hall that morning, in defiance of Philip's advice and my own common sense, I wrapped my cloak more securely about me and instructed Timothy Plummer to lead the way.

There could not have been a more marked contrast between the cold, dark street without, roofs and window panes drummed by the onset of a thin, lashing rain, and the great hall of Crosby Place.

The leaping flames of a huge fire burning on the hearth sent shadows flickering across the richly carved ceiling and the delicate tracery of the musicians' gallery. High walls and spacious, lofty windows spoke louder than words of the modern approach to building, and of the fortunes to be made in the wool trade. Sir John Crosby was a man of substance and intended that the world should know it.

The hall was empty except for two young people who were playing spillikins in front of the fire. The elder was a very pretty, dark-eyed girl some twelve or thirteen years of age, the younger a sturdy boy of about ten. It was nearly seven years since I had seen them last, but they were both instantly recognisable; the girl because she was so like her father, the boy on account of the strong resemblance he bore to his physically more powerful uncles, the King and the Duke of Clarence. These were Richard of Gloucester's two bastard children, the Lady Katherine and the Lord John Plantagenet.

They glanced up as Timothy Plummer and I entered, brushing the rain from our cloaks, smiled and then continued with their game. But within seconds, a large, comfortable-looking woman, who was plainly their nurse, bustled in and began to shepherd them away.

'Time for bed,' she said as they protested. 'You can play again tomorrow.' And she swept up the spillikins, dropping them into a capacious pocket. 'Make your courtesies to Master Plummer and the gentleman.'

But this they had already done without any prompting, and allowed themselves to be hustled through a door and out of our sight. I stored up the incident to relate later to Adela; a moment to treasure and remember in old age, when two scions of a royal Duke made obeisance to a common chapman.

> When Adam delved and Eve span,
> Who was then the gentleman?

Timothy indicated that I should take a seat near the fire while he went to find the Duke, but I preferred to stand. When he had disappeared through the same door as the children, I noticed how quiet it was. In a great household there was usually constant noise and movement, but today it was as if someone had died and everyone was already in mourning.

The door opened once again and Richard of Gloucester came in.

31

Four

H e was wearing a long, green brocade robe, trimmed with sable, over hose and a shirt bleached so white that it made his skin appear the colour of old parchment. I thought that I had never seen him look so fragile. He had always been small of stature and of slight physique, two facts that belied the depth of his determination never to give in to the ill-health that had dogged him since he was a child; but that evening, he seemed sick in mind as well as body. The almost black hair and dark eyes were lacklustre, and his nervous habit of twisting the rings on his fingers more pronounced. We were the same age, twenty-six, but I felt myself to be many years younger than Richard of Gloucester.

He gave me his hand to kiss and sat down; then, bidding me be seated in a chair opposite his own, he smiled, and, as always, that smile revealed a different man, infusing his rather austere features with warmth and kindliness.

'Thank you for coming, Roger,' he said, although he must surely have expected me to obey his summons. An attendant entered, carrying a silver flagon and two crystal goblets which he placed on a small table at the Duke's elbow, before making a stately exit. 'Will you take some wine? This is an excellent malmsey, although a little too sweet for my taste, I must confess. My bro . . . Some people, I know, prefer it for that reason.'

'I'll take your word for it, my lord. I know nothing of wines.' I accepted the brimming goblet with its silver-gilt rim engraved with a scene of Bacchanalian revels, and waited for him to fill his own.

When he had done so, 'To the absent,' he said quietly, raising it in salute.

'To the absent,' I repeated, avoiding his eyes.

'You must be wondering why I've sent for you,' he went on, after a moment's hesitation. 'I understand from Timothy Plummer that your wife is with you here, in London. I'm sorry to intrude upon your visit like this, but I have need of your special powers.'

Richard of Gloucester was a man liked, in many instances loved, by everyone who took the trouble to know him properly. All the same, in spite of his gentleness and thoughtfulness towards friends and servants, there was a ruthless streak in his nature. When he decided that he wanted something done, no consideration for the convenience or feelings of others would deter him from getting his way.

After a few seconds, while he contemplated the crackling flames on the hearth, he raised his eyes to mine.

'You attended the Duke of York's wedding yesterday. I saw you, outside Saint Stephen's Chapel.' He did not wait for my affirmation before continuing, 'You therefore cannot have failed to notice Mistress Jane Shore.'

'I saw a woman I was told was Mistress Shore. She was dressed in a pale blue gown that seemed to sparkle as she moved.'

'I couldn't say,' was the terse reply. 'I took no notice of what she was wearing.'

The Duke plainly disapproved of the King's chief leman, as he no doubt disapproved of all Edward's other mistresses, and of the sybaritic life that had turned his adored eldest brother from the magnificent, clean-limbed hero of his youth into the man he was today; still immensely tall, still golden-haired, but running to fat, the blue eyes dimmed by boredom and excessive drinking, the once handsome features blurred by too much good living, the sharp mind blunted by constant flattery from sycophantic courtiers. I reflected, as I had done once or twice before, that there was a deep-rooted streak of puritanism in Richard of Gloucester's nature that no doubt made him many enemies. His ability to see things only as good or evil, right or wrong, could one day cause him great suffering, if, that is, it had not done so already.

He interrupted my train of thought to ask, 'What else do you know of Mistress Shore?' While I cudgelled my brain to remember what Jeanne Lamprey had told me of the lady, the Duke went on, obviously not expecting an answer, 'She is the daughter of a mercer called Lambert, and she married a goldsmith by the name of William Shore.' He refilled both our goblets. 'She was not, however, the only female of the Lambert family to marry into that particular trade. It seems that a cousin of her father's also married a goldsmith, one Miles Babcary, who still owns a shop in West Cheap. This couple – so my information runs – had an only child, a daughter who, in due course, married a man, whose name I can't remember.' The Duke was growing impatient, wanting to be done with the tale. 'The long and the short of it is, Chapman, that some months ago this girl – or woman, as I think she now is – was suspected of murdering her husband. She was never arrested, never charged with the crime – partly, I am told, for lack of evidence; and partly, I suspect, because of influence brought to bear by Mistress Shore upon the King. But the taint of suspicion still surrounds her, poisoning her life.'

There was another silence as the Duke's attention again began to stray, the expression on his tired face becoming ever more haunted.

I cleared my throat. 'And Your Highness wants me to discover the truth of this matter, if I can?'

'What? Oh . . . Yes! That's why I sent for you, Roger. Mistress Shore is very unhappy that her cousin is still being whispered about by her neighbours.'

My thoughts were racing. Why was the Duke of Gloucester interesting himself in this affair? He disliked the King's mistress, so why was he hoping that I might be able to clear the name of one of her kinswomen? What did any of it matter to him, especially at a time when he had far greater worries to occupy his mind?

But of course! Fear for the Duke of Clarence was the reason. He was convicted but not yet sentenced. There was still time for clemency on the part of the King. And what my lord of Gloucester needed above all else was as many voices as possible raised on Clarence's behalf; as many people as he could muster to plead for the Duke with King Edward in order to counteract the influence of the Queen and her family. And who would be listened to with more sympathy than a favourite leman? But first he had to find an inducement, a lure, in order to persuade Jane Shore to embrace his brother George's cause. So if, at his instigation, I could clear her kinswoman of the suspicion of having murdered her husband, then he would have the necessary bait.

Duke Richard laughed suddenly. 'Your face, Roger, is as easy to read as an open book. You've guessed, I think, why I'm asking for your help in this matter.'

I gulped down the rest of my wine, half rose and replaced the empty goblet on the table beside him, then subsided again into my chair.

'But what if this cousin of Mistress Shore *is* guilty of murdering her husband, my lord? What then? What good will that be to you?'

He sighed, pushing the curtain of hair out of his eyes. 'Then at least we shall know the satisfaction of having brought a criminal to justice,' he said heavily. And when I did not answer, he asked, 'Well? Will you do this for me?'

'Do I have a choice, my lord?'

'You always have a choice, Roger. You know that.'

But I was not so certain that I did. People of the Duke's standing never realise how used they are to being obeyed until someone challenges their authority. Not that I was about to do so. For one thing, my loyalty to Richard of Gloucester was as strong as ever, my affection for him undiminished; for another, however hard I tried, I could never quite suppress the feeling of excitement that invariably overwhelmed me when presented with a challenge to what the Duke had flatteringly called 'my special powers'. Wherever there was a mystery, I could not rest until I had solved it.

I thought guiltily of Adela. I had come to London to show her the city, and now here I was proposing to desert her for part of that time; maybe a great deal of that time. I thought even more guiltily of the Lampreys, and wondered if Jeanne would be kind enough to take my abandoned wife under her wing. I could imagine all too well what Margaret Walker would say when we returned to Bristol and the truth was revealed.

This reflection prompted me to say, 'My lord, my wife and I are due to leave London a week today with the carter who brought us here. If it should happen that I've not solved this problem by then . . . ?'

'You will stay until you have done so, and I shall make all necessary arrangements for you and your wife to be conveyed home to Bristol once the matter is successfully concluded. Before you leave Crosby Place tonight, Timothy Plummer will take you to see my treasurer, who will ensure that you have sufficient money for any extra expense you may incur. Now, is there anything else you wish to ask me?'

I glanced at him to see if he were serious; then protested indignantly, 'My lord, you have told me practically nothing! Merely that there is a goldsmith living in West Cheap whose daughter is suspected of murdering her husband. What is this woman's name? What were the circumstances of the husband's death? Who else might possibly have had a reason for killing him? How many people are there in the household? And how am I to make their acquaintance?'

The Duke laughed again, but there was neither mirth nor warmth in the sound.

'You must forgive me, Roger. My wits are gone wool-gathering.' He thought for a moment before enquiring, 'Where are you staying in London?'

'At the sign of Saint Brendan the Voyager, in Bucklersbury, not far from West Cheap.'

'Ah! Then someone will call upon you there sometime tomorrow morning, to conduct you to Mistress Shore's house in the Strand. She is the best person to tell you anything you need to know.' A faint spasm of distaste contorted his features. 'I will make all the necessary arrangements tonight.' He rose to his feet and I rose with him. He held out a hand once again, but when I would have kissed it, he stopped me and gripped one of mine instead, as if I were a friend. 'Do your best for me, Roger. As you've guessed, I need Mistress Shore's help in . . . in a certain matter.'

Mistress Shore lived in one of the magnificent houses that border both sides of the Strand, hers being one of those whose gardens run down to the river. The young man, dressed in the Duke of Gloucester's blue and murrey livery, who had presented himself at the Voyager soon after dinner that

36

morning, was obviously expected, and had no difficulty in gaining entry for the pair of us.

When I had returned to the inn the previous evening and told Adela all that had passed between the Duke and myself at Crosby Place, she had made no difficulties and uttered far fewer recriminations than I felt I merited. For this, two reasons were, I think, responsible. Firstly, in her condition, she was finding London noisier, busier and more tiring than she had expected; secondly, she had become close friends with Jeanne Lamprey, who was proving a restful and sympathetic companion, solicitous, as only another woman can be, for Adela's welfare. A very early morning visit by myself to their old clothes shop in Cornhill had put both Jeanne and Philip in full possession of the facts, and provoked the latter into lecturing me on the folly of not heeding good advice when it was offered.

'I warned you, Roger, not to attend the Duke of Clarence's trial! You'd already been spotted once by my lord of Gloucester at the wedding. To risk bringing yourself to his notice for a second time was the purest folly. You've got no more than you deserve.'

Jeanne told him to hold his tongue and promised to take care of Adela during those hours that I should necessarily be forced to spend in West Cheap. And I had a suspicion that both she and my wife continued to relish this glimpse into the lives of those normally so far above them, and were not altogether displeased by the turn of events.

The Duke of Gloucester's envoy and I were shown into a lofty hall where, surprisingly, a homely spinning wheel stood close to the hearth on which a bright fire burned, welcome on such a cold and cheerless winter's morning. An embroidery frame and coloured silks lay scattered over the central table of carved and polished oak, while an ancient, moth-eaten dog was ensconced in one of the hall's three armchairs, dribbling contentedly into a red satin cushion. My companion, to my amusement, eyed it askance. Like me, he had no doubt expected the King's favourite mistress to own an elegant little greyhound, bedecked in a jewelled collar and velvet coat.

My heart began to warm towards Mistress Shore, even

before she put in an appearance. But when she finally arrived, hot, somewhat flustered and full of apologies for her tardiness in receiving me, I knew that whatever the Duke of Gloucester felt about this woman, I liked her, and was willing to serve her for her own sake, as well as his.

The young man who had brought me to the house made me known to Mistress Shore and then, with a bow and a flourish, took his leave. When he had departed, she gave me a conspiratorial smile.

'Now we can be comfortable.' She looked me up and down. 'You're very good looking,' she said, but without any hint of invitation or coquettishness in her tone. 'You remind me of the King when he was younger.'

I could feel the hot blood rising in my cheeks. 'Y-you're very kind,' I stammered.

She only smiled and shook her head. 'Shall we have some ale? I prefer ale to wine. His Highness says that that's because I have low tastes, and of course, he's perfectly right.' She giggled.

I thought her enchanting, and could see why most men – with one very notable exception – would find her so. Jane Shore had a happy disposition.

After she had called a servant and given orders for the ale to be brought, she grew serious, settling herself in one of the two unoccupied armchairs and inviting me to sit in the other. She patted the ancient dog's head as she passed, and he briefly opened a bleary eye and twitched his ragged stump of a tail before going back to sleep again.

'His Grace of Gloucester tells me that you are a solver of mysteries,' she said. 'He has told you a little, has he not, about my kinswoman, Isolda Bonifant?'

'A very, very little,' I replied earnestly. 'That is why I am here this morning, to learn, I hope, a great deal more from you.'

The ale arrived and she poured it into two pewter beakers, wishing me good health before she drank. 'It was fate,' she said, 'that brought you here; fate that the King should have discussed my cousin's plight with his brother. I hope that you will be able to help Isolda, Master Chapman, for it's no pleasant thing for her to have neighbours, and even friends, whispering about her behind her back. Which she knows they must do by the way they grow embarrassed in her company, or avoid her altogether if they can.'

'That I can well imagine. Now then, if you please, will you tell me the background to the story?'

It was a straightforward enough tale. As Duke Richard had said, a cousin of Mistress Shore's father, one Susannah Lambert, had married a goldsmith, Miles Babcary of West Cheap. The couple had had only one child, Isolda, born in June, 1448, the year after their marriage. This girl, according to my companion's account, had never been pretty, even as a child, and had grown plainer as she grew older, a fact which had made it difficult to find her a husband. She was also, it appeared, fiercely independent, the mother having died when her daughter was only thirteen, and Isolda having assumed the role of woman of the house from that day forward.

Two weeks after her twenty-fourth birthday, she had finally married. Her husband, Gideon Bonifant, was ten years older than his bride and of inferior status, having been no more than assistant to an apothecary in Bucklersbury before the wedding. But Miles Babcary had been so relieved to see his only child settled and happy at last that he had, as well as welcoming Gideon into his home, also taken him on as a partner, patiently teaching his new son-in-law the business of goldsmithing from the lowliest task to the most complex. Master Bonifant had proved himself to be an apt pupil and the business throve, the one sadness being that after five years of marriage there was no sign of a grandchild for Miles; no immediate heir after Isolda to inherit his shop and his money.

The Babcary household, as well as an apprentice and maid-of-all-work, also consisted of Miles's niece and nephew, his younger brother Edward's orphaned children. Edward Babcary had died at the battle of Tewkesbury fighting for King Edward in the spring of 1471, and his wife had died of plague two months later. At that time, Christopher Babcary had been thirteen years of age, his sister only eleven, and with typical generosity, Miles had offered them the shelter of his roof. His nephew he had taken on as a pupil in the shop, while Eleanor Babcary had proved a useful assistant to Isolda in the running of the house. Even after Isolda's marriage the following year, no serious changes were deemed to be necessary, and the domestic and business arrangements of the Babcary household had carried on in much the same way as before, except that with both his son-in-law and his nephew learning the trade, Miles had needed only one apprentice.

And so matters had continued for the next five years, until the autumn of 1477.

'I have to admit,' Mistress Shore said, her colour slightly heightened, 'that although I used to be a frequent guest of my father's cousin and his daughter, I have lost touch with them of late, for the past three years in fact, since . . . since I came to live here, in this house,' she finished.

I nodded understandingly: she had had less to do with the Babcarys since becoming the King's mistress. But she was not a woman who would ever consider herself of so elevated a status that she would ignore her kinsfolk completely. Some contact had been maintained with the family, and when Isolda Bonifant had been suspected of murdering her husband, Mistress Shore had brought all her considerable influence to bear upon the King in order to ensure that no charge was brought against her cousin.

'For I didn't, and still don't, believe Isolda guilty of such a crime,' she said belligerently, jutting her chin and daring me to question her judgement. 'There has to be another explanation, and if people weren't so bigoted, they'd see that for themselves. Friends and neighbours who've known her all her life must know that she isn't capable of killing anyone. It isn't in her nature.'

Such blind faith made me uneasy. 'How did Master Bonifant die?' I asked.

'He was poisoned.' Mistress Shore sounded defiant, as well she might. 'Oh, I know what you're thinking! That poison is a woman's weapon.'

'It's easier for them to use than either the dagger or the cudgel,' I pointed out. 'On the other hand, I've known women who have resorted to both those methods, and men who have administered poison. They say it's a favourite means of despatching enemies in Italy. Do you know what poison was used?'

Mistress Shore hesitated. 'I think it was aconite, monkshood, or so Miles Babcary informed me. I'm not sure how he knew. I suppose the physician or the apothecary who was called recognised certain symptoms.'

'Undoubtedly. I believe it causes burning pains in throat and stomach, and the victim has great difficulty in swallowing. The muscles of the neck stiffen, and after ten minutes or so, breathing becomes impossible.'

Jane Shore gave a little shiver. 'How horrible! But there were other people in the house as well as Isolda. It might have been one of them. I believe that Christopher Babcary didn't get on well with Master Bonifant. They had had many disagreements.'

'Do you know why?'

My hostess did not reply at once, looking down at her hands, clasped in her lap. Finally, after a few moment's silence, during which the only sounds to be heard were the old dog's wheezy snores and the crackling of the fire on the hearth, she raised her head and looked me in the eyes.

'Master Chapman, I must be honest with you. The King doesn't wish me to be too closely concerned in this business. Until my kinswoman's name is cleared, he prefers that I have nothing to do with the Babcary household.' She sighed. 'I can understand that. He feels that he has done enough by bringing his influence to bear and preventing charges being brought against Isolda. Therefore, if I give you my cousin's direction in West Cheap, you would earn my deepest gratitude if . . . if—'

'If I were to confine all my enquiries to the family, and not bother you until I have reached a conclusion,' I finished for her.

She smiled mistily at me. 'Indeed, I feel ashamed of making this condition, but I cannot bring myself, at this difficult time, to go against His Highness's wishes.'

'And how will the Babcarys like me poking and prying about? Do they even know of my existence?'

'Yes. Yes, they do, and all of them are anxious for your assistance. They want to know the truth as much as I do.'

41

It occurred to me that there must be one person who already knew the truth and whose welcome would be a sham: the murderer. But I said nothing. Instead, I rose, kissed the little hand that was offered me and promised Mistress Shore that I would do everything in my power to discover who had really killed Gideon Bonifant.

Five

I recognised the place at once. It was the house where Adela and I had seen the lazy apprentice being scolded from an upper window by his bespectacled master.

Following Mistress Shore's directions, I had walked almost to the end of West Cheap, where, at the Church of Saint Michael at Corn, it joins Paternoster Row to the south and the Shambles to the north.

'Look for a shop and dwelling close to the Church of Saint Vedast,' she had instructed me. 'A representation of two angels is painted on the plasterwork between the third-storey window and the roof. I sent to my cousin this morning to warn him of your arrival. You will be expected.'

So there I was, a pallid winter sun struggling to break through the leaden clouds, my cloak and boots splashed with mud and filth from carts driving too near the central gutter, my ears deafened by the babel of street cries – 'Hot sheep's feet!' 'Ribs of beef!' 'Clean rushes!' 'Pots and pans!' 'Pies and pasties!' and dozens more. Every few yards of my journey from the Strand, hands had clutched at my sleeves and whining voices had assailed my ears, pleading for alms. Some beggars were hale and hearty, others hideously disfigured, either by nature or by the cruelties of civil punishment and war, and all excited pity. I gave what I could, but there were too many suppliants, and eventually I had been forced to ignore their importunities. I reached my journey's end with some relief and entered the shop.

A long counter faced me as I stepped inside, and beyond this was the workroom. A youth, the same boy I had seen three evenings since, was working the bellows at a furnace built into a wall, while the same elderly man was admonishing him in an exasperated tone.

'No, no, no, Toby! A light pressure, if you please! You want to fan the coals gently into flame, not blow great clouds of smoke out through the vent to choke the passers-by! Good God, lad, don't you ever attend to any of the instructions that you're given?'

Another man, not so very much older than the apprentice, was hammering out a piece of gold on an anvil, which stood on a bench in the middle of the room. As I watched, he laid down the hammer and picked up a pair of tweezers, beginning to pull and tease the hot metal into shape. Near at hand lay a chisel and a rabbit's foot, while further along the bench were what looked like a pair of dividers, a saw, a file and a number of small earthenware dishes. An array of other tools was ranged along a shelf to my right.

It was the older man, whom I rightly guessed to be Miles Babcary, who saw me first, bustling forward in the hope of a sale, his face falling ludicrously as soon as he noted my homespun apparel.

'Master Babcary?' I asked, holding out my hand. 'I'm Roger Chapman. Mistress Shore told you, I think, that I should be coming?'

I judged him to be about sixty (he later told me that he had not long celebrated his fifty-eighth birthday), a ruddy-cheeked, somewhat corpulent man with thinning grey hair in which gleams of chestnut brown could still be seen. His pale blue eyes, magnified by the spectacles perched on the bridge of his nose, blinked at me, owl-like, but at my words, his kindly features brightened.

'So she did! So she did! Walk around the counter, Master Chapman. You are more than welcome. We shall be very glad, believe me, to have this hateful business cleared up once and for all. You can have no idea what it's like for my daughter to be whispered about behind her back.'

'Master Babcary,' I warned, 'I may not be able to arrive at any firm conclusion. Or . . .' I hesitated. The elder of the two younger men had now drawn near and was listening intently to our conversation. I continued, 'Or I might reach the wrong conclusion as far as you're concerned.' I saw from Miles Babcary's slightly puzzled expression that he did not fully

44

understand my meaning, and I began to flounder. 'What I mean is . . . What I am trying to say . . .'

The young man came to my rescue. 'Are you suggesting, Chapman, the possibility that my cousin Isolda might really have poisoned her husband?'

Both his age and a fleeting likeness to Miles told me that he must be the nephew, named by Mistress Shore, if my memory served me aright, as Christopher Babcary. I nodded, and there was an immediate explosion of protest from his uncle.

'No, no! I won't have it! My dearest girl could never have done anything so terrible! Master Chapman, you are here to prove her innocence.'

'I will if I can, sir,' I assured him. 'But you must have realised by now that if Mistress Bonifant isn't guilty, then someone else is.'

Again, I encountered that bewildered stare, and again it was Christopher Babcary who interpreted my meaning.

'What the chapman is saying, Uncle, is that if Isolda didn't murder Gideon, then someone else in the house must be the killer; one or the other of us who was present here that day, at Mistress Perle's birthday celebration.'

This idea, although I could see that it was not a new one to the nephew, plainly had not occurred before to Master Babcary. So absorbed had he been in trying to prove that his daughter was not a murderess that the implication of her innocence had quite escaped him. For a moment he looked as if he might burst into tears, but then pulled himself together, his face taking on a mulish expression.

'I – I want Isolda exonerated,' he stuttered at last. 'She didn't do it. I know she didn't. She loved Gideon, whatever he might have said to the contrary. I'm sorry, Christopher, my boy, if it means that you and others fall under suspicion. But if it's of consolation to you, I don't believe that anyone who was present here that day is guilty, either. In fact, I'm very sure no one is.'

Christopher Babcary glanced at me, then back at Miles. 'But it stands to reason, Uncle, that one of us must have poisoned Gideon. Besides himself, there were nine of us in the house that evening, and apart from those nine, no one else could have put the monkshood in his drink. The shop was locked and shuttered as soon as the guests had arrived.'

Miles Babcary put a hand to his forehead, growing more confused by the minute. One half of his mind could not help but acknowledge his nephew's logic, but the other half refused to accept it. If Miles could have his way, Gideon Bonifant's murder would prove to have been an accident or suicide; or, better still, the handiwork of a passing stranger who had mysteriously managed to gain access to the house.

I said gently, 'Master Babcary, we cannot continue to stand here in the shop where every passing fool can gape at us through the open doorway. Can we be private? In spite of talking to Mistress Shore, I am still ignorant of many details concerning this murder.'

'Yes, yes! Of course! But you must wait a few moments, if you please. Toby, is the gold melted yet? If so, bring it over here immediately.'

The boy lifted a pot out of the furnace with a pair of tongs and carefully transported it to the work bench, his tongue protruding from one corner of his mouth, his young body taut with concentration as he tried not to spill any of the precious liquid. Meantime, Miles Babcary had drawn towards him a thin sheet of copper on which innumerable circles were shallowly engraved; and within each circle a bird or a flower, the figure of a saint, a face or the wheel of fortune was also scored into the metal. It was plainly a mould of some sort, but what purpose was served by the final product – delicate, paper-thin, filigree golden medallions – I could not imagine.

Christopher Babcary, noting my puzzled frown, enlightened me.

'They are sewn on women's gowns. They make the material shimmer as my lady walks.'

'So that's what it was,' I said. 'I'm remembering how Mistress Shore's robe glittered at the Duke of York's wedding.'

'As did every other lady's gown, I should imagine,' Christopher amended. 'We and the rest of the goldsmiths hereabouts sold out of our entire stock of medallions during the preceding weeks.'

46

His uncle, meanwhile, had been filling the circular moulds with the molten gold, the surplus being caught in a narrow runnel fixed to the edge of the bench. The boy addressed as Toby began to scrape at the lumps and flakes as they hardened, gathering them up and carefully depositing them in some of the earthenware bowls.

'Where does the gold come from?' I asked.

'Mostly from Hungary and Bohemia,' Miles Babcary answered, removing his leather apron and hanging it up on a nail. 'These days, it's brought into the country in the shape of coins, which are thought preferable to the old-fashioned ingots . . . Well now, Master Chapman, perhaps you'd like to accompany me upstairs where we can be comfortable, and I'll tell you all you need to know about this unfortunate affair.'

He paused long enough to issue instructions to his nephew and the boy, Toby, on what needed to be done during his absence, then led the way through an inner door to a passage-way beyond. Here, to our right, a staircase spiralled upwards, while, straight ahead, lay what I supposed to be the kitchen quarters. As if to prove my assumption correct, a young girl appeared, entering from the yard at the back and carrying across her shoulders a yoke from which two buckets were suspended, some of their contents spilling on to the flags in great splashes of clear, sweet water.

'Ah! Meg!' Miles Babcary beckoned her forward. 'This is Roger Chapman who will be in and out of the house and shop for a while. He may want to ask you some questions, but there's no cause to be afraid of him. Just tell him what you know. He won't get angry or hurt you.'

The girl unhitched the yoke from her shoulders, lowering it and the buckets to the ground before approaching us with such caution that she literally inched her way along the wall, arms outstretched, fingers splayed against the stone.

'She's very wary of strangers,' Miles informed me, but not loud enough for the girl herself to hear. 'She's a foundling, and was, I'm afraid, mistreated at the hospital on account of her appearance. She's also slow of speech and understanding.' He tapped his forehead significantly. 'You have to be patient with her.' He added as an afterthought, 'Meg Spendlove's her name.'

I held out my hand and said gently, 'I'm pleased to make your acquaintance, Mistress Spendlove.'

Her only answer was a goggle-eyed stare. She was so small and thin that it was impossible to be certain of her age, and I doubted very much if even she knew how old she was. (Although Master Babcary told me afterwards that they thought her to be in her sixteenth year as, according to the nuns of the hospital, she had been abandoned, at only a few days old, in the same month that Queen Margaret had invaded in the north.) She was unprepossessing to look at, someone at sometime having broken both her nose and jaw, and the bones having knit together very badly. Because of this, her mouth hung almost permanently open, and when it was shut, she breathed in a painfully wheezing fashion. Contrary to expectation, however, there was a hint not only of intelligence but also of shrewdness in the dark brown eyes, if you took the trouble to look for it.

'You're a good girl,' Miles said, patting her shoulder. 'Try to remember what I've just told you concerning Master Chapman. Now, off you go and finish your work or you'll have Mistress Bonifant on your tail, and you don't want another scolding, do you?'

The girl shook her head and went back to pick up her pails, disappearing with them through a second door which, as I later discovered, led into the kitchen.

My host and I proceeded up the twisting stairs as far as the first-floor landing, where two doors were set in the wall, side by side. Miles pushed open the right-hand one, ushering me into what was plainly the family living-room. It was as spacious as the narrow confines of the building would allow, and was, I guessed, the largest chamber in the house. A solid oaken table stood in the middle of the rush-strewn floor, a leather-topped bench, piled with brightly coloured cushions, occupied the window embrasure, and a corner cupboard displayed not the usual collection of silver and pewter ware, but, as was only to be expected, items of gold taken from Master Babcary's stock. A fire burned brightly on the hearth, a good supply of logs stacked close by, ready to replenish it when necessary. Two armchairs, several stools and a carved wooden chest, which stood against one wall, completed the furnishings.

'Sit down. Sit down, Master Chapman,' my host invited, with that repetition of speech which I was soon to learn was characteristic of him. I had hardly done so, drawing up a stool to the fire, glad to warm my cold hands at the comforting blaze, when the door opened and someone else came into the room; and before I could turn my head, Master Babcary continued, 'Ah! Here's my daughter.'

Isolda Bonifant was not as I had imagined her. Mistress Shore had described her as being plain; plain enough, in fact, to find difficulty in attracting a husband. And indeed, no one could have described her as a pretty woman. Her best feature was a pair of deep blue eyes that returned my gaze with a candid stare, but no trace of resentment at my obvious curiosity. Otherwise, it was a strong, almost mannish face with thick, dark eyebrows, a high-bridged nose and a stern, unsmiling mouth. And yet I was immediately attracted to her. She reminded me in some way of Adela, a woman who, once she had committed herself, would give you her full loyalty and support. I could understand why her father thought her innocent of this terrible crime.

I pulled myself up short with a silent admonition. I knew, none better, that first – and sometimes even second and third – impressions could be deceptive. Master Babcary was making me known to his daughter, and I rose from my stool to return her greeting.

'Mistress Bonifant,' I said, bowing. 'God's peace be with you.'

'I hope it may be,' she answered frankly, advancing into the room. She looked me up and down. 'You're a very strange chapman. I've never met one before who is intimate with princes and the King's chief whore.'

'Isolda!' Her father's reprimand was harsh. 'You won't talk like that, if you please, while you're under my roof. Mistress Shore is your kinswoman by blood and mine by marriage. She has done, and is doing, her best to help us. I wish you will remember that without her assistance you could well have been accused of Gideon's murder.'

Mistress Bonifant shrugged. 'Perhaps it would have been better if I had been. At least, by now, I would either have been proved innocent or be dead.' She moved further into the room, coming to stand beside me, and I saw the dark shadows beneath her eyes. 'But that still doesn't explain how the chapman here is acquainted with our cousin.'

And so, not for the first time, and certainly not for the last, I gave brief details of my history and the circumstances that surrounded my friendship with the Duke of Gloucester. As always, my listeners expressed surprise that I had not chosen to better myself by taking advantage of the Duke's ever increasing cause for gratitude; and, as always, I reiterated my reasons for not doing so.

'I like my independence too much, the freedom of being my own master. I want no one set in authority over me.'

Master Babcary admitted that he could see the force of such an argument, and Isolda also conceded that, were she a man, she might feel the same way. Having said this, she begged me to be seated again and brought forward another stool for herself, placing it alongside mine.

'Well, and what conclusions have you come to regarding the murder of my husband, Master Chapman?'

'Good Heavens, girl!' her father protested. 'He hasn't been in the house but half an hour, and as yet knows very little of what happened last December. I brought him up here for some peace and quiet and in order to make him acquainted with the facts.'

'Then I shall stay to help you.' And Isolda sat down with a rattle of the household keys fastened to her belt.

Miles Babcary must have seen the expression on my face, for he said nervously, 'Do you think that a good idea, my dear? You are, after all, the one most nearly concerned and . . . and . . .' His eyes rolled in my direction, seeking guidance.

Mistress Bonifant laughed suddenly, sounding genuinely amused. 'And you think it would be better if I didn't remain to plead my own cause?'

Miles Babcary and I assented with almost one voice.

'Very well then,' she agreed, rising to her feet, but just at that moment the door opened for the second time and a young girl came in.

I judged her to be some sixteen or seventeen years old, about the same age as I had learned Meg Spendlove to be, but

there all similarity ended. There could not have been a greater
contrast than between those two. One was plain – some might
even call her ugly – unloved and had probably never known
an act or word of simple human kindness until she had
come to this house to work. The other was a beautiful,
blue-eyed, creamy-skinned peach of a girl, obviously cher-
ished by all who knew her. Miles Babcary's face lit up at
the mere sight of her face, and Isolda went forward to kiss
her cheek.

'Nell, my love, you must be chilled to the marrow. Was it
very cold outside? Come to the fire and warm yourself.'

At the same time, Miles Babcary turned to me and said,
'This is my niece, Eleanor. You have already met her brother,
Christopher, downstairs. Nell, my sweetheart, this is Roger
Chapman who has been sent to us by Mistress Shore. He
has agreed to try to solve the mystery of poor Gideon's
death.'

Eleanor Babcary gave me a smiling, incurious glance,
putting back the hood of her cloak to reveal an abundance
of chestnut-brown hair. An effort had been made to tame
it into two long plaits that hung down over her shoulders,
but a profusion of little curls were everywhere escaping their
confinement, tendrils that she vainly, if absent-mindedly, tried
every now and again to smooth into place.

'I wasn't at all cold,' she said in answer to Isolda. 'This
lovely fur-lined cloak that you and Uncle Miles gave me for
Christmas has kept me warm.' She reached out to take one
of Master Babcary's hands in hers, pressing it gratefully to
her cheek.

My host's smirk of pleasure reminded me of nothing so
much as a callow schoolboy who has been praised by a
favourite tutor, and my suspicions were confirmed that Eleanor
Babcary was the darling of the household. What I was not so
sure of was whether she was aware of this fact, or if she used
the knowledge for her own advantage. Only time would tell.
What was plain, however, was that Isolda, like her father,
doted on her cousin, and somehow I did not think her a lady
who would be easily fooled by a pretty face and a charming
manner.

'Was Mistress Perle at home?' Miles Babcary demanded.

51

'Did you speak with her? Did she agree to take supper here this evening?'

'I saw her, yes, and spoke with her.' Eleanor tenderly squeezed her uncle's hand which she was still holding in one of her own. The blue eyes filled with facile tears that spilled over and ran down the velvety cheeks. 'But she still refuses to eat with us, Uncle. She repeated that she thinks it better that she sees us as little as possible until this business of Gideon's death is satisfactorily resolved. Those were her very words: I took particular note of them. "Until this business of Gideon's death is satisfactorily resolved."'

Disappointment and bewilderment were visible in every line of Miles Babcary's face. 'Why does she persist in this answer?' he asked angrily of no one in particular. 'It's over a month and a half now since the murder, and still she refuses to set foot across my threshold. Why?'

Neither of the women seemed inclined to answer this question, Eleanor looking sympathetic, but vacant, Isolda closing her lips tightly as if there was much she could have said, but chose not to do so. It was left to me to offer a solution.

'Master Babcary, your nephew said in my hearing that your son-in-law died during Mistress Perle's birthday feast, so I presume that the celebration took place in this house?'

My host nodded. 'That is correct. It was the fourth of December, the feast of Saint Barbara, after whom Mistress Perle is named, and I had invited her to sup with us that evening.'

A slightly foolish smile curled his lips and he sighed sentimentally. I began to understand his attachment to this Mistress Perle. My guess was that he had been courting her, hoping to make her his wife, and that the lady had not been unwilling. Her present rejection of him was therefore all the harder to bear.

I said gently, 'Don't you think that her reluctance to see you might be the result of your fierce protestations concerning your daughter's innocence? As Master Christopher was saying to you a short time ago: if Mistress Bonifant didn't commit the murder, then someone else who was in the house that evening did. It follows, therefore, that Mistress Perle may feel herself to be the object of your suspicion.'

Master Babcary's florid countenance turned pale. 'She couldn't possibly think such a thing! She couldn't!' But a moment's consideration showed him the truth of my words. He grabbed my arm and shook it. 'Master Chapman, you must find out what really happened! Come! Draw closer to the fire and I'll tell you about the events of that evening.'

Six

The two women left us, Eleanor allowing herself to be led away by Isolda without once questioning the older woman's decision. Yet again, I wondered if she were always this docile; and if so, did she resent the fact that uncle and cousin seemed to treat her as though she were still a child?

'Now,' said Miles Babcary as the door closed behind them, 'you've met all the members of my household, Master Chapman – all those who remain, that is. But I don't need to remind you that until the evening of the Feast of Saint Barbara, last December, there was another, my son-in-law, Gideon Bonifant. He—'

'Did you like him?' I asked, interrupting my companion's flow of words and thus flustering him. I have often found this a useful tactic for getting at the truth.

'What?' Miles stared at me, mentally thrown off balance. 'I . . . He was . . . Why should I not like Gideon?' was the belligerent response. He fidgeted uncomfortably for a moment or two before adding, 'To be honest, he was not someone you could like or dislike with any great fervour. He was not a man anyone could get to know very well. His emotions were always kept strictly in check, and what sort of a husband he made I have no idea. But he seemed to make Isolda happy, and that was all that mattered to me.'

'Mistress Shore hinted that perhaps Gideon was not a good enough match for your daughter. An apothecary's assistant, so she said, from Bucklersbury.'

'Well, well, and what if he was?' Miles let his irritation show at this second interruption. 'You've seen Isolda. As you can guess, she didn't attract men easily, even when young. You know that she's . . . that she's not a handsome woman. To be truthful, she's plain. She's very plain. Added to which,

54

she has an independent turn of mind, which is not surprising when you consider that she has been sole mistress of this house since the age of sixteen. That was when my last housekeeper left me because, she said, she and Isolda could no longer share the same roof without falling out every day.'

I asked curiously, 'And yet – forgive me if I am being too bold – you are thinking of marrying again?'

This time, Miles's annoyance was palpable. 'Master Chapman, it is only just over two weeks since I celebrated my fifty-eighth birthday. I am not yet in my dotage. I am still a virile and active man. A comfortable and well-run home is not the only consideration for someone of my age and appetites. I must admit that until Mistress Perle was widowed two and a half years ago, the thought of remarriage had not entered my head. But I have known and been fond of Barbara for a very long time; and once her period of mourning was over and she was able to take up the threads of her life again, I realised that my liking for her had turned into something stronger. And from one or two very broad hints that she dropped, I had every reason, until recently, to believe that she was entertaining similar thoughts about me. I talked the matter over with my daughter and Gideon, and told them that if Mistress Perle should do me the honour of agreeing to become my wife, I would buy her house in Paternoster Row and give it to them to live in. They seemed agreeable enough. I think Isolda, particularly, was beginning to feel it time that she had an establishment of her own.'

'Mistress Perle and her husband had no children?' I enquired, although I had already guessed the answer.

'No, none.' Miles's irritation increased still further. 'But why am I telling you all this? What has it to do with Gideon's death?'

'In a case of murder,' I assured him apologetically, 'there is no saying what might eventually prove to be of importance in solving the crime. Please forgive me if I have probed too deeply into matters that you feel do not concern me.'

He appeared somewhat mollified by this explanation, although a little resentment still lingered.

'Very well! Very well! Let us now return to the evening of Gideon's death. As I have already told you, it was Mistress

Perle's birthday, December the fourth, the Feast of Saint Barbara, and I had invited her to celebrate the occasion here, with my family; the family that I hoped would also soon be hers. She was only too happy to agree, provided that she could bring with her her two great friends and neighbours, Gregory and Ginèvre Napier.'

'Ginèvre Napier!' I exclaimed. 'And she lives in Paternoster Row? Then I know the lady. Or perhaps I should rather say that I met her once, some years ago, when I was enquiring into the disappearance of two children from their home in Devon. I came to London to speak to Mistress Napier, who had been a friend of the children's mother.'

'Well, well! Goodness me! Upon my soul! Upon my soul! Here's a coincidence!' Master Babcary exclaimed. 'If it is indeed the same person.'

'A lady,' I replied, selecting my words carefully so as not to give offence, 'past the first flush of youth, but determined to hold the ravages of time at bay.'

'That's her! That's her!' my host declared. He added, not bothering to pick and choose *his* words, 'A painted hussy I've always thought her, no better than she should be. And so I've often told Mistress Perle, for it troubles me that Barbara should make a companion of such a woman, although I believe the Napiers were very kind to her during Edgar Perle's last illness. But Barbara is unpersuadable in the matter, and continues to be close friends with the couple. It's the only subject on which we don't see eye to eye, so I suppose I can't complain. Man and wife will never agree on everything – if, that is, we ever become man and wife,' he finished gloomily.

'Tell me about the evening of the murder,' I invited.

'That's just what I've been trying to do for the last ten minutes,' he retorted indignantly, 'only you keep on interrupting me, Chapman.'

I said I was sorry, hoping that he would not detect the insincerity in my tone. 'Pray continue, sir.'

'Very well! Very well! Mistress Perle, Ginèvre and Gregory Napier were to share our supper with us, and the shop was shuttered and locked before they arrived. Being December, it was almost dark by four o'clock, and I felt that I should lose very little custom by closing an hour or so earlier than usual.

It was, in any case, very nearly time for the curfew bell.' He took a breath and then continued, 'The meal had been laid here, in this room, with the best napery and cutlery and the set of silver plates that I made for my poor wife when first we were married. The very *finest* silver, you understand, from the mines at Kuttenberg, which lie somewhere between Prague and the borders of Muscovy, or so I'm told. And, as on all festive occasions, each member of the family had his or her especial goblet.'

'Especial goblet?' I queried.

For answer, my companion got to his feet, went to the door and opened it. 'Isolda!' he shouted. 'Come here, if you please. I want you!'

There was a short delay, then I heard the patter of feet descending the second flight of stairs from the floor above. Isolda's voice asked, 'What's the matter, Father?'

'The key, girl! The key to the corner cupboard, let me have it.'

There was the chink of metal against metal as Isolda slipped the key from the ring attached to her girdle; then, having come back into the room and again shut the door, Miles proceeded to unlock the fretted panels of the corner cupboard, behind which could be seen the gleam of gold and silver. He stooped to one of the lower shelves and, when he stood upright once more, he was holding a crystal goblet with a silver foot and stem and a carved golden rim, very like the one from which I had drunk at Crosby Place. He carried it over to the fire and handed it to me.

'This is mine,' he said, resuming his seat. 'If you look carefully, you will see amongst the chasing around the lip my initials, M.B.'

Turning it slowly and reverently between my hands, watching as the flames from the fire struck myriad rainbow-hued sparks from the crystal bowl, while a hundred reflected lights burned deep in the heart of the golden rim, I saw amidst the carved bunches of grapes, gambolling nymphs and trailing swags of vine leaves the intertwined initials M and B, just as my host had claimed.

'I see them,' I said. 'Master Babcary, this is as beautiful a piece of craftsmanship as I have ever beheld.'

57

A faint flush of pleasure mantled his cheeks, although he must have been used to such praise, and from far greater connoisseurs of the goldsmith's art than I was.

'It's one of six,' he told me. 'And I hope that one day it will be one of seven.' He went on, by way of explanation, 'When I was first married, I embellished two goblets as a wedding gift for my wife; one with her initials carved into the rim, the other with mine. Then, when Isolda was born, I decorated another such goblet for her as a christening present. When my nephew and niece were orphaned and came to live with me, I did two more, and, finally, the following year, one for my son-in-law. Susannah's I have put away at the back of the cupboard and no one uses it now, but I am hoping to replace it soon with one bearing the initials B.B. For Barbara Babcary,' he added, in case I was in any doubt as to his meaning.

'And each member of the household uses his or her own goblet,' I murmured.

'Not every day! They are not for everyday use,' he reproved me. 'They are taken out only on special occasions.'

'And Mistress Perle's birthday was just such an occasion,' I suggested.

'Of course! The five goblets were set out on the table along with others that I keep for guests.'

'I understand. Pray continue,' I urged.

'After the shop was closed for the night, and all the merchandise removed from windows and locked away, we retired to our bedchambers to change into our Sunday clothes before the guests arrived; all, that is, except my daughter, who was still downstairs in the kitchen, helping Meg prepare the food. It . . . it was very unfortunate that this should have been so, but you've seen Meg Spendlove, Master Chapman, and can probably guess that she is not the most reliable of servants. But Isolda won't hear of turning her out, and says it's not important that Meg is simple because she – Isolda – prefers to keep an eye on everything herself.' He sighed. 'And that is true. My daughter is a most efficient housekeeper.'

'You say you all retired to your bedchambers. Where are these rooms situated, sir?'

My host bent down and threw another log on the fire. Some resin caught alight and flared up in a bright blue flame.

'My chamber is on this floor, next to the room we are now sitting in. Isolda's room – and Gideon's room as it also was then, of course – is on the next floor at the front of the house, immediately overhead, while my niece, Eleanor, sleeps in the bedchamber behind it, above mine. Finally, the two rooms on the third floor, beneath the eaves, are occupied by my nephew at the front and Tobias Maybury, my apprentice, in the little attic at the back. Meg has her own bed in a cupboard in the kitchen.'

'And do you know at what time Mistress Bonifant eventually came upstairs to change her gown?' I asked.

My companion's mouth suddenly shut like a trap and he began drumming with his fingers against the arms of his chair. He looked distressed and uncomfortable, and, to my mind, was silently debating whether or not to lie.

I leant forward. 'Master Babcary,' I pleaded, 'you must tell me the truth if you want my help in finding an answer to this mystery. Concealing what really happened won't benefit either you or your daughter, and falsehoods may result in my pointing the finger of suspicion at an innocent person. I feel sure you wouldn't want that.'

For a moment or two he made no answer, merely passing his tongue between his lips as if they needed moistening. At last, however, he said reluctantly, 'I heard Isolda come upstairs just as our guests knocked at the outer door. She must have come in here to check that all was well, because as I quit my room she left this one. We passed each other, she going towards the upper flight of stairs as I was going towards the lower.'

'Did she say anything?' I asked.

Again there was that hesitation while he once more considered the advisability of a good round lie. But he decided, sensibly, against it.

'Isolda told me that everything was ready, that the table was set and that she had poured wine into the goblets so that we could drink Mistress Perle's health as soon as we were all assembled. She said that there was only the food to bring up from the kitchen, and she would help Meg with that whenever we decided to sit down to eat, but she thought I might want to give Barbara her birthday present first.'

'Did you make any answer?'

Master Babcary lifted suspicious eyes to mine, patently uneasy that I had made no comment on the information I had just been given.

'I think I agreed with her, then went downstairs to the shop to let in our guests.'

'Did you meet anyone coming up?'

Master Babcary shook his head. 'No, I told you that with the exception of Isolda, everyone had already retired to his or her room to change into Sunday clothes.'

'Not everyone,' I pointed out. 'Meg Spendlove was still below.'

'Oh, Meg! Meg doesn't count, surely! What reason would she have to murder Gideon? Besides, as I said, her bed is in the kitchen. She'd have no reason to go upstairs until the food was called for.'

'In a case of murder,' I retorted, 'I've found it wise to discount no one. Meg might have had some cause to dislike your son-in-law, hate him even, that the rest of you know nothing about.'

My companion shrugged and got up to light the candles in a branched candlestick of latten tin that stood in the middle of the table. The January day was growing dark outside, with rain now drumming steadily against the window panes. 'Oh, as to that,' he replied, resuming his seat and drawing it a little closer to the fire, 'I can tell you that there was no love lost between them. Gideon was a man who put great store by good order and hard work. Now, Meg is hard-working enough, and more than willing to do her fair share of domestic chores if supervised and treated kindly, but she tends to be untidy and careless if left to her own devices. Her slatternly ways irritated my son-in-law, sometimes beyond endurance, and he could never understand Isolda's tolerance in the matter. There were disagreements between them on the subject. I won't call them quarrels, because Gideon was a difficult man to quarrel with, simply folding his lips and walking away when any one of us did something that angered him.'

'And had there been any unpleasantness between him and Meg in the days before the murder?' I asked.

My host frowned. 'I don't think so; nothing, at least, that I can recollect. But then, I have so many calls upon my time,' he added self-importantly, 'that I probably wouldn't remember. You must quiz the women about that sort of thing. Those events loom larger in their lives than they do in men's.'

'But was there any chance,' I persisted, 'that while you were welcoming your guests and letting them into the shop Meg could have crept upstairs and put poison in your son-in-law's wine? For I am assuming that that was what happened, that the monkshood was put into Gideon's cup as it stood, unattended, on this table.'

Master Babcary shivered and then nodded, his pomposity draining away as he contemplated the terrible climax of that December evening.

'I can't honestly say that I saw Meg during the time before Mistress Perle and I, together with Master and Mistress Napier, came up here to the parlour. But that doesn't mean,' he added musingly, 'that she couldn't have slipped upstairs and down again without anyone noticing, for we stood a few minutes in the shop exchanging greetings while they all took off their cloaks, and the two women removed their pattens.' He looked a little ashamed of this sudden about face, but I could well understand that he would rather the blame for the murder was laid at Meg Spendlove's door than at his daughter's.

'What happened next?' I asked. 'Who was here and who was absent when you and your guests entered this room?'

Miles screwed up his face in an effort of concentration. 'Gideon was here and Toby – Tobias Maybury, my apprentice – and . . .' he paused, willing himself to remember. 'And Nell and Christopher. Isolda made her entrance a few moments later. As I've told you, she had been the last one to go to her room to change.'

'So what happened next?' I prompted, as Miles seemed disinclined to proceed with his story.

He shivered and held his hands again to the flames. 'Next, I gave Mistress Perle her birthday gift. A jewelled girdle,' he went on unnecessarily, as though anxious to postpone reaching the awful moment of the murder as long as possible, 'of pale blue leather, studded alternately with Persian sapphires and Egyptian turquoises. She was delighted with it' – as well she might be, I thought – 'and I could see that Mistress Napier was very envious of her friend.' (A fact, I decided, that must have given the gift added value in the eyes of Barbara Perle.)

'And then,' I said, 'presumably you all drank Mistress Perle's health?' My companion nodded mutely. 'And that was when your son-in-law died?'

'Yes.' Miles's voice was so low that I had to strain my ears to catch the word.

'Can you remember exactly what happened?'

'I shall never forget it as long as I live.' He raised his eyes from contemplation of the fire, where a woodlouse was just escaping as fast as its legs could carry it from the terror of the flames, and looked directly into mine. 'I went to my accustomed place at the head of the board and raised my goblet. "To Mistress Perle," I said. "May she have long life and happiness."'

'I'm sorry, but I must interrupt you yet again,' I apologised. 'Do you always sit in the same order around the table?'

'We are creatures of habit,' he said, 'as, in my experience, are most families. Every household has its own little rituals, its simple jokes and allusions that mean nothing to outsiders.' Master Babcary was more astute than he looked. 'When we are on our own, I always sit at the head of the board, with Isolda at the foot. My nephew sits to my right, beside Tobias, and opposite him, to my left, his sister. When . . . when Gideon was alive, he sat on the same side of the board as Nell, between her and his wife. But that evening, with company present, Isolda had arranged the table so that she was on my right hand, and, alongside her, Gideon and then Nell. Mistress Perle was seated to my left, Gregory and Ginèvre Napier, in that order, to *her* left. Christopher was at the foot of the table. Toby, as on all occasions when we entertained, would take his meal with Meg, downstairs in the kitchen.'

'So it was Isolda who directed you where to sit?' I asked, and Miles Babcary reluctantly agreed. 'You said she also set the table, so would she have made sure that each of the family goblets was correctly placed?'

Once again, a muttered and reluctant assent was wrung from my host, and I felt that it was hardly surprising Mistress Bonifant had been suspected of her husband's murder. Indeed, the surprise was that, even with the power of the King being brought to bear on her behalf, she had never been charged with the crime. On the other hand, there was one vital question that I had not yet posed, and the answer to it might make a world of difference. I was not, however, ready to ask it for the moment.

'You all went to the table and took your places, after which you raised your goblets, already filled with wine by your daughter, and proposed the birthday toast to Mistress Perle. What then, sir?'

'What then? Why, we drank, of course.'

'Did Master Bonifant collapse at once?'

'Not immediately. We all sat down – we had been standing to drink Barbara's health, you understand – except Isolda, who left the room to go down to the kitchen. The rest of us began to talk: Master Napier and I about the new tariffs that the Poitevins have imposed on the exports of silver from Melle; and the women about such items of gossip as were current last December, whatever they may have been. Gideon was exchanging a few remarks with Christopher, which surprised me because they had been somewhat at loggerheads for the past few months, when suddenly he struggled to his feet, trying desperately to get his breath. Neither could he swallow; his throat and lips were stiff as boards and his face was turning blue. He tried to speak, but all that came out was a terrible croaking sound. I'll never forget it. It will haunt me until the day I die.' And Miles Babcary covered his eyes with his hands.

'What did you do?'

'What could any of us do? Mistress Perle was almost fainting in horror, and I had to give her the better part of my attention. It was Mistress Napier, I think, who told her husband to go for the apothecary who lives in Gudrun Lane. She has a cool head on her shoulders, I'll grant you that. Before he could leave the room, however, Isolda and Meg came in carrying the trays of food. It took them a moment or two to understand what was happening but, as soon as they did, Meg screamed and dropped her tray with an almighty crash, exactly as one would expect her to behave.'

'And Isolda,' I asked, 'what did she do?'

There was a silence of several seconds, then Miles said

slowly, 'She just stood there, as though turned to stone, while Gideon raised his hand and pointed a finger at her, his eyes filled with horror and absolute terror. Then he pitched headlong across the table. By the time the apothecary was fetched, he was dead.'

Seven

A log crackled, the flames leapt up the chimney and shadows were sent scurrying and curtseying across the tapestried walls. After a moment's silence, I cleared my throat and asked the question that had been gnawing away at the back of my mind for the past half an hour or more.

'Master Babcary, was there – *is* there – any good reason why your daughter should be suspected of murdering her husband? So far, you have painted the picture of a couple happily, or at least contentedly, married, even if that marriage was not a love match.'

'Who says it was not a love match?' My companion's bottom lip jutted dangerously.

'Are you claiming that it was?' I demanded, meeting his attack with counter-attack, a strategy that I have frequently used to good effect.

The lip was withdrawn, indicating defeat. 'Perhaps not,' he conceded. 'But they both liked each other well enough. It's true that Gideon drove a hard bargain; an equal partnership in the shop, although he knew nothing of goldsmithing, and senior status to Christopher, who had been learning the trade for a full year before Gideon's arrival in the house.' Resentment coloured Miles's tone and, as if suddenly aware of it, he made an effort to laugh off his son-in-law's presumption. 'Of course, there was nothing in that, when all's said and done! He was Isolda's husband, and would one day inherit the shop and everything in it in her name. It was only natural that he would have to learn what was what, and that he should expect to be more important to me than my nephew.'

Nevertheless, you did not like him the better for it, I thought to myself. Aloud, I asked, 'Was your daughter happy that matters should be thus arranged?'

'She wasn't consulted,' Miles replied simply. 'Her assured inheritance of all that is mine was a part of her dowry, along with the sum of money I settled on her and Gideon at the time of their wedding. These are men's concerns, not women's. She was sufficiently content to be married at last, after years of being a maid.' He tried to compose his features into an expression of acceptance for a situation that had plainly irked him. Miles had not cared for his son-in-law, I decided, however much he might have tried to persuade himself and the world otherwise.

'You haven't yet answered my question, sir,' I reminded him, as a further squall of rain spattered against the windows.

'Question? What question?' Brooding upon Gideon's short-comings, he had forgotten what it was that I had asked him.

'Was there any good reason why Mistress Bonifant should have been suspected of murdering her husband?'

Once again, the short-sighted, pale blue eyes looked into mine while their owner debated whether or not to tell me the truth.

'There was none on her part,' Miles answered at last. 'Isolda's affection for Gideon in the weeks and months leading up to the murder appeared to be what it had ever been, I'll swear to that. And so will everyone else in the house.' Or incur his undying displeasure was implicit in his tone, although the words remained unspoken.

'In that case, what can you tell me about Master Bonifant? Did you have any reason to believe that his affection for your daughter had altered in any way? Did he ever give you any hint that all might not be well between them?'

Rain pattered down the chimney and hissed among the burning logs like a plague of snakes. The silence stretched, thin as a tautly drawn wire, but at last Master Babcary shrugged resignedly.

'Gideon had told me some weeks, maybe a month or so, before the evening of his death that he suspected Isolda of cuckolding him with another man.'

I was betrayed into a gasp, hastily suppressed. 'And did he happen to mention this other man's name?' I asked.

'No, not directly, but he did tell me on a separate occasion that he had overheard Christopher boasting to his sister of being in love with an older woman, and that he – Christopher, that is – was almost certain that his love was requited.'

I thought about this. 'You were not the only person in whom Master Bonifant confided his doubts about your daughter and nephew, obviously.'

'Why do you say that?' Miles's tone was accusatory. 'Have you been talking to other people before you came here?'

I shook my head. 'Only to Mistress Shore, but you know about that. No, I'm judging by the fact that if you had been the sole recipient of Gideon's confidence, his accusation would not have become generally known. You would have said nothing that would in any way have incriminated your daughter, and certainly not once your son-in-law had been murdered.'

'Why should I? I had no idea if the slander were true or false,' was the indignant rejoinder. 'Would you expect me to repeat something detrimental about my own child for which I only had Gideon's word?'

'I'm not blaming you,' I said hurriedly. 'I have a daughter of my own, and whatever might be right in the eyes of God or the law, I know that I could never do anything that might harm her.'

'Not even if you thought she had committed some great sin?' Miles Babcary asked in a voice so low that I almost failed to hear him.

'No, not even then,' I admitted, 'for that's the nature of the tie between my child and me.' He nodded to show that he understood, and I continued, 'So who else did your son-in-law confide in?'

'In Gregory Napier, the last person in the world I should ever have wished to be privy to my family's affairs.' Miles spoke bitterly, and I could see that his hands had begun to tremble. 'There were also one or two others who came forward to say that Gideon had made them free of his suspicions. One was his former master, Ford, the apothecary, whose shop is in Bucklersbury.'

'And what was Mistress Bonifant's response to these accusations?'

'She just laughed at them. She said they were absurd and that we must be making them up. At first, she didn't seem to grasp how serious they were, especially after Gideon had been poisoned.'

'And when she did?'

'She was completely bewildered, poor girl. She couldn't begin to imagine why Gideon would have wanted to spread such lies about her, and demanded to know the identity of the man with whom she was supposed to have been unfaithful.'

'And when it emerged that it was her cousin, what did your nephew have to say?'

Master Babcary rubbed the side of his nose with his finger. 'Kit denied it furiously. He also denied that he had ever told his sister that he was in love with an older woman, and that the woman might be in love with him. Nell, of course, upheld his story.'

'Of course! But did you believe her?'

Master Babcary pursed his lips. 'Ye-es,' he said, but with a lack of conviction that made me raise my eyebrows. Reluctantly he confessed, 'Nell has led a very sheltered life, first with her father, then with me. She is inclined to get flustered when she is hostilely questioned, or feels herself under threat in any way.' He stared long and hard into the burning heart of the fire. 'Sometimes, she sounds as though she's lying when she isn't. There are people like that, you know,' he added eagerly. 'She's very shy.'

I agreed that there were indeed people in whom the mildest interrogation aroused the strongest sensation of guilt, even when they were entirely innocent of any wrongdoing. Eleanor Babcary could well be one of them, but it was also possible that, on this particular occasion, she might *not* have been telling the truth in order to protect her brother. I suspected from his general demeanour that her uncle had thought her denial less than ingenuous. But when I suggested this possibility to him, Miles sprang hotly to her defence.

'I'll swear that she wasn't lying. You don't know that girl as I do, Master Chapman. She is as open and as honest as the day. She abhors untruths, I tell you. She simply gets confused, as I have already explained, when faced with a barrage of questions.'

'And who questioned her?'

'One of the Sheriff's officers, naturally, for of course we

68

were obliged to send for the Law as soon as we realised that my son-in-law had been poisoned. The officer wasn't as gentle with Nell as he might have been, and consequently her attitude persuaded him that she was lying.'

'But she stuck to her story?'

'Oh, yes! That, more than anything, convinced me that she must be telling the truth.'

I refrained from pointing out that if Eleanor Babcary abhorred untruths, as her uncle had just maintained, he would have needed no convincing: he would have known for a fact that his niece was not lying. Moreover, I believe that the person has not been born who is totally incapable of telling a falsehood. Surely, if for no other reason, we all instinctively make the effort to protect those whom we love.

The door opened and Mistress Bonifant's voice sounded calmly through the gloom, unperturbed by the fact that she knew we must have been talking about her.

'It's nearly four o'clock, Father. Will Master Chapman be staying to supper?'

'I – er – I have no idea, my dear.' He turned to me. 'Master Chapman, would you care to share our evening meal with us? You would be very welcome.'

'I was unaware that the day was so far advanced,' I said, getting to my feet. 'Thank you for your offer, Mistress Bonifant, but I must go back to the Voyager and take supper with my wife. This visit to London was to have been a holiday for both of us, and I cannot neglect her any further this evening. Tomorrow being Sunday, I shan't disturb your Sabbath peace, but, with your permission, Master Babcary, I'll return on Monday and question the other members of your household.'

'If you think you can solve the riddle of my son-in-law's death, we shall be glad to see you,' he answered heavily. He glanced somewhat shamefacedly at his daughter, where she still stood framed in the open doorway. 'I'm sorry, my dear, but I've had to tell Master Chapman everything.'

'If by that you mean that Gideon seems to have gone around accusing me of adultery,' Isolda replied evenly, 'it's only what I should have expected you to do, Father. There's no need to apologise. Thanks to the testimony of Gregory Napier and

Master Ford, the apothecary, everyone in Cheapside has heard about it.'

I half expected her to plunge into a hot denial of her late husband's allegation, but she did no such thing, and I began to realise that heat and Isolda Bonifant were strangers to one another. She was a woman of even greater self-control and self-containment than my Adela but, then, according to Master Babcary, Gideon had been of a similar temperament, and they seemed to have been eminently well suited to one another. It was possible, however, that one of them had been acting a part.

I took my leave of Mistress Bonifant and was conducted downstairs again by my host. As we turned towards the inner shop door, Meg Spendlove emerged, and at the sight of me, she shied like a startled horse. The tin tray she was carrying by her side clattered against the wall, and her thin, white face puckered as though she were about to burst into tears.

'There, there, my good child,' Miles Babcary said soothingly, 'that will do. There's no need to be frightened. No one's going to hurt you. Have you taken Master Kit and young Toby their ale? That's all right, then. Off you go to the kitchen before something boils over and puts out the fire.' He added, so that only I could hear, 'Not an infrequent occurrence, I do assure you, Master Chapman.'

Christopher Babcary and Tobias Maybury were still at their work, the interior of the shop lit now by lamps and candles, the flames reflected a hundred times over in the depths of the various gold and silver objects and precious gems. Many more of the sparkling golden medallions had been made, ready to be bought and sewn on the silk and velvet gowns of London's wealthiest ladies, so that they could ripple with light whenever they moved. No doubt, I thought bitterly, there was some sumptuary law that restricted the medallions' use to noblewomen only, but then I had to smile as I considered that probably no such law was necessary. For what good would these fragile, wafer-thin golden discs be to women who wore homespun and coarse, thickly woven linen?

Master Babcary was looking around in obvious satisfaction, his troubles momentarily forgotten. He was a man who plainly loved his trade, and who was never happier than when he was in his workshop. He would have had little time, then, for a man like Gideon Bonifant, who seemed to have regarded the art of goldsmithing merely as a means of making money. And as if to confirm that impression, Miles had taken my arm and was drawing me towards a small table where a coronet of entwined gold and silver ivy leaves was taking shape.

'For my kinswoman, Mistress Shore,' he said, picking it up and holding it lovingly between both hands, 'to be worn next week at the Westminster Tournament, in honour of the new little bride and bridegroom. It is to be set with these Scottish pearls and Egyptian emeralds.' He sighed wistfully. 'I would have designed a grander circlet if only she would have permitted it. But Jane gave strict instructions that I should make nothing for her that would in any way outshine the jewels to be worn by the Queen or any of Her Highness's sisters.'

He replaced the coronet on the table and linked one of his arms through mine, giving it a little squeeze, well away by now on what was obviously his favourite hobby horse. 'One of the finest examples of the goldsmith's art that I have ever had the privilege of seeing was the wedding coronet of our own Princess Margaret, when she married the Duke of Burgundy ten years ago this summer. Alas, I had no hand in the fashioning of it – I only wish that I had – but it was put on display with other items of her dowry, including all her jewellery, in the Goldsmiths' Hall in the weeks before her wedding. It was small and was meant to perch on the top of her head to show off that beautiful long, fair hair of hers. It was made of gold and decorated with enamelled white roses, rubies, emeralds and sapphires. In the front was a diamond cross and a huge pearl set in another white rose; and all along the lower edge, "C"s and "M"s were wrought in gold and linked by lovers' knots. Oh, it was a splendid piece of work, Master Chapman, I can tell you! It made me proud of my calling and of my fellow goldsmiths who had made it.'

I encountered Christopher Babcary's amused glance, and he winked at me.

'I think the chapman wants to be off, Uncle. It's wet and dark outside. He's wanting the comforts of the Voyager, I reckon.'

'Of course! Of course! My boy, you should have said. But beauty delights me.'

71

He led me towards the street door and the display booth, where the glitter of precious metal still enlivened the darkness. Soon everything would be taken inside and safely locked away for the night but, for the moment, the windows of the goldsmiths' shops in West Cheap continued to sparkle like so many heavenly constellations.

As I was about to escape into the murk of the January evening, Master Babcary grabbed my arm and detained me yet again.

'My father, you know,' he said, his eyes glowing with excitement, 'saw the crown brought to this country by King Richard's first queen, Anne of Bohemia, at the end of the last century. He told me that it was the most exquisite thing he had ever laid eyes on in the whole of his life. He said it was six inches tall at its highest point, straight-sided and set with the most glorious array of jewels: scores of diamonds, rubies and sapphires and more than a hundred pearls.' Master Babcary's transports suddenly died away in a heavy sigh. The light left his eyes and his shoulders sagged. 'It's gone from these shores now, alas! It was given away by the usurper, Henry of Bolingbroke, as a part of his daughter's dowry when he married her to Ludwig of Bavaria.'

'Uncle!' Christopher Babcary had come to stand beside us and slipped an affectionate arm around the older man's shoulders. 'Master Chapman needs to be off, and we have to start packing up for the night. Besides, it's suppertime and I'm ravenous. My stomach is positively rumbling with all those delicious cooking smells wafting in from the kitchen.'

My host was contrite. 'You must forgive me, lad. My family have heard all my tales so often that they derive no pleasure from hearing them any more, so a stranger is a godsend to me. Well, well! We shall see you again on Monday then.' He shook my hand vigorously and swung round on his heel, immediately berating the unfortunate apprentice for some sin of omission or commission, I wasn't sure which.

Christopher Babcary grinned as he opened the outer door. 'You musn't mind Uncle Miles,' he apologised quietly. 'His enthusiasm for his work can become a little wearisome after a while, and you have to ask him – politely, of course, but firmly – not to repeat all the anecdotes that you've heard a hundred times before. But don't you worry! I'll make sure he doesn't bore you too much while you're here.'

I thanked him, but assured him that I really didn't mind. 'How did his son-in-law take Master Babcary's stories?'

Christopher's face lost its animation. 'Gideon was never one to wrap things up in clean linen. He would tell my uncle bluntly to hold his noise; that he had no interest in what he was saying. Indeed, Gideon made no secret of the fact that he found goldsmithing itself extremely irksome. He once told Uncle Miles to his face that he would sell the shop as soon as he was master here.'

I nodded. I should have liked to continue the conversation, but instinct told me that it was not the right time. Christopher wanted to be away to his supper, and I needed to go back to the inn to find out how Adela was faring. I therefore bade him goodnight and stepped out into the wind and the rain.

Both had increased in intensity during the last few minutes, and there was also a hint of sleet in the air. The cobbles gleamed wetly between the piles of refuse that had mounted up everywhere during the day, and their surface was treacherous and slippery. I trod warily, using my cudgel as a walking stick rather than holding it at the ready as a weapon. A sudden, particularly fierce gust of wind almost tore my cloak from my back, and I clutched at it with my free hand, holding the edges together at the neck as best I could, but unable to pull up my hood, which now lay, a soggy weight, across my shoulders. I silently cursed Master Babcary for delaying me, but reflected yet again on how much he and Gideon Bonifant must secretly have disliked one another. To be compelled to live and work together, day in, day out, under the same roof, and, at the same time, be forced to present a complaisant face to the world for Isolda's sake, must have been purgatory for both of them. Had it eventually been enough of a spur to drive Miles Babcary to murder?

I was too tired and too preoccupied with the elements to give the idea further consideration just then, and I pushed on along West Cheap in the direction of the Poultry. The rising storm had driven most people to seek either permanent or temporary shelter indoors, and there were only two or three other intrepid walkers like myself still battling against the squalls of wind

73

and rain. Many of the wall cressets had been doused or blown out, but shafts of light from shops and houses slabbed the darkness.

I was approaching the entrance to Gudrun Lane, a gaping mouth of blackness on my left, illuminated solely by a lamp hanging high over the doorway of a stable. As I pressed forward, my head bent against the ever increasing force of the wind, I was suddenly convinced that, out of the corner of my left eye, I had seen a movement – someone or something had retreated into the alleyway. Common sense told me that there was little significance to be attached to this fact: a man, a child, a dog, a cat was taking cover from the storm. But I discovered that for no apparent reason I was nervous. Fear slithered across the surface of my skin.

I had suddenly recollected that halfway along its length, Gudrun Lane was connected, by a little street running at right angles to it, to Foster Lane. And Foster Lane, at its southern end, joined West Cheap by the church of Saint Vedast and Master Babcary's shop. I also remembered something else that I had lost sight of during the last two or three hours, whilst making the acquaintance of Miles Babcary's family and servants: a member of that household could well be a murderer who would be terrified that I might discover the truth about him or her. Had someone left the house as soon as I had taken my own departure, hurrying by that circuitous route to waylay me at the entrance to Gudrun Lane?

I spun round, my cudgel gripped firmly in my right hand and raised to do whatever combat was necessary. My heart began beating faster as I entered that black void of the lane, lit by its solitary beam of light from overhead.

Eight

K eeping close to a row of three-storeyed houses that made up the left-hand wall of Gudrun Lane, I crept forward, my cudgel at the ready, my feet squelching through puddles and piles of garbage. Once, a thin cat, disturbed from its scavenging by my approach, shot across my path with a screech of fury, making me start back and almost knocking me off balance, my heart pounding so hard that I was scarcely able to breathe. Another time, a dog, as wet and bedraggled as I must have looked myself, came sniffing and snapping around my ankles, until I kicked it away with a curse. But apart from these two incidents, nothing broke the silence except for the drumming of the rain and the gusting of the wind.

I was beginning to doubt the existence of this alley that connected Gudrun and Foster Lane – how did I know about it, anyway? I must, at sometime or another, have been this way with Philip Lamprey during one of our forays into the city – when suddenly, there it was, to my left, as narrow and as noisome as memory had painted it. I hesitated for a long moment before turning the corner, every muscle tensed in readiness for a sudden assault upon my person. But nothing happened. No one was lying in wait for me, and the wet cobbles stretched away into the darkness, lit by the pallid gleam of a torch fixed to the wall of one of the cottages and set in a sheltered nook, out of reach of the wind. The piles of rubbish were even higher here than in West Cheap, and I had to step with extreme caution so as not to lose my footing.

Beyond the range of the torchlight, I paused again, convinced that I had heard a noise some little way ahead of me: a cough, perhaps, or a sharp intake of breath.

'Who's there?' I called, but there was no reply. Seconds

later, a huge rat scuttled close to one of my boots and disappeared into another mound of offal and rotting vegetables a few yards behind me.

Three or four more paces brought me into Foster Lane. I turned left towards the looming bulk of Saint Vedast, and within moments was back in West Cheap, standing outside Master Babcary's shop. I could hear voices from within raised in cheerful conversation, and the sudden peal of a woman's laughter, but the shutters were up and there was nothing, no movement of any kind, to suggest that anyone was lurking in the surrounding shadows. Either whoever had come after me, with the intention of warning me off, had then thought better of it, or I had been a victim of my own overheated imagination. I was reluctant, however, to admit that it might be the latter.

The storm had abated somewhat, and I was gripped by a burning desire for the warmth and safety of the Voyager – its ale, its excellent food and the company of my wife. Moving as far into the centre of the thoroughfare as I dared without danger of stumbling into the open drain, I strode out as fast as I could, looking straight ahead of me and ignoring as much as possible all the black, gaping mouths of the streets and alleyways on either side of the road. Ten minutes later, I reached the Great Conduit and the entrance to Bucklersbury.

'You've had a long day,' Adela observed.

She was curled up on the bed, watching me devour a huge, steaming hot meat pie, together with a bowl of dried peas and onions. Both dishes had been served, on the orders of Reynold Makepeace himself, in the warmth and comfort of our room. My wife, who had eaten her supper before my arrival, assured me that she was feeling a great deal better, and insisted that we talk about the rigours of *my* day – although I fancied that there was an unusual touch of acerbity in her tone.

'As a matter of fact, I have had a very tiring few hours,' I answered defensively. 'First, if you remember, I had to visit Mistress Shore at her house in the Strand—'

Adela, who had indeed forgotten this fact, immediately interrupted. 'Tell me all about it!' she commanded.

And I was allowed to go no further with the account of my doings until I had described my meeting with the King's mistress in the the minutest detail. Adela was particularly taken with my description of the old dog on his red satin cushion, and at once pronounced Mistress Shore to be a woman very much after her own heart.

'Jeanne Lamprey tells me that she's popular both with the common people and at court.' Adela tilted her head to one side. 'So why doesn't the Duke of Gloucester care for her, do you suppose?'

I stared consideringly at my plate. It was a question that had been nagging away at the back of my own mind ever since my meeting with the King's mistress and the realisation that she was, in truth, as kind and as merry and as unassuming as her reputation made her out to be. Why then did the man I admired – worshipped, almost – above all others obviously have so little liking for her?

'I think,' I said at last, raising my eyes to my wife's, 'that Duke Richard regards Mistress Shore in the same light as he regards members of the Queen's family, the Queen herself, Lord Hastings and so many others who surround the King. He sees them all as responsible in their various ways for his brother's physical and moral decline. Oh, Edward's handsome enough even now, I grant you, but seven years ago, around the time of the battle at Tewkesbury, he was magnificent; lean as a greyhound, strong as an ox and with a mind sharp enough to outwit all those powerful barons who had robbed him of his throne and driven him into exile.

'But now, while he'll never be fat on account of his great height, he's growing corpulent, he has a double chin, he's a pensioner of King Louis of France – a fact of which the Duke of Gloucester bitterly disapproves – and, if the gossips are to be believed, he devotes more time to pleasure than the Council Chamber. And to top everything else, he seems, finally, to have turned against his brother, George of Clarence.'

'Your Duke sounds to me a rather puritanical young man,' Adela observed dryly, wriggling into a more upright position on the bed, her back supported by the banked up pillows. 'Almost a prig, but not above overlooking Mistress Shore's faults – real or imagined – when he needs to make use of her and of her influence with the King.'

I resented any criticism, however oblique, of the Duke of Gloucester.

'He's trying to save his other brother's life,' I protested vigorously. 'Surely a compromise with his conscience is justified under such circumstances.'

'It depends what the Duke of Clarence has done to turn the King so irrevocably against him at last.' Adela gave her sudden, disarming smile. 'But don't let's quarrel when I haven't seen you all day, and when I'm unlikely to see much of you for as long as it takes you to resolve this mystery. What happened at the goldsmith's? Do you have any idea as yet whether or not the daughter really committed the crime?' She patted her stomach. 'Tell your son and me all about it.'

'It might be another daughter,' I said, somewhat rattled by her insistence that the child she was carrying was a boy. 'What I want is a girl who looks like you.'

'It's a boy,' was the confident answer. 'And Margaret agrees with me.'

'I don't see how you can possibly be so sure,' I retorted, and was rewarded with what I called her 'knowing' expression – a slight smile of contempt for my male ignorance, accompanied by a look of pity. A shake of her head implied that it would be fruitless to continue a discussion in which I was so plainly at a disadvantage.

As I had come to realise over the years that all pregnant women, however rational in other ways, adopt this omniscient attitude towards the mysteries of childbirth, especially when addressing a man, I let the subject drop and launched into a recital of everything that had happened at Master Babcary's shop.

'So you see,' I said when I had finished, 'there are still many enquiries to make before I can offer an opinion as to Mistress Bonifant's guilt or innocence. To begin with, apart from the family and servants, there were three other people present in the house on the night of Gideon's death – three neighbours to whom I have not even spoken as yet.'

Adela reached over and took the bowl containing the remains of the dried peas and onions from the tray on my knees, and began scooping the vegetables into her mouth with the wooden spoon provided.

'I can't help it,' she laughed, noting my raised eyebrows, 'I'm hungry all the time. The trouble is that, although I know peas and onions will probably give me a violent colic later, I can't resist eating them. But go on. What do you make of the story that Gideon Bonifant was spreading just before his death? The story that Isolda was unfaithful to him with her cousin, this – this—'

'Christopher Babcary,' I supplied. I propped my chin on my hands and stared into the heart of the small sea-coal fire where the flames burnt blue and yellow, and for whose warmth and light and comfort we had agreed to pay the landlord a small extra daily charge. 'Why would a man spread such a story if it weren't true, particularly as he and his wife seem to have spent five reasonably contented years together?'

Adela put the now empty bowl back on the tray and shifted her position in order to make herself more comfortable.

'On the other hand,' she said after a moment or two, 'even if we accept that the story is true – and, as you say, a man doesn't claim to have been made a cuckold without good reason – infidelity doesn't necessarily turn a woman into a murderess.' She chewed her bottom lip thoughtfully. 'You say that both Isolda and her cousin deny the charge that Gideon levelled against them?'

'Yes, but they have to, don't they, unless they wish to brand themselves poisoners in the eyes of the world? They'd be fools to admit it.'

'But if Mistress Bonifant *did* kill her husband, how did she hope to get away with it if he had already told people about her infatuation with Christopher Babcary?'

'Because she had no idea that he'd done so. Her father confirms that he never mentioned Gideon's accusations to Isolda. And the other people in whom her husband confided – his old master, the apothecary, and Master Napier – were hardly likely to have confronted her with the story.'

Adela rubbed her stomach and grimaced. 'That's true,' she

agreed. 'But what about this cousin? Was he never suspected of being the murderer?'

'He might have been, I suppose, in due course. But Mistress Shore seems to have implored the King for his intervention too rapidly for the Sheriff's officers to have levelled accusations at anyone, or for any kind of investigation to have got under way. King Edward, not wishing, I imagine, for his chief leman to be implicated, even by association, in anything so sordid as murder, halted all enquiries immediately. But it's not so easy, of course, to stop the whispering of neighbours and erstwhile friends, as it is to give orders to officials. And so here I am, once more embroiled in what, in a very roundabout way, has become the Duke of Gloucester's concern.'

Or God's, I added silently. For it wasn't Duke Richard who had brought me to London at this particular time. It was the Almighty yet again, manipulating my thoughts and desires; or, at least, if not mine, then Adela's. But I was learning at last not to feel resentful – well, not too resentful – for I had come to appreciate that I might find my day-to-day existence very humdrum without these adventures of mine.

I emerged from my brief reverie to realise that Adela was speaking, echoing something of my own uneasiness.

'. . . but you mustn't lose sight of the fact, Roger, that *somebody* committed that murder, whether it was Isolda Bonifant or no. And whoever it is, is probably very frightened by your investigation and the possibility that you might discover the truth.'

'Only "might"?' I protested, quizzing her and laughing at her discomfiture. 'No, no! You're quite right, my love! It would never do for a wife to be too confident of her husband's abilities, or she would cease to have the whip hand.' Then, seeing that my teasing was genuinely distressing her, I plunged, without thinking, into an account of what had occurred on my way back to the inn.

But this, of course, only served to worry her even further, as I ought to have known it would.

'Do you really believe that you were being followed?' she demanded anxiously.

I shook my head. 'I honestly don't know. I could find no evidence of it, and yet—'

'And yet?' she queried, her voice trembling a little.

'And yet, at the time, I was certain that I had heard or seen something suspicious. And when I remembered that connecting alleyway between Foster and Gudrun Lane, I was conscious that anyone from the Babcary household could have caught up with me without following me directly from the shop. But I might have been mistaken. There are sufficient cats and rats foraging among the rubbish to account for any number of apparently mysterious movements and noises. I mustn't let my imagination run away with me.'

But my wife remained unconvinced. Once it had dawned on her that a murderer was still at large, and that I might pose a danger to him or her, she was unable to be easy in her mind. I could see her wrestling with the urge to demand that I disoblige the Duke of Gloucester and give up my enquiry into the killing of Gideon Bonifant. But Adela was also wise enough to know that even if she prevailed this once, she was unlikely to do so the next time – or the next.

So she contented herself with giving me a wintry smile and saying, 'Take care! You already have three, and will soon have four, people dependent on you for their daily bread. None of us can afford to lose you.'

I rose to my feet, stretching and yawning. 'It's nice to know that I'm appreciated as a breadwinner, if nothing else,' I grinned.

I was rewarded with a look of deep hostility. 'You know perfectly well what I mean.'

'Of course I do.' I sat down on the edge of the bed and put my arms around her.

'What will you do tomorrow?' she asked, slewing round to kiss my cheek. 'You said you've promised the Babcarys that you won't disturb their Sabbath peace.'

'Neither shall I.' I returned her kiss. 'But I've a fancy to see this Master Ford, the apothecary who was Gideon Bonifant's former master. Undoubtedly, he will go to church. But which one does he favour, I wonder.'

There were at least four churches of importance in the area, any one of which Master Ford might attend, although none in Bucklersbury itself.

In adjoining Needlers Lane stood the churches of Saint Pancras and of Saint Benet Sherehog. Walbrook, at the eastern end of Bucklersbury, boasted Saint Stephen Walbrook, while Saint Mary Woolchurch served the inhabitants of the Stock's Market and the Poultry.

'Where does Master Ford, the apothecary, worship of a Sunday?' I asked Reynold Makepeace after breakfast the following morning.

He scratched his nose while giving the matter his full consideration.

'Now there you have me, Master Chapman, for I don't know, I'm sure. Wait here a moment and I'll enquire in the taproom. Someone there might be able to help you.'

He returned a few minutes later, however, shaking his grizzled head.

'I'm afraid no one seems to know for certain, although Peter Paulet, who lives in Soper Lane, thinks he remembers that the late Mistress Ford used sometimes to worship at Saint Mary Woolchurch.'

I thanked him for his trouble and enquired about the exact location of Master Ford's shop.

'Now that I can tell you,' my host said with satisfaction, wiping his hands on his best Sunday linen apron. 'You'll find it on this side of the street, at the Walbrook end, almost directly opposite a large stone-built house on the southern side, called the Old Barge. A strange name for a house, you might think, but ships used to tie up there before that part of the Walbrook was paved over. But Master Ford's shop won't be open today, if, that is, you're needing any remedies from him.' The kindly face clouded with anxiety. 'It's not Mistress Chapman, is it? If there's anything wrong, you must let me send for the local midwife. She'll be by far the best person to advise you.'

'No, no! My wife is in excellent health,' I assured him, which was true except for a somewhat disturbed night, the result of Adela's craving for dried peas and onions. 'I just wanted a word with Master Ford about – about something,' I finished lamely.

Fortunately, Reynold Makepeace was not a curious man, and made no attempt to discover why I had this sudden urge to speak to one of the Bucklersbury apothecaries, or, indeed, how I even came to be aware of his existence. He simply nodded and hurried away to attend to his customers in the taproom, one or two of whom were vociferously demanding his services.

Quarter of an hour later, my wife and I left the inn, walking eastwards towards Walbrook. The storm of the previous evening had, thankfully, blown itself out, giving way to a cold, but not frosty, morning, and a thin sun struggled to break through the leaden clouds. Adela, wrapped in her thick woollen cloak with its fur-lined hood, a garment purchased especially for this visit to London, assured me that she was as warm as it was possible to be in January, while her pattens kept her feet out of the mud and rubbish. (For being Sunday and a day of rest, there were no street cleaners to remove yesterday's accumulated filth. Cleanliness and godliness, alas, do not always go hand in hand.)

The clamour from the bells was deafening, for London, or so I'm told, has well over a hundred churches within its walls, not to mention those proliferating outside its pale. Adela had to raise her voice to make herself heard.

'Why do you wish to speak with this Master Ford?'

'If Gideon Bonifant was once his assistant, he must know something about the man. Anything he can tell me might prove useful. Wait!' I paused, gripping her arm and pointing to the opposite side of the street where Bucklersbury ran into Walbrook. 'That big house must be the one that Landlord Makepeace mentioned. And Master Ford's shop, he said, is almost directly opposite.'

This information, however, was not as valuable as it at first seemed, for the frontage of the Old Barge was the width of at least four or five shops on the northern side of the street, three of them belonging to apothecaries. But even as we watched, people began leaving home for church in answer to the bells' summons. A family of six – father, mother and four children – emerged from one of the apothcaries' shops, setting off westwards, in the direction of Needlers Lane, while from another, a middle-aged couple headed for Saint

Stephen Walbrook. Minutes later, a tall, thin man appeared in the remaining apothecary's doorway, turned smartly to his left and had vanished round the corner into Walbrook before I had time to gather my wits together.

'That must be him,' Adela hissed, nudging me painfully in the ribs. 'Reynold Makepeace told us, if you remember, that Master Ford is a widower, and both of the other two men had wives.'

'I think you're probably right,' I nodded. 'And that's the way to the Stock's Market and Saint Mary Woolchurch, where, again according to Master Makepeace, the late Mistress Ford sometimes worshipped.'

'Then what are we waiting for?' my wife demanded, slipping her hand once more within my arm. 'In that case, that's where *we* shall worship.'

'And we'll probably have the added pleasure of seeing Jeanne and Philip as well,' I said.

For I had recollected that Saint Mary Woolchurch was also adjacent to the old clothes market, and consequently was the church most often attended by the Lampreys. (Although they did occasionally honour Saint Benet Fink, on the corner of Fink's Lane, with their presence.)

Adela's step quickened at the prospect of a possible meeting with our friends, even though she expressed doubt about finding them very easily amongst the attendant congregation. But in this she was wrong, for almost the first people we encountered in the crowded nave, standing at the back near one of the pillars, were Jeanne and Philip Lamprey, both of whom greeted us as if they had not seen us for a month, instead of only the previous day.

Once the Mass had started, and I could whisper in Philip's ear without being overheard by all around us, I asked him if he knew Master Ford, the apothecary. Philip nodded.

'Is he here?'

My friend craned his neck and stretched up on his toes in an effort to see over the heads of all those in front of him. Finally, he gave a grunt of triumph.

'I can just see the top of his hat. It's the one he wears every Sunday. I recognise the feather coiled around the brim. Why do you want to know?'

I countered with a another question of my own.

'Are you well enough acquainted with Master Ford to introduce me to him when the service is over?'

Philip rolled suspicious eyes towards me. 'Not really, but that needn't stop me. However, that's all I'm doing. I've already told you once, Roger, you're not involving me in any of your schemes. They're usually far too dangerous.'

Nine

M aster Ford seemed a little disconcerted to be claimed as an acquaintance by Philip Lamprey for, as Philip bluntly informed him, he had not been in Master Ford's shop above twice in his life, those being the only two occasions on which he had previously spoken to the apothecary.

'But I've often seen you among the congregation here, and Mistress Ford, also, when she was alive.' My friend's tone was hearty as he pumped the other man's hand up and down. Philip was doing his best for me, even if he did not wish to get involved.

Jeanne went one better. Put in the picture by my wife, she bewildered Master Ford still further by inviting him to take his dinner with us at the Voyager, where, in a whispered conversation during the service, I had invited the Lampreys to eat with Adela and myself. Quick to follow this lead, I added my entreaties to hers, but decided to be honest with the apothecary and give him a chance to decline should he wish to do so.

'Hmmph,' he grunted when I had finished a somewhat halting explanation. 'I wondered how long Mistress Shore and her kinsfolk would be content to let the matter of poor Gideon's murder rest, before trying to find out the truth.' We began to move slowly towards the church porch, impelled forward by the crowd of people surrounding us. 'It's all very well the King bringing pressure to bear on the Sheriff's officers to proceed no further with their enquiries but, in the end, it's always unsatisfactory not knowing what really happened.' The nostrils of his long, thin nose, set in the middle of his long, thin face, flared in disapproval.

We emerged into the Stock's Market to discover that the day had grown brighter, the sun forcing its way through a break in the leaden clouds and diffusing sufficient warmth to dry the slimy cobbles.

I turned once again to my new acquaintance. 'What's your answer, then, Master Ford? Will you give us the pleasure of your company at dinner?'

He hesitated, but only for a second: Reynold Makepeace had a well-deserved reputation for serving some of the best food for streets around.

'Thank you,' he said in his courteous, rather stately fashion. 'I should be pleased to accept your kind invitation.'

His tone was still a little wary, but who could be surprised at that? To be accosted by two complete strangers and two known to him only by sight, and, in addition, be pressed into dining with them, must have been a bewildering experience. But I suspected that dinner at the Voyager, even with four unknowns, was preferable to his own lonely table. Besides, it turned out that he was well acquainted with Reynold Makepeace, and the pair of them greeted each other with the easy familiarity of old friends.

By the time we had walked the length of Bucklersbury, it was past ten o'clock, and the long trestles and benches of the Voyager's dining parlour were already filling up. In deference, however, to the fact that Adela and I were guests at the inn, and that I was known to have some connection with His Grace of Gloucester, the landlord ushered the five of us into a private room overlooking the main courtyard, and saw to it that we received the best and promptest of attention. (The look he gave Philip was a puzzled one, unable, probably, to reconcile this pock-marked, unsavoury-looking individual with my more noble connections.)

We ate boiled beef with buttered vegetables, a curd tart accompanied by a dish of raisins steeped in brandy, and a sweet cheese flan, all washed down with the Voyager's best home-brewed ale. It was a dinner to remember, as, indeed, I have remembered it down through the years with pleasure and nostalgia. (Food today isn't what it was. There's no flavour to anything any more, although my children – quite wrongly, it goes without saying – attribute this fact more to my age and loss of taste than to the inferior quality of the viands.)

During the course of the meal, I was able to talk to Master

Ford, who was seated next to me, about Gideon Bonifant and the murder.

'Gideon was my assistant for only a year before he married Isolda Babcary and went to work for his father-in-law,' the apothecary said, between mouthfuls of boiled beef and buttered vegetables. 'The marriage was a great stroke of good fortune for him, and raised his prospects beyond anything he could otherwise have hoped for. Indeed, until Mistress Babcary took a fancy to him, Gideon had no prospects that I could see, and seemed destined to remain my assistant for the rest of his life. After all, it seemed highly unlikely that anyone in the local community of Isolda's standing and expectations would ever glance in his direction.'

'On the other hand,' I interrupted, 'is it not true that Isolda Babcary had met with no success in finding a husband before she met Gideon Bonifant? I've met the lady, and while I should be reluctant to describe her as ugly, she is certainly no beauty. Moreover, as her father was at pains to inform me, she is of a very independent disposition. And the combination of lack of good looks and strong-mindedness seems to have deterred the other men of her acquaintance from proposing matrimony, even though, or so I imagine, she was possessed of a substantial dowry.'

Master Ford, with great dignity, wiped a dribble of gravy from his chin and ladled another helping of boiled beef and vegetables on to his plate. He then turned his head slowly in my direction, staring reproachfully down that long, patrician nose of his.

'Are you suggesting that Gideon was prepared to overlook these defects in Isolda Babcary in order to avail himself of her fortune?' he demanded.

'Well, he wouldn't be the first man to have done so,' Philip cut in, waving his knife and spoon excitedly in the air and saving me the trouble of replying. 'There's many a poor man who's improved his lot by marrying for money. And no shame to him for doing so, either! It isn't something I'd be happy to contemplate, but the poor must look out for themselves in any way they can. That's my motto!'

'I daresay!' The apothecary's expression grew even more disapproving. 'But Gideon Bonifant was a very pious, very

God-fearing man who told his rosary several times a day and always said his prayers before going to sleep at nights. He was not the sort of person to put financial considerations above all others.'

Philip grimaced. 'Sounds like a bit of a dullard to me,' he sniggered.

He was seated opposite me, next to his wife, and I kicked out with my foot in an effort to restrain him. Unfortunately, from the spasm of pain that contorted Jeanne's features, I realised that I had missed my target. Turning back to Master Ford, I hastily changed the subject.

'You say that Master Bonifant had worked as your assistant for only a year before he married Isolda Babcary, yet I recall Mistress Shore telling me that he was ten years older than her kinswoman at the time of the wedding. And Isolda herself was twenty . . . ?'

'Twenty-four.' Master Ford nodded. 'Yes, you are quite correct. Gideon had turned thirty-four when they married. So you see,' he added, directing a censorious glance at Philip, 'he was not a youth to have his head turned by the prospect of wealth and social betterment. He did not marry Isolda Babcary for her money.'

Philip snorted and opened his mouth, doubtless to say what I felt inclined to say myself, that advancing years might have made Gideon more, rather than less, desperate to improve his lot. But I refrained and looked at my friend, silently imploring him to do the same. To my great relief, he got my message and addressed himself once more to his plate.

'The point I am trying to make,' I said, turning yet again to our guest, 'is that Master Bonifant was not a *young* man when he first went to work for you. He must have been at least thirty-two or maybe thirty-three years of age. Do you know anything about his life before that date?'

The apothecary laid his spoon and knife together on his empty plate and, for a moment or two, allowed his attention to wander to the curd tart and sweet cheese flan that one of the inn servants had just placed on the table, together with the brandy-soaked raisins and a jug of fresh ale. Once having satisfied himself of their excellence, he politely gave me all his attention.

'Gideon was not a native of this city,' he said. 'He had lived, until such time as he came to work for me, in Southampton. But the unexpected death of his young wife, some months earlier, had given him a distaste for the place. So he left, and set out for London, in an effort, I imagine, to put the tragedy behind him.'

I stared in surprise at my informant. 'Master Bonifant had been married before? Neither Mistress Shore nor Master Babcary told me that he was a widower.'

The apothecary looked somewhat nonplussed by this remark, then shrugged.

'Perhaps,' he suggested, 'they saw no need to mention it. After all, it's hardly relevant to his death. Nevertheless, I feel sure they must have known. I can't believe that Gideon would have kept the fact a secret.'

'No, indeed,' I answered thoughtfully.

Adela glanced up from her plate and laughed. 'My husband likes to know every little detail, Master Ford, whether it has any bearing on his enquiries or no.'

'He's just plain nosy,' Philip said, 'and it can land him in a lot of trouble.' He added feelingly, 'It can land other people in a lot of trouble, as well.'

'Each fact, however irrelevant it appears, may be of importance,' I retorted sententiously. 'But pray continue, Master Ford. How did Master Bonifant come to be in your employ? Had he been an apothecary's assistant in Southampton?'

'So he told me, and I saw no need to doubt his word. He seemed to know the business, and quickly proved to my satisfaction that he could mix lotions and make up unguents as well as I could myself. He knew the properties of all the different herbs, and was good at discussing the ailments, as well as the necessary remedies, with my customers, particularly the older ones. He had, in fact, become invaluable to me during that short twelvemonth, and I was extremely sorry to part with him when the time came for him to marry.'

'How did you meet him, and what happened to your previous assistant?' I asked.

Master Ford managed a thin-lipped smile. 'I see what your friend means about your nosiness. Are such facts really important in attempting to solve the mystery – if indeed there *is* a mystery – of Gideon's murder?'

'Probably not,' I admitted. 'But as I have already pointed out, I cannot tell what might be of value and what might not. And it's true, I'm curious by nature.'

'"Nosy" was what we said,' Philip grinned.

With an effort of will, I ignored him, but I was beginning to tire of his pleasantries. Leaving my curd tart untouched on my plate, I twisted my head even further in Master Ford's direction, in spite of the fact that such a posture was giving me a severe pain in my neck. 'I'd be grateful for an answer to my question.'

The apothecary sampled the sweet cheese tart and it seemed to have a mellowing effect upon him.

'My previous assistant was my wife,' he explained. 'She had inherited her considerable knowledge of ailments and their treatments from her father, who was also an apothecary, and so I had never had need of any other help in the shop. She had been dead only three or four months when Gideon came asking me if I was in want of an assistant.' Master Ford heaved a sigh. 'The similarity of our situations, both of us so recently bereaved, may, originally, have inclined me to employ him, but I never had any cause to regret my decision.'

'Of all the apothecaries in London,' I asked, 'how did he come to pick on you? There must be a dozen in Bucklersbury alone.'

Master Ford shook his head sadly, as though he were dealing with an idiot child. 'I was not the first shop at which he had offered his services. Gideon told me later that he had, in fact, been trudging around the city for several days. It was, oddly enough, the apothecary in West Cheap, in Gudrun Lane, who advised him that I might be glad of his assistance.'

'Why do you say "oddly enough"? What was strange about the apothecary in Gudrun Lane?'

'Jeremiah Page was summoned to the goldsmith's house the night that Gideon died.'

'Ah, yes!' I refilled my beaker with ale and finally managed to consume a mouthful or two of curd tart. 'I remember Master Babcary mentioning that fact.' I frowned. 'Why was an apothecary sent for and not a physician?'

Master Ford shrugged. 'That I cannot tell you. I wasn't there. You must ask members of the household for an answer. Maybe there's no physician who lives close enough at hand. Maybe those present weren't sure that Gideon was really dead, and hoped that an apothecary might have an antidote to revive him. Maybe . . . But I repeat, I wasn't there. I don't know what anybody said or thought. I only heard the rumours and the stories that circulated afterwards.'

'You were shocked by the news of Gideon Bonifant's murder?'

'Of course I was shocked.' Master Ford hesitated a moment or two before continuing, 'Shocked, but not altogether surprised.'

'And why was that?' I queried, although I could guess the answer.

The other three had by now finished their meal and, with nothing else to distract them, were listening intently to the conversation.

Master Ford, who had also eaten his fill, eased his thin buttocks into a more comfortable position on the bench and pressed a thumb and forefinger to the bridge of his nose as though considering his reply. At last he said, 'A few weeks before his death, Gideon confided in me his suspicion that his wife was being unfaithful to him with her cousin, Christopher Babcary.'

'And you believed him?'

Once again, the apothecary hesitated over his answer. 'At the time, I thought him completely sincere in his belief, but mistaken.'

'Why did you think him mistaken?' Jeanne Lamprey wanted to know.

Master Ford spread his long, thin hands, with their elegant, tapering fingers.

'I don't know Christopher Babcary all that well, you understand. I've only spoken once to him at any length, and that was at Gideon's wedding to Isolda. He was some fourteen years of age then, all spots and pimples as such callow youths generally are. But I've caught sight of him many times since, when I've been in West Cheap, and over the past five and a half years, he's grown into a good-looking young fellow.

92

'Now, it seemed to me, when Gideon first told me of his suspicions concerning him and Isolda, highly improbable that such a man, who cannot lack for female companionship, would fall in love with a woman older than himself by some ten years, and one, moreover, who is so plain that she found it difficult to get herself a husband in the first place.' Master Ford bit his lip. 'But I should have had more faith in Gideon's knowledge of the pair. I repeat, he was a God-fearing man and would never have made such an accusation lightly.'

'You think then that Mistress Bonifant is guilty of her husband's death?'

'Either she alone or she and her cousin together.' Master Ford turned to stare defiantly at me. 'Don't think me ignorant of the details of the murder. I made it my business to find them out. I was fond of Gideon – or as fond as I could be after only a year's close acquaintance. He was not a man anyone could get to know easily, for he was reluctant to talk freely about himself. His grief at the death of his first wife went too deep for idle prattle, and I honoured him for that. I understood his reticence. I'm just sorry that chance put Isolda Babcary in his way.'

'How did that happen?' I asked.

The apothecary shook his head. 'I don't know. All I do know is that one day she came into the shop asking for Gideon. I called him from the back room where he was mixing up some lotions for me, and I could see at once that they were no strangers to one another. The only thing that surprised me, as it appeared to surprise Gideon, was that she had come seeking him out. I thought it unmaidenly and forward.'

'Did you think then that romance might be in the air?'

'It was the last thought to cross my mind. She was twenty-four years old and plain. She had nothing to recommend her to a man like Gideon.'

'Except her money and the fact that her father was a goldsmith in West Cheap,' Philip said, unable to resist the temptation to say his piece yet again.

'Philip! Hold your tongue!' Jeanne was before me with her admonition. 'Nevertheless,' she went on, smiling apologetically at Master Ford, 'you must admit that there is some truth in what my husband says.'

'Well . . .' Won over by her charm, the apothecary wavered. 'Maybe Gideon was a little flattered at being singled out by a woman of standing and fortune. But I'd be willing to swear to his sincerity when he told me that he was extremely fond of her. He said she had a sweet and pious nature, and that in his estimation that was of far greater importance than her lack of physical beauty.'

I could see that Philip was about to make some jibe or other, but Jeanne forestalled him.

'Indeed, I must confess to feeling precisely the same way when I married my husband,' she said, causing Philip's jaw to drop open in astonishment at such an unexpected broadside. But her remark, cruel as it may have been, had the desired effect of ensuring his silence.

I carefully avoided looking at Adela, who was shaking with suppressed laughter, and kept my eyes fixed firmly upon the apothecary, who had obviously seen nothing amusing in Jeanne Lamprey's remark.

'Did you remain friendly with Master Bonifant after his marriage?' I asked.

'We were always on speaking terms,' the apothcary answered slowly. 'If we met one another in the street, we exchanged more than the time of day. Gideon would enquire after my health, and I after his and that of Mistress Bonifant. And in the first year or so succeeding the wedding, he would occasionally visit my shop, rather than the one in Gudrun Lane, if he or his wife needed any medicaments. But, understandably, as the years went by, those visits grew less and less until they ceased altogether. Latterly, I saw nothing of him unless, by chance, we met out of doors.'

'Why do you say "understandably"?' I wanted to know.

Master Ford shrugged and once again regarded me as though I were slightly simple.

'Because,' he explained slowly and clearly, 'Gideon became a part of the Babcary household. He was learning the goldsmith's craft from his father-in-law and had no more interest in the apothecary's trade. I didn't blame him. He didn't wish to be constantly reminded of his lowlier past.'

'Did it surprise you that he and Isolda had no children?'

'No, it didn't!' Master Ford exploded angrily. 'I never

thought upon the subject. It's God's will that many couples remain childless. It was His will that my dear wife and I should have no progeny. Really, Master Chapman, your curiosity gets the better of you and I think, if you and your friends will excuse me, that I shall be going.' He rose from the bench and made courteous bows to both Adela and to Jeanne. 'Thank you for a very fine dinner, but now I must be on my way.'

He was gone before I could do anything to stop him. I heard his voice upraised in the passageway as he took his leave of Reynold Makepeace.

'Well,' remarked Philip with great satisfaction, 'you can't pretend that it was *my* fault Master Ford went away. That was entirely your doing, Roger! You asked one question too many as you always do. That long nose of yours is still getting you into trouble.'

I nodded in vexation. 'I should have guessed that he and Mistress Ford were childless when there was no mention of a son or daughter.'

'You weren't to know,' Adela soothed, patting my arm. 'So! Did your questions yield anything apart from the fact that Master Bonifant had been married before?'

I considered her question. 'Oh, I think so. I know now that Gideon was a pious, God-fearing man—'

'Or passed as one,' Philip sneered, his experience of life before he met and married Jeanne not having made him think very highly of his fellow creatures in general.

'Or passed as one, as you say,' I agreed. 'And he certainly showed very little gratitude to the man who had given him both shelter and employment when he was destitute in London. Master Ford should surely have been treated as a friend after the marriage put Gideon on an equal footing with him.' I sighed. 'But apart from his accusation against his wife and her cousin, I know as yet of no other reason why anyone should wish to murder Gideon Bonifant.'

Ten

W e spent the rest of the day in the company of the Lampreys, sitting for a while longer, after Master Ford's departure, over our ale at the Voyager, and then, when the weather improved still further and the afternoon became dry and bright, we went for a walk at Adela's request.

'For I shall be nothing but a bladder of wind if I sit here any longer,' she protested, 'like one of those footballs that boys kick around in the streets.' She eyed me with mock severity as she rose to her feet. 'Here I am, barely three months pregnant, and already this child is causing me more discomfort than Nicholas did in nine. He's going to take after his father, a restless soul.'

'As long as he isn't as nosy,' Philip said, and I forced myself to laugh, although I could feel my hackles rising. My old friend was becoming a regular source of irritation to me.

We walked the length of Walbrook and down Dowgate Hill to the Baltic Wharf, where the great foreign ships from that northerly region of Europe drop anchor near the Steelyard to unload their cargoes of timber and furs and dried fish. There were plenty of people about, some still dressed in their church-going clothes, ready to be pleased by the unexpected and fragile burst of good weather.

A couple standing near to us on the dockside, and talking loudly enough for the woman's part in the conversation to be easily overheard, had apparently made the journey to Saint Stephen's church at Westminster that morning in order to see the little Duke and Duchess of York at Mass. It seemed, however, that the newly-wed children had been the two persons of least interest to the lady, whose discourse was all of fashion and of what had been worn by which dame of consequence, with disparaging remarks falling as thick as leaves in autumn

– much to the fascination of my wife and Jeanne Lamprey who had edged closer to the couple in order not to miss a word.

The speaker, although she was at present swathed in the concealing folds of a dark woollen cloak, plainly considered herself enough a woman of the *beau monde* to pass such strictures, and oozed self-satisfaction. Her companion, whose back was towards me, also seemed happy with her company if his over-zealous attentions were anything to judge by. From where I was standing, I could just make out his companion's features beneath her hood: a handsome, world-weary face, the thin cheeks too pale even for the January cold, and undoubtedly daubed with the white lead used by the more sophisticated women of our society to conceal the effects of sun and wind on their complexions.

Eventually, Philip and I, weary of contemplating the ships, gestured to our still eavesdropping wives that we should move on and, as they reluctantly obeyed our summons, the couple also decided that they had remained stationary long enough. The man swung round, offering the woman his arm, and I came face to face with Christopher Babcary.

'Master Chapman!' He greeted me without enthusiasm, but, at the same time, was obviously gratified to be seen with such a companion. He made no effort to introduce the lady, however, and was beginning to walk away when he paused and turned back. 'We shall meet again tomorrow then, in West Cheap, unless, that is, you've changed your mind.' Abruptly, he released himself from the woman's clasp and stepped closer to me, lowering his voice so that only I could hear his words. 'And wouldn't it be wiser if you did so? All these questions can do no good: they only stir up trouble for Isolda. She's had enough to bear since Gideon's death, with all the hints and whispers and rumours circulating amongst our neighbours.' He suddenly turned aggressive and added violently, 'Leave us alone, Chapman, or you may live to regret your interference.'

He spun on his heel and rejoined his companion who had been waiting for him with ill-concealed impatience. She said something to him that I could not catch, but from his hangdog expression, it was plainly a reprimand.

'Bad-tempered harpy!' Philip grunted sourly, staring after

their retreating backs. 'But there! If the lad fancies that sort of woman, what can he expect? Who is he? One of the Babcary family I should guess.'

'You would guess correctly,' I answered, also watching the couple's progress towards Dowgate Hill, the lady still visibly incensed and refusing, with much head tossing, to take her escort's hand. 'That's Christopher Babcary, the goldsmith's nephew.'

Adela came to stand beside me, slipping her hand into the crook of my arm.

'So that's the man accused by Gideon Bonifant of cuckolding him, is it?' she enquired, having overheard my answer. 'Well, if that's the kind of woman young Master Babcary prefers, I can't imagine, at least not from your description of Isolda, that he would entertain anything but a cousinly affection for her.' My wife went on thoughtfully, 'Of course, that doesn't mean to say that Gideon was wrong in his assumption that his wife was betraying him with another man. He might simply have picked on the wrong person. You'll have to bear that in mind when pursuing your investigations, Roger.'

I bit my tongue and maintained my composure with an effort. First, I had been forced to endure Philip's jibes about my 'nosiness', and now here was Adela telling me how to conduct my business, instructing me in what I should do well to remember. It only needed Jeanne Lamprey to add her mite for my cup of humiliation to run over.

Jeanne was busy keeping an eye on the weather, which was changing yet again, black clouds piling up the Thames from the east, bringing with them a freshening wind and a smell of sleet and rain in the air.

'We'd better make for shelter,' she decided, pulling up the hood of her cloak and holding it firmly together under her chin. 'Adela shouldn't be out in a storm, Roger, not in her delicate condition.'

I made no answer, except to put an arm around my wife. It seemed that I was not to escape advice on how to be either a solver of mysteries or a good husband, and I found myself looking forward to the morrow when I could once more be my own man.

We parted from the Lampreys on the corner of Bucklersbury,

Philip having promised to fetch Adela early next morning and to escort her to their shop. There, in return for all their kindness, she would spend the time before dinner helping Jeanne to sort and mend the old clothes collected by Philip over the past few days and now ready for reselling.

'And after we've eaten,' Jeanne said, reaching up to kiss Adela's cheek, 'provided that Philip can manage on his own for a while, and if you feel fit enough, I'll take you to see the wild animals in the Tower.'

Adela thanked her, returning the kiss, and a few moments later, we were hurrying along Bucklersbury, making for the inn as fast as we could, the icy spears of rain already beginning to sting our faces. Once within the comfort of our room, we lit the candles and closed the outer shutters against the cold, shaking the dampness from our cloaks and hanging them from the wall pegs to dry.

'And now,' said Adela, seating herself on the edge of the bed and eyeing me accusingly, 'what was Christopher Babcary whispering to you on the quayside, there? And you needn't think to lie to me, either, Roger. I couldn't hear what he was saying, but I could see by the expression on his face that he was giving you some kind of warning.'

'Not a warning exactly,' I muttered. 'But I admit he was trying to persuade me to change my mind. He thinks that my questioning could do Mistress Bonifant more harm than good. And he's right, of course, if she should prove to be guilty of her husband's murder.'

'Was that all he said?' My wife regarded me with her clear, unwavering gaze.

I sighed. I had discovered very early on in my married life that it was almost impossible to lie to Adela. 'No, he advised me to leave the family alone or I might live to regret my interference.'

'But you won't take his advice, of course.' It was a statement, not a question.

'My dearest, I can't,' I protested, sitting beside her on the bed and putting my arms around her. 'I can't possibly disoblige the Duke.'

'Can't or won't?' she asked, but immediately turned to plant a kiss on my lips. 'Forgive me, I shouldn't have said that. I don't know what's got into me lately. It must be my condition, I'm allowing myself to become a prey to odd humours and fancies and doing what I said I'd never do. I'm interfering.'

I held her closer, murmuring endearments. I knew that I was at fault, that I should have refused the Duke's commission. I ought not to be abandoning her in a strange city, dependent for amusement on two comparative strangers. But I was as selfish then as I am today (or, at least, so my children tell me). Once presented with a mystery, I could no more leave it unresolved than I could grow wings and fly.

The next morning, after breakfast, I saw Adela off to Cornhill in the company of Philip Lamprey, and then, with an uncontrollable lightening of the heart and a spring in my step, set out myself for West Cheap.

The sky was leaden grey, there was a sprinkling of snow on the ground and the wind was bitter, but nothing could diminish my spirits at the sheer pleasure of being on my own again, of being my own master, of being able to order my own actions exactly as I chose. The world about me was already humming with activity: church bells were tolling, street cleaners shovelled yesterday's steaming refuse into their carts, traders took down shutters and opened up their shops, pedlars and piemen shouted their wares, lawyers, in their striped gowns, hurried past on their way to Saint Paul's. As I was caught up and borne along on this tide of humanity, I was prodded into the realisation of just how good it was to be alive, and I thought with sudden poignancy of those prisoners, like the Duke of Clarence, languishing in prison, many under sentence of death. But it also reminded me of how wrong it is to rob another human being of the life that God has given to him or her; the life that is our pathway to heaven.

I experienced a stab of guilt. Since my brief conversation on Saturday with Christopher Babcary about the murdered man, and now after talking to Master Ford, I had begun to feel a certain antipathy towards Gideon Bonifant, resulting almost in indifference as to the identity of his murderer. But even supposing those feelings concerning him were justified, murder was never warranted, however unpleasant the victim might have been. And all I could reasonably say of Gideon just at present was that he seemed to me an ungrateful, rough-tongued man, with an eye to his own advancement by any means at his disposal. But of how many hundreds of others could that also be said? It did not mean that any one of them could be killed with impunity and nobody care.

The furnace had already been lit in Master Babcary's workshop by the time that I arrived, and young Tobias Maybury was assiduously working the bellows, forcing the flames to leap higher and higher up the chimney. Christopher Babcary was seated at the bench in the middle of the room, burnishing a golden belt buckle with his rabbit's foot, and brushing the tiny particles of loosened metal into his leather apron. Master Babcary himself was standing at the long bench, which also served as a counter on which to display the finished goods, thoughtfully rubbing his chin as he alternately scrutinised Saturday's batch of golden medallions and a lump of amber that either he or one of the other two had begun to chisel.

At my entrance, they all looked up from their work, the apprentice, after a cursory glance, returning to his bellows. Christopher Babcary gave me an enigmatic stare before resuming his polishing, and only Master Babcary evinced any pleasure at seeing me again. He left his bench and came towards me, hand outstretched.

'Master Chapman! You've kept your word and come back to us, then.'

'Did you doubt that I would?'

'No, no! At least, I didn't. However, Kit, there, thought that you might have had second thoughts, didn't you, lad? I don't know why.'

His nephew grunted something unintelligible without pausing again in what he was doing, but it seemed to satisfy his uncle. The older man turned back to me.

'Well, I don't suppose you need to talk to me for a second time, Master Chapman. You heard all I had to say the day before yesterday. But of the rest of my household, who would you like to speak to first?'

I hesitated about making demands, and had rather hoped that Miles would have made his own suggestion. Having been invited to state a preference, however, I said reluctantly,

'With your permission, sir, Mistress Bonifant would seem the obvious choice.'

My host nodded vigorously. 'Precisely my own conclusion. So I've told Isolda to hold herself in readiness in the upstairs room. She's there now, I believe, so you can go up straight away.' His face assumed an anxious expression. 'I'm sure she'll be able to convince you of her innocence.'

I made no answer to this last remark, but with my hand on the latch of the inner door, I paused and turned round.

'Master Babcary, who do *you* think murdered your son-in-law?' I asked.

The question took him by surprise, as I had intended that it should.

'Wh-what do you mean?' he stammered.

'You don't deny that Master Bonifant was poisoned?'

'N-no! Of course I don't.' He began to fidget uncomfortably. 'What's this all about? I don't understand. What are you getting at?'

'I'm asking for your opinion – if, that is, you truly believe your daughter to be innocent – as to who you think the real murderer might be. Surely you must have some suspicions of your own.'

'No,' he snapped, the good-humoured smile vanishing from his face. 'I suspect no one.'

'To suspect no one is to suspect everyone,' I pointed out gently, 'including Mistress Bonifant.'

Miles Babcary was no fool: I could see by the expression in his eyes that he was perfectly capable of following my logic, but he was not prepared to admit it.

'I don't know what you mean,' he shrugged. 'You're talking in riddles.'

To continue to press him would have been foolish and only antagonise him further, and as master of the house I needed his goodwill. Besides, I should be no more successful in getting him to admit to his suspicions, if he had any, than I had been on Saturday. I felt sure that he was as uncertain of his daughter's innocence as he was of anyone else's guilt, but he was never going to say as much to me. For the time being, I must leave well alone.

'Forgive me, sir,' I apologised, 'I didn't mean to upset you.

I'll go up now and talk to Mistress Bonifant.' But once again I paused and called across to Christopher Babcary, 'I hope you and your lady got home safely yesterday without either of you getting too wet.'

He replied briefly that they had, while his uncle raised his eyes to heaven.

'And which lady is this, pray?' Miles asked. 'No, don't bother telling me, boy, for I'm sure I shall be none the wiser.' He shrugged and turned back to me. 'I've never known such a lad for fancying himself in and out of love every few weeks or so. First it's one woman, then it's another. I suppose that one of these days he'll decide it's time to settle down and make up his mind who it is he really wants to marry, but not just at present.' He took a pace towards me, lowering his voice. 'Which is why that story my son-in-law was putting about in the months before his death was so much moonshine.'

But was it? I wondered, as I climbed the stairs to the first-floor landing. Might not Christopher Babcary, at one time, have fancied himself in love with his cousin? He appeared to like older women, if the lady I had seen him with the previous day was anything to judge by. On the other hand, not only were Isolda Bonifant's looks against her, but the familiarity of living under the same roof with someone, each day and all day, year in and year out, seemed to me to make this an unlikely possibility.

Yet I knew from past experience that I could rule nothing out, that the improbable happened in life far more often than one imagined. Perhaps young Master Babcary's fancy had once strayed towards Isolda, and perhaps she had been flattered by his unexpected attentions. On the other hand, she must have known of his reputation for fickleness. How could she not have, living in the same house and watching him grow up? Would she, therefore, have allowed herself to succumb to his charms? But maybe she had genuinely fallen in love with him, and could not help herself.

But as yet there was no answer to any of these questions, and I knew that neither Isolda nor her cousin could be expected to admit to betraying Gideon, even supposing there was any truth in the accusation. Yet why should Gideon Bonifant lie? No man worth his salt wants to appear as the cuckolded husband, and is

103

therefore hardly likely to make up such a story. But he could have been mistaken in the identity of Isolda's lover, a person in whom I was beginning to believe. Her plain features may well have proved a barrier to the finding of a husband when she was a maid, but five and a half years of marriage could have given her a confidence and an air of invitation lacking in a single woman.

I stood still for a moment at the top of the first flight of stairs, looking at the two doors facing me. The left-hand one, if I remembered rightly, led into Master Babcary's bedchamber at the back of the house; the other, beside it, opened into the family living-room, where they spent their evenings and the long winter hours of darkness together. Above me, on the second and third floors, the rest of the household slept; close quarters for five people, six when Gideon had been alive, and that was without including the little maid, Meg Spendlove, whose domain, waking and sleeping, was the kitchen.

I walked the few paces along the landing to the second door, then raised my hand and knocked before lifting the latch and going inside.

Isolda Bonifant was seated to the left of the fireplace, in one of the two armchairs, and her cousin, Eleanor Babcary was seated in the other. I was somewhat taken aback not to find my quarry alone, but the younger woman immediately rose to her feet and began to edge towards the door.

'I'm just going,' she said nervously.

'Oh, sit down again, Nell,' Isolda scolded, half amused, half irritated. 'Master Chapman won't eat you, you goose! Besides, he'll want to talk to you as well as to me. He can talk to us both together.'

I didn't know what to say. The last thing I wanted was to have the older woman prompting her cousin, putting words into her mouth, which would almost certainly be the case if Eleanor Babcary stayed. I glanced from one to the other, thinking, not for the first time, what cruel tricks nature could play. The Babcary blood, which they both shared, gave them a certain similarity of feature, enough at any rate to suggest that they were related. Yet Eleanor, with her creamy skin, blue eyes and profusion of curly auburn hair, was extraordinarily pretty – some might even think her beautiful – while Isolda could never be described as anything but plain. And the Lambert blood, which bound the latter to Mistress Shore, had also worked in her disfavour. Yet her candid blue gaze, her strength of character, her direct mode of speech, gave her, to my mind at least, an attraction that the gentle, timid charm of her cousin did not. But I suspected that not many men would agree with me.

Eleanor, obviously used to obeying her cousin, but sensing that I wished her to go, hesitated, unsure what to do. Her long, slender fingers played nervously with the pendant that she wore, twisting it round and round on its thin gold chain.

'Nell, sit down!' Isolda commanded. 'And stop fiddling with that thing around your neck. It's so delicate that you'll break it, if you're not careful. Draw up a stool, Master Chapman, and ask us what you want to know.'

I did so reluctantly, as Eleanor Babcary, with equal reluctance, resumed her seat by the fire, but perched on the very edge, as though ready for instant flight. I could see the pendant clearly now, a fragile circle of gold holding a true lover's knot set with tiny sapphires.

'That's very beautiful,' I said.

'It was a present from all of us on her seventeenth birthday, last October,' Isolda told me. 'My father made it, but we all had a hand in it somewhere. Even I was allowed to help in a very small way, although my big hands are so clumsy that Gideon was doubtful about letting me anywhere near it. He—' She broke off, staring in dismay at her young cousin's trembling underlip. 'Nell! Dearest! What's the matter? What have I said to upset you?'

She had half risen from her chair and would have gone to Eleanor, but the younger woman was already on her feet.

'It's nothing! Nothing!' she protested, in a voice choked with sobs. Then she fled from the room, and we heard the patter of her feet as she ran upstairs, followed by the slam of her bedchamber door.

Isolda slowly sank back into her seat. 'Now what on earth's got into Nell?' she wondered.

Eleven

There was a moment's reflective silence while Isolda Bonifant and I were busy, each with our own thoughts. I had no clue to my companion's, for her face gave nothing away but, for my part, I was wondering what had been said to provoke such a violent reaction on the part of the younger woman. Had it been the mention of Gideon? Had Eleanor Babcary been fonder of her cousin's husband than she had a right to be? Or was it simply that the manner of his death had distressed an impressionable young girl to such a degree that any allusion to him upset her? But the answer, of course, was not apparent and would have to wait until I knew more about her.

I decided to make no mention of the incident. There was no point in wasting my time listening to Isolda's lies and prevarications.

'Mistress Bonifant,' I said, leaning across and reclaiming her attention with a gentle tap on the arm, 'your father has made me free of his recollections concerning the evening of your husband's death. Will you now give me yours?'

She had jumped at my touch, startled out of her reverie, blinking at me for a second or two as though uncertain where she was.

'Master Chapman! I'm sorry, I was daydreaming. Firelight sometimes has that effect on me.' She drew a deep breath and smiled bravely. 'Please forgive me. What is it that you want to know?'

'Will you tell me what you remember about the evening Master Bonifant died?'

'Very well,' she agreed after a slight hesitation. 'What exactly has my father told you?'

'I'd rather hear your version of events first, if you please, independently of his.'

She sighed and looked down at her hands, which were clasped loosely together in her lap. Absent-mindedly, she began to twist her wedding band round and round on her finger.

'It was Mistress Perle's birthday,' she began at last, 'which is also her saint's day – December the fourth, the feast of Saint Barbara. My father had asked her to celebrate the occasion here, with all of us, and I think she would have agreed at once but for the fact that she wanted her friends and neighbours, Gregory and Ginèvre Napier, to be of the party.' The heavy lids were suddenly raised and the cool blue eyes looked directly into mine. 'Perhaps you may have realised for yourself, since your talk with my father, that he is hoping to make Mistress Perle his wife.'

'Master Babcary admitted as much. He also told me that, if such an event took place, he intended to buy the Widow Perle's present home in Paternoster Row for you and your husband to live in. He believed you both to be happy with such an arrangement. Indeed, he implied that you, in particular, were more than happy, that it was your wish to have an establishment of your own.'

Isolda cradled her chin in one hand, supporting her elbow with the other.

'I shouldn't have objected,' she agreed after a moment's contemplation of the fire. 'That is to say,' she added honestly, 'I couldn't possibly have remained here if Father had married again.' Once more she raised her eyes to mine. 'I've been mistress of this house too long – ever since the age of sixteen or thereabouts – and I couldn't share the management of it with another woman.'

My curiosity got the better of me. 'What would you do if Master Babcary and Mistress Perle were to be married sometime in the future?'

Isolda smiled serenely. 'I should hold my father to his promise and remove to Paternoster Row, taking poor little Meggie with me. She'd never suit Mistress Perle's notion of a kitchen maid, and, in any case, Barbara would undoubtedly bring her own highly competent servants with her. And I should ask Nell to live with me – that is, until she gets married. Which she undoubtedly will, because she's so beautiful.'

'Does she not care for Mistress Perle, either?'

My companion threw back her head and gave a hearty, full-throated chuckle.

'Nell likes everyone,' she said, dropping her hands back into her lap. 'But you're quite right with your "either", Master Chapman. I'm not enamoured of my father's choice of bride. Did I make it that apparent?'

I shifted uncomfortably on my stool. 'Well—' I was beginning awkwardly, but Isolda cut me short.

'You mustn't worry about it,' she assured me. 'People are always telling me that I'm not good at concealing my feelings. But please don't mistake me. I know nothing against Barbara Perle. The truth is that I'm piqued because I never thought my father would consider marrying for a second time. Now, what else did you wish to ask me?'

'Well, I know from Master Babcary that Mistress Perle finally agreed to his suggestion that she celebrate her birthday here, on condition that she could bring her friends, Gregory and Ginèvre Napier with her . . . Your father doesn't care for the Napiers, particularly the lady, does he?'

'No, indeed! If, that is, one can call her a lady!' Isolda gave me a sidelong, somewhat shamefaced grin. 'Now I'm being catty, Master Chapman. But you must make up your own mind when you see her. As you say, Barbara won the argument, and consented to my father's proposal.'

'The three guests arrived, or so I understand from Master Babcary, sometime around four o'clock, after the shop was barred and shuttered for the night. Prior to that, the merchandise had been removed from the windows and locked away, and then everyone but you retired to change into their Sunday clothes. Where were you, Mistress Bonifant?' I enquired with an assumed ignorance.

'I was still in the kitchen,' was the somewhat tart reply, 'cooking the food. My father had insisted that we have all Barbara's favourite dishes and, as there are quite a goodly number of them, I had spent most of the day there. Meg was helping me, but her assistance is often more of a hindrance than otherwise.'

'And, earlier, you had come upstairs to this room to lay the table. You had unlocked that cupboard over there and put out the special family goblets, each with its identifying set of initials worked into the gold around the rim. And you had filled them with wine.'

She did not respond immediately, and I began to wonder if she were going to answer at all. For a while, the only sounds to be heard were the crackling of logs on the fire and the rustle of the wall tapestries as they billowed in a sudden draught. From below, Master Babcary's voice was raised, calling for Meg Spendlove, but after that all was quiet again until Isolda suddenly swivelled in her chair to face me.

'Damning, isn't it? Enough, probably, to have brought me to the stake but for my cousin's intervention on my behalf with the King. Yet the fact is that I often filled our cups with wine – or ale, or water, or whatever else we were drinking – before we ate, because it meant that I could then top up the pitcher, so saving us from the annoyance of having to send down to the kitchen for more drink during a meal. And, in addition, on that particular evening, I wanted us all to pledge Mistress Perle's health as soon as we were assembled.'

'And afterwards, when you had finished laying the table, you returned to the kitchen?' She nodded. 'But when you eventually came upstairs again to change your gown, did you go straight to your bedchamber?'

'No, I came in here for a last look round, just to make sure that I'd forgotten nothing. I knew how much the occasion meant to my father.'

'And did you encounter anyone else while you were doing this?'

'Yes, my father himself. He was coming out of his room just as I was leaving this one. His bedchamber, as you probably know, is next door, so we passed one another on the landing. I told him that everything was ready and he grunted. He was in a hurry to get downstairs. I think he said that the guests had just arrived.'

So far, her story tallied in most essentials with that of Master Babcary. Either they were both speaking the truth, or they were in collusion, and adept at telling lies.

I asked abruptly, 'What did your husband think of your father's intention to remarry?'

She seemed somewhat put out by this change of direction,

but gave the impression of answering as openly and as honestly as she could.

'Gideon was a little – what can I say? – a little worried by the idea at first. But when my father explained to him that I should in no way be the loser by the marriage – that although he would have to make provision for his wife, the shop and all its contents would still be left to me – my husband grew more reconciled to the match.' She added hastily, 'You must understand that Gideon was only concerned with protecting my interests.'

I assured her that I did. And she might well have been right: I was in no position, just then, to judge the truth of her assertion, even though I might doubt it.

'How did Master Bonifant get on with the rest of the household?' I asked, startling her once again and making her uneasy.

'He – he got on well enough, why do you ask?' And when I refrained from answering, she added defensively, 'Gideon was a very reserved man, who only made friends with difficulty. Even after five and a half years of marriage, I can't pretend that I ever really knew what he was thinking. Nevertheless, he was a kind husband: considerate, f-faithful.' She stumbled slightly over the final word.

I pretended not to notice. 'What about your cousins?' I queried. 'Was Master Bonifant fond of them? Were they fond of him?'

There was another infinitesimal pause before Isolda could bring herself to reply.

'The three of them rubbed along together, but I don't know that there was any deep affection on either side.' She scratched one cheek consideringly. 'You have to remember that when Gideon came to live here, after our marriage, Kit wasn't quite fourteen years of age, while Nell was only eleven. They were children in the eyes of a man of thirty-four, and so they have remained ever since.'

I thought that while this might well be true on Gideon's side, Eleanor Babcary, whose flower-like innocence made her appear a lot younger than her years, was now a young woman of seventeen and, after her outburst just now, I couldn't help wondering yet again what her feelings had been towards her cousin's husband.

110

'What about the young apprentice?' I asked. 'Tobias, isn't that his name? And your maid, Meg Spendlove, how did Master Bonifant get along with them?'

'Oh, come now!' Isolda was incredulous. 'You can't possibly imagine that either of those two had anything to do with Gideon's death!'

'I rule no one out who was in the house that evening. Someone killed your husband, Mistress Bonifant and, if, as you claim, it wasn't you—' I broke off, shrugging.

She looked unhappy and began to fidget with the leather girdle that encircled her waist. It was fully a minute before she answered, and I had time to wonder what her response would be. Eventually, she gave herself a little shake and sat up straighter in her chair.

'So be it,' she sighed. 'I didn't murder my husband, Master Chapman, however black things might look against me, so I'll tell you what you want to know.'

'To be honest with you,' I said, 'your father has already informed me that Master Bonifant found Meg's slatternly ways difficult to tolerate, and that you and he had had differences of opinion on the subject.'

My companion seemed vexed, but admitted reluctantly, 'Father's right. Gideon was extremely neat and orderly in all his ways. A girl like Meg was bound to irritate him, and he couldn't understand why I didn't dismiss her and employ someone more efficient.'

'Why didn't you?' I queried.

Isolda was indignant. 'Meg has been with us since we took her from the Foundling Hospital when she was ten years old. And if you had seen her then, you'd know how happy and well fed she is now, in spite of her appearance. I could no more turn Meggie into the street to fend for herslf than I could Eleanor.' She looked away from me, staring once again into the heart of the fire, and added in a low voice, 'I know what it is to be plain and unattractive.'

I was at a disadvantage. If I refuted her statement, my protests would ring hollow, and the more I tried to convince her of their sincerity, the less I would be believed. It was better, I decided, to say nothing on the subject.

111

Instead, I asked hurriedly, 'Do you know if Master Bonifant had had cause to take Meg to task shortly before he died?'

Her head turned sharply in my direction, and I could see the answer in her face.

'Who told you?' she demanded accusingly. 'Was it Father?'

'No, nobody told me. I merely drew a bow at a venture.' And the arrow, I added to myself, has found its mark.

Isolda tapped one of her feet angrily, annoyed with herself for falling into the trap.

'Yes,' she conceded at last. 'There had been an unpleasant scene between my husband and Meg some few weeks before the murder.'

'What was it about?' I prompted when she seemed disinclined to continue.

My companion slumped back in her chair as though suddenly very tired.

'It was the occasion of Nell's last birthday feast,' she said wearily, 'on the thirty-first of October, All Hallows' Eve. I wasn't very well that day, and had left the setting of the supper table to Meg while I lay down upon my bed. Woman's trouble,' she added, looking me straight in the eyes before I could embarrass her by asking a tactless question. 'I had given her the key of the corner cupboard and told her to be especially careful when putting out the gold and crystal goblets. (I have discovered over the years that if you trust Meg to do something, she will give of her best. What she resents most is being treated as though she's a fool.)

'I had gone over with her again and again where everybody sat, so that each person would get his or her own goblet. But, unfortunately, Meg still managed to make a mistake, although, as I insisted at the time, she could be forgiven for it. She had mixed up Gideon's and Christopher's goblets, but the initials G.B. and C.B. are very alike, especially with all that carved foliage surrounding them.'

'But Master Bonifant was angry with her?'

Isolda frowned. 'He was excessively angry for a man who normally showed his displeasure merely by folding his lips together and walking out of the room. He ranted and raved, saying the most appalling things to poor little Meg, just as though all the frustration of years had suddenly burst into

112

the open. I can remember Father and Nell and Kit, and even Toby Maybury, staring open-mouthed, as though they couldn't believe their ears; as though Gideon had suddenly taken leave of his senses. Of course, after a few minutes, when he saw how everyone was looking at him, he took himself in hand, calmed down and apologised to Meggie.'

'And how did she react to this burst of temper?'

'Very much as you might expect. There were floods of tears and instant denials. But then, that's Meg's way of dealing with every unpleasant situation in which she finds herself. Nothing is ever her fault, but always that of some other unidentifiable person.'

'Did she accept Master Bonifant's apologies?'

Isolda smiled sadly. 'Of course not! He had always made his disapproval of her plain, although in his customary austere fashion, and, as a consequence, *she* had never liked *him*. She was, I think, even a little afraid of him. But,' my companion added hastily, seeing the trap into which she was falling, 'her dislike was not enough to make her poison him, if that's what you're thinking.'

I said nothing in response to that. A simple soul like Meg Spendlove was just the sort to harbour a grievance and brood upon injustice. For most of her short life she had been the butt of other people's unkindness, and it would not be surprising if, one day, a particular act of hostility had proved too much for her. Had she, after weeks of turning the incident over in her mind, found herself, on the occasion of Mistress Perle's birthday, with the opportunity to get rid of her tormentor once and for all, and taken it? But that posed another problem. Where had she obtained the poison?

That question, however, would have to wait. 'What were your feelings,' I asked Isolda Bonifant, 'about your husband's uncharacteristic outburst?'

She answered, this time without any hesitation whatsoever. 'I thought it all part of a general deterioration in Gideon's health that had been worrying me over the preceding two or three months.'

'He was ill?' Master Babcary had mentioned nothing of this. 'What was the matter with Master Bonifant? Had anyone else noticed that he was ailing?'

'No, I don't think so.' Isolda answered my last query first. 'It wouldn't have been so obvious to other people. But Gideon hadn't been eating as well as usual. He had always been a hearty trencherman, even though he put on no flesh to show for it, yet for many weeks before his death, he had started to leave food on his plate at every meal. It's true that Kit remarked on the fact to me one day, asking what was wrong with Gideon's appetite, but I don't think he assumed it to be a sign of poor health, only that my husband was preoccupied about something or other.'

'You thought differently, however?'

'I might not have done so had it not also been for his broken nights. Gideon had always been a sound sleeper, but quite suddenly, about the same time that he started losing interest in his food, he began to be very restless. I would wake in the small hours to find him gone from my side, and when I went to look for him, he was prowling about the house, unable, he said, to sleep.' She had a drawn, unhappy look that I had noticed once or twice before during the course of this conversation. 'But when, on the first occasion that this happened, I begged him to come back to bed and to tell me if there was anything troubling his mind, he answered with such savagery, at the same time raising his hand as though ready to strike me, that I never interfered again. When I woke and he wasn't there, I just waited until he returned. And I learned to pretend to be asleep when he did so.'

'Did these nightly wanderings occur very often?'

'With increasing regularity. To begin with, I suppose I would find him gone perhaps once in a couple of weeks. But later, it was almost every night.'

'And he never hinted at what was worrying him?'

Isolda shook her head, avoiding my eyes.

'But I know now, don't I? Father has told you what Gideon was saying about me.'

'About you and your cousin Christopher, yes!' There was another long pause, this time while I plucked up courage to ask the necessary question. 'Mistress Bonifant,' I said at last, '*was* there any truth in your husband's accusation?'

'Of course not!' Her tone almost scorched me with its furious denial. She went on, more calmly, 'Oh, Kit likes women, but not my sort of woman. I agree that he prefers them to be older than himself but, apart from the fact that he has always looked upon me as another sister, he is only attracted by worldly and sophisticated women. They flatter him and persuade him that he, too, is worldly and sophisticated – but I suspect that they make use of him. And behind his back, they're probably laughing at him.'

I thought she could well be correct. But there was another question, more difficult than the first, that I must now put to her.

'Were – were there any grounds for your husband's suspicion that . . . that he was being betrayed?'

Isolda turned once more to look at me, and her eyes widened, but whether in anger or astonishment I was unsure.

'By me? With another man, you mean?' And when I nodded, she burst into mocking laughter. 'Master Chapman, are you blind? I'm a plain, some would say an ugly, woman, who had enough difficulty in finding *one* man who wanted to bed me. Where would I have found another?'

Such candour was endearing – if it were genuine.

'You do yourself a great injustice,' I said, repairing my earlier omission, 'and I will repay your frankness with some of my own. You are not beautiful, not even pretty, but there are many men who would find you easy to love. So I ask you again, did Master Bonifant have any reason for his suspicions?'

Isolda drew a deep breath. Then, 'No,' she answered a trifle unsteadily, 'he did not. I swear to you that whatever grounds he thought he had for suspecting me of infidelity, they were entirely false. Where they could have come from, I have not the least idea – unless some secret enemy of mine, or of his, put them into his head for his or her own wicked purpose.'

Twelve

'Do you know of such an enemy?' I asked after a few moments, when Isolda's last words had had time to sink in.

She shook her head. 'No, although it's not for want of thinking about it. But no particular person springs to mind. Of course, it would be foolish to presume that Gideon and I were loved, or even liked, by all our acquaintances, or even by all those who professed themselves to be our friends. Yet I'm unable to think of a single soul who would wish either of us so ill that he or she would be prepared to tell a lie that could result in so much distress and misery.'

'Nevertheless, somebody did just that.'

She sat forward in her chair, stretching her back as though it were aching. 'I know,' she answered quietly. 'That's what I find so frightening.'

'And your husband never mentioned this accusation to you? Did you indeed know nothing of it until after Master Bonifant's death?'

'Gideon never said a word to me. Had he done so, I should have been able to refute the accusation. And I hope that I should have been able to set his mind at rest.' She shivered and held out her hands to the blaze. 'That's what disturbs me most, Master Chapman, that he seems to have had such belief in this tale, accepted it so readily, that he never even asked me to prove my innocence.'

I nodded sympathetically. If she were telling the truth, this omission of Gideon's did appear odd, to say the least of it. But was she telling the truth? I had only her word for what had passed between herself and her husband. I should never now hear his side of the story.

116

'What did you do that evening,' I asked, 'when you had changed your gown?'

'I came downstairs, naturally, to this room, to join in the celebration.'

'And who was here when you entered?'

'Everyone – except Meg, of course. She was still down in the kitchen.' Isolda ticked off the assembled company on her fingers, screwing up her eyes a little as she once more conjured up the scene in her mind. 'My father, Mistress Perle, Gregory and Ginèvre Napier, both my cousins and, of course, Gideon. Oh yes, and our apprentice, Tobias Maybury,' she added on a faint note of surprise. 'I recall wondering at the time why he was present.'

'Shouldn't he have been?'

'If it had been a normal mealtime, with just the family, yes. He always eats with us. But not when we entertain. Then he has his food downstairs in the kitchen, with Meg. And I remember now . . .'

'Go on,' I urged as her voice tailed away into silence. 'What do you remember?'

'Oh, it probably means nothing,' she protested, 'but it occurred to me that he looked . . . well, flushed, as if he were feeling guilty about something or other. It was probably my imagination, for he didn't remain long in the room after my arrival, and he seemed perfectly himself when I saw him some fifteen minutes later, down in the kitchen. He and Meg were whispering and giggling together. At least,' she amended, 'Toby was giggling. Meg, come to think of it, looked rather flushed and indignant.'

'I see. Now, according to Master Babcary, you instructed everyone where to sit.'

Isolda smiled thinly. 'So I did, because I had laid the table and knew where I had placed each person. Yes,' she continued, bitterly, 'I can quite see why suspicion points so heavily in my direction.'

I was unable to reassure her. 'Pray continue,' I entreated. 'What happened next?'

'We all took our places around the table to drink Mistress Perle's good health. Oh, but I'm forgetting. Before we did so, Father presented Barbara with her birthday gift, a leather girdle

117

studded with sapphires and turquoises. It's very beautiful and very costly and would, I think, have apprised us of Father's intentions towards her, had we not known them already. Neither Gideon nor Kit, as I recall, looked as though he much approved.'

'After which you all drank the lady's health in the wine already poured out by you?'

'Yes.'

'And then?'

'And then I went down to the kitchen to help Meggie bring up the trays of food.' Isolda took a deep breath to steady her voice. 'As I re-entered this room, Master Napier was just coming out. He looked grey and sweating, and I thought he'd been taken ill, but I know now, of course, that he was going for the apothecary in Gudrun Lane. I didn't realise at first what was happening, until I saw Gideon. He was standing beside his chair, struggling desperately for breath. His face was turning blue. He couldn't speak, and his lips and throat seemed so stiff that he could neither swallow nor talk. All he could do was to make a terrible croaking sound.' Isolda covered her face with her hands and remained like that for several seconds. When she raised her face again, however, it had been wiped clean of all emotion. 'Meggie screamed and dropped her tray, while Gideon . . . Gideon raised his hand and pointed at me.' She shuddered. 'Dear Mother in Heaven! I'll never forget his eyes. They were so full of hatred.'

By eleven o'clock, dinner had been eaten and cleared away, the men coming upstairs from the shop one at a time: first Master Babcary, followed by his nephew and, lastly, by the apprentice, Toby Maybury.

I had found it strange eating with the family and not being relegated, as I usually was, to the lowlier company of the kitchen. But as someone known to be in the employ of Mistress Shore and, even more importantly, in that of the Duke of Gloucester, I was treated as a guest rather than as a nosy, interfering pedlar – although I suspected that the Babcarys were beginning to regard me in that light.

Eleanor had reappeared at dinnertime, looking pale and wan, but with an unimpaired appetite. She ate daintily, but heartily, making short work of a plate of mutton stew and dumplings, three honey and saffron tarts and a mazer of ale. All the same, she managed to convey the impression that she had just risen from her sickbed and was treated accordingly, with much tenderness and loving affection, by her cousin, brother and uncle. In these circumstances, I felt I must delay questioning her until such time as she was showing a more robust face to the world, and consequently requested that I might be allowed to talk to Meg Spendlove.

'Then speak to her in the kitchen,' Isolda advised me. 'Meg won't be happy anywhere else. Not that I think you'll get very much out of her, even there. She's very wary of strangers, particularly of men.'

We were once more alone, the men having returned to the workshop and Eleanor Babcary having withdrawn again to her bedchamber, complaining of a headache.

'I'll do my best to overcome her prejudice,' I said. 'But before I go downstairs in search of her, there is one thing, Mistress Bonifant, that I have so far failed to ask both you and your father. How do you think the monkshood was obtained? Would you or any other member of the household know?'

Isolda hesitated, then answered reluctantly, 'My father, who's not so young as he was' – I couldn't help reflecting how indignantly Master Babcary would have taken issue with this statement – 'uses an oil, made chiefly from the root of the monkshood plant, to ease his aching joints. Long hours bent over his workbench has given him rheumatic pains in his arms and back. This liniment, provided for him by Master Page of Gudrun Lane, gives him great relief when rubbed well into his shoulders and the surrounding flesh.'

'And who performs this service for him?'

The colour crept up under her skin and then receded, leaving her very pale.

'I do sometimes,' was the reply. 'At other times, it's Kit.'

'But everyone in the house is aware that Master Babcary uses this embrocation?'

'I suppose so.'

'And also that it is extremely poisonous?'

She nodded. 'Master Page made it plain both to Father and to me that it could prove fatal if swallowed, and we

119

naturally made sure that the other members of the household were also told. And because of that warning, Father always keeps the bottle containing the liniment locked in a cupboard in his room.'

'And where does he keep the key to this cupboard?'

Isolda bit her lip. 'In a little wooden box in the chest at the foot of his bed. Unfortunately,' she added, 'everyone knows that it's there and which cupboard it unlocks.'

'So anyone could have taken the bottle and poured some of the contents into Master Bonifant's wine?'

'Yes, I'm afraid that's true.'

I thought about this. 'My mother used to use a liniment made from the root of the monkshood plant,' I said after a short silence, 'for her rheumatics, and my recollection of it is that it had a pungent smell. Why, I wonder, did Master Bonifant not notice it as he drank?'

Isolda began to collect the dirty dishes together and stack them in a pile. After a long moment, she replied, without raising her eyes from what she was doing, 'The oil was very potent, and Apothecary Page warned us that even a drop could prove fatal. Kit and I were to wash our hands thoroughly every time we so much as touched it, and we were never to use it if we had a cut or scratch or any kind of abrasion on our skin. So I suppose it needed only a very small amount to kill Gideon. And the wine itself had a strong bouquet.' She gave an uncertain little laugh and finally met my gaze. 'You see, I'm being perfectly candid with you, Master Chapman.'

Was she also being very clever? I asked myself, but was unable to make up my mind.

'I appreciate your frankness, Mistress Bonifant,' I replied. 'After the – after your husband's death, did you or Master Babcary check the bottle containing the monkshood oil to see if any of it was missing?'

'We did, but it was impossible to tell. The bottle is of thick, smoked glass with a very tiny neck. And, as I told you, only the smallest drop would have been necessary to kill Gideon. Why do you ask?'

'Because it occurs to me that it may not have been your father's liniment that was used. If, for instance, the murderer was from outside this house, then the poison must have been obtained elsewhere.'

Isolda gave me a quick, sidelong glance. 'You're thinking of Barbara Perle and the Napiers. But what motive could one of those three possibly have had for wishing my husband dead?'

'That I don't know at present, but there may have been a reason. And now, if you'll allow me to carry that tray downstairs for you, I'll speak to Meg Spendlove.'

Isolda shook her head. 'You'd do better to let me come with you and introduce you properly as a friend. Besides,' she added, picking up the heavy wooden tray, loaded with its stacks of dirty dishes, as though it were a featherweight, 'I don't trust you with your hands full on that twisting stair. You're more than liable to drop the lot. In domestic matters, men are clumsy creatures – or, at least, so they pretend.'

On which slightly sour note, she led the way down to the kitchen where Meg Spendlove was already scouring out the cooking pots ready for the preparation of the evening meal.

The maid's eyes had widened with fright as soon as she saw me, and she retreated to the opposite side of the stone bench on which she was working when Isolda explained that I wished to talk to her about the murder.

'I don't know anything, Missus,' she muttered. 'I wasn't there.'

Isolda lowered her burden on to one end of the bench and put water to heat over the fire in order to wash the dirty plates.

'No one's accusing you of anything, Meggie,' she said soothingly, adding, with a significant glance in my direction, 'Master Chapman knows that you had nothing to do with Master Bonifant's death. He just wants to ask you a question or two. Now, sit down quietly on that stool and listen to what he has to say. Don't be afraid. I shall be right here, beside you.'

I would far rather have spoken to Meg alone, but I had enough sense to realise that without Isolda's comforting presence I should probably get nothing out of her at all. It was therefore the lesser of two evils, and I resigned myself to putting up with a certain amount of interference from my hostess.

'Meg,' I said gently, not quite sure where I should begin,

121

'what . . . what were your feelings about Master Bonifant?' She stared at me blankly. 'Did you like him?' I asked.

I had expected prevarication, and was unprepared for her blunt, 'No! I didn't. I hated him.'

'Now, Meggie dear!' Isolda interrupted hurriedly. 'You know that's not true. You didn't always get on well with him, I agree, but you didn't hate him.'

'Yes, I did,' was the uncompromising retort. The little face was suddenly filled with loathing. 'I'm glad he's dead. I thank God every night for it when I say my prayers.'

There was no arguing with such conviction, and Isolda stood, irresolute, not knowing what to say for the best, nor how to put Meg on her guard for what she probably guessed would be my next question.

'Did you know that the liniment used by Master Babcary to ease his aches and pains is poisonous?'

Meg nodded vigorously, a belligerent gleam in the brown eyes.

'Yes, 'cause Missus Isolda told us all when the 'pothecary first brought it to the house. And I know where it's kept, and where the key to the cupboard is.' Having made this admission, however, all her bravado seemed to desert her and she burst into noisy sobs. 'But I didn't kill Master Gideon. I didn't! I didn't!'

Isolda flew to her side, putting a protective arm around her shoulders.

'Of course you didn't, Meggie! Nobody would ever accuse you of such a thing, would he, Master Chapman?' And she stared at me defiantly, daring me to contradict her.

This assurance seemed to have the opposite effect on Meg to the one intended, and the sobs grew louder. I had to wait several minutes for the noise to abate, but the delay afforded me an opportunity to ignore Isolda's question without her realising it.

'Meg,' I said, even more gently, when the fit of crying had eventually subsided, 'I know that you and Mistress Bonifant spent most of the day in the kitchen, preparing the food for Mistress Perle's birthday feast but did you, for any reason, go up to the parlour after the table had been laid?'

'I've already told you that she didn't,' Isolda put in quickly.

I tried to recollect whether she had done so or not, but I need not have worried. Meg Spendlove was too simple to take a hint.

'I didn't go up *after* the table was laid,' she answered, frowning slightly. 'But I did go up with the Missus aforehand. She said if I was good, she'd let me put the special cups on the table. Missus told me where to put them, so I shouldn't get 'em mixed up again.'

Isolda sighed resignedly. 'She loves those goblets. She likes to look at the carving around the rims, the clusters of grapes and vine leaves, the nymphs and shepherds dancing.' She glanced at the girl and shook her head. 'Why did you have to go and blurt that out, Meggie? No one need have known you were there.'

Meg seemed puzzled. 'Toby knew,' she said. 'He peeped round the door while you were telling me where to put the things on the table.'

It was Isolda's turn to frown. 'I didn't know that. I didn't see him.'

'You wouldn't. You had your back to him,' Meg answered. 'But I saw him and he saw me. He winked at me, then went away again.'

'Was he there for long?' I asked. 'Long enough, say, to overhear what Mistress Bonifant was saying and to watch where you placed the goblets?'

'I dunno. I suppose so.' Meg had stopped being frightened and was beginning to grow surly at all this questioning.

But I hadn't quite finished with her yet.

'Later on,' I said, 'after Mistress Perle and her friends had arrived, Toby came down to the kitchen to have his supper with you, as he always did when there were guests. Mistress Bonifant has told me that when she entered the kitchen, you and he were whispering together. Toby was laughing. What were you talking about?'

The colour surged into her face. 'Nothing!' she exclaimed fiercely. 'Anyway, I can't remember.'

'Then how do you know that it was nothing? Something must have amused Toby,' I urged. 'What was it?'

Meg's face, from which the tide of red had now receded, became expressionless. 'Can't remember,' she repeated.

'Try,' I pleaded.

Meg simply shrugged her thin shoulders and looked away.

Isolda smiled mockingly. 'Master Chapman, you might as well save your breath. You'll get no more out of her now that she's made up her mind not to tell you. She can be as obstinate as a mule.'

I had no doubt that she was right. I have invariably found that simple people, like Meg Spendlove, possess tremendous strength of will and determination.

'Did you poison Master Bonifant, Meg?' I asked abruptly, hoping to catch her off her guard.

She thrust out her underlip and her eyes sparked with anger. 'No! But I wish I had,' she answered.

There seemed nothing more to be said. Meg was in a thoroughly recalcitrant mood and I should get no more from her. I could have persisted, but it would have done no good. I glanced at Isolda, who gave an almost imperceptible, discouraging shake of her head.

'We'll leave you alone then, Meggie,' she murmured. 'I'll come back later and give you a hand with the dirty dishes.'

'No need to,' Meg replied, her tone surly. 'I can do them on my own.'

'Well, at least she isn't frightened of you any longer,' Isolda smiled as we left the kitchen. There was a crash from somewhere behind us as an iron cooking pot was carelessly dropped on the stone-flagged floor and we both laughed. 'Now, what do you want to do next? Do you wish to speak to Toby Maybury? If you'll return upstairs, to the parlour, I'll see if Father can spare him from the workshop.'

'I do want to speak to him,' I agreed, 'but I also need to speak to both your cousins.'

Isolda pursed her lips. 'I suppose Nell *might* be feeling well enough to answer a few questions by now,' she said doubtfully. 'I'll ask her if you like. But don't be surprised if she declines. She's not very strong, you know. She has always suffered from delicate health.'

It was on the tip of my tongue to protest that a girl who had such a hearty appetite was probably as strong as a packhorse, but I restrained myself. I should gain nothing by antagonising these people, and it was obvious that Eleanor Babcary was a privileged person in the household.

'I should be very grateful for your help in this matter, Mistress Bonifant,' I said. 'I should like to have a word with Mistress Eleanor, if I may. Master Toby can wait a while.'

Isolda accompanied me up the first flight of stairs, leaving me outside the parlour to continue on up to the second storey, where her cousin's bedchamber was situated next to her own. I pushed open the door, closing it carefully behind me, and once again approached the fire, thankful for its warmth after the dank chill of the kitchen.

I sat down in the armchair, recently vacated by my hostess, and stared into the heart of the flames. So far, I had no idea who had killed Gideon Bonifant, but was very much inclined to think that Isolda was innocent of the crime. Yet I was well aware that this was to ignore the most telling evidence, and was simply because I liked her. Moreover, I knew that my judgement was often at fault, and on several occasions before this, I had been drawn to women who had turned out to be far more evil than any man. Her apparent frankness might mean that she was just a clever dissembler, and it was therefore vital that I remain on my guard where Isolda was concerned.

I had guessed that Eleanor Babcary would take some persuading to leave her bed, but it now seemed a very long time since my hostess had left me at the parlour door. I got up from my chair, stretching my arms and legs, which were beginning to ache from inactivity, unused to this cloistered, sedentary life. I turned my back to the fire, letting its heat seep into my bones, and it was while I was standing thus that I suddenly realised how quiet, all at once, the house was. It was true that the door of the room was closed, but surely I had previously been able to hear some sounds through it. But now there was nothing; not so much as the echo of a distant voice, not even the creak of a floorboard. I could hear no footfall from the rooms overhead, no faint crash from the kitchen regions.

The hairs began to rise on the nape of my neck, and I again felt as I had done the night before last, on my way back to the Voyager. It was as though some evil presence was very close at hand, and I reflected with dismay that I had left my cudgel downstairs, in the shop. So I clenched my hands into two sizeable fists and rocked forward on the balls of my feet, ready to launch myself at whatever was threatening me.

The silence seemed as impenetrable as ever. Then the latch of the door was slowly lifted.

Thirteen

Yet again, my worst fears were not realised. It was Eleanor Babcary who entered the room, closely followed by Isolda. I breathed a sigh of relief, but, at the same time, wondered why my imagination was playing me such tricks.

It was plain that Eleanor had accompanied her cousin against her will. There was a pout to the soft lips, a sullen expression in the blue eyes that clearly indicated her reluctance, and I wondered what arguments Isolda had used to cajole her into talking to me. Perhaps she had pointed out that it would be wiser to submit to my questioning now and get it over with, than to wait in uneasy anticipation of the ordeal still to come.

'I hope you're feeling better, Mistress,' I said with as much concern as I could muster, convinced in my own mind that there was nothing really wrong with the girl except for an irritation of nerves which I could not, at present, explain. 'Won't you sit down?' And I pointed to the armchair nearest the fire.

She glanced over her shoulder at Isolda, who nodded encouragement.

'Do as Master Chapman says, Nell. I'll sit here, opposite you, and then you'll have no need to be afraid.'

'I hope Mistress Babcary knows better than to be afraid of me,' I responded with some asperity. 'I've done nothing that I'm aware of to inspire fear in any member of this household.'

'You're looking for the truth concerning a murder,' Isolda answered drily. 'That's enough, surely, to frighten us all.' She moved to the other armchair and sat down.

Her cousin followed suit, but held herself erect, fidgeting nervously, as she had done earlier, with the pendant around

127

her neck. I drew forward a stool and seated myself midway between the two women.

'Mistress Babcary,' I invited, 'tell me all you can – anything that you remember – about the evening that Master Bonifant died.'

Eleanor's story, told haltingly, agreed with both her cousin's and her uncle's version of events, and was recounted with almost no prompting from the former, and with very few glances in her direction.

Eleanor had, she said, gone up to her bedchamber to change from her workaday into her best clothes at the same time as the other members of the family – excepting, of course, Isolda – and had returned here, to the parlour, to see Mistress Perle presented with her birthday gift and to drink her health.

'Mistress Bonifant was late putting in an appearance because she had been delayed in the kitchen,' I pointed out. 'What did you all talk about while you were waiting for her arrival?'

The younger woman furrowed her brow. 'I can't remember. Mistress Napier spoke to me, but I have no recollection of what she said, because I wasn't listening to her very closely. Toby was winking and mouthing something at me from behind her back, but I couldn't make out what it was he was saying.'

I leant forward a little, my interest quickening. 'Winking and mouthing, was he? And did you ever find out what it was that he'd been trying to tell you?'

Eleanor shook her head. 'I never asked him.' Her face grew bleak. 'With everything that . . . that happened afterwards, I'd forgotten all about it until now.' She had at last stopped tugging at her pendant and was gripping the arms of her chair so hard that the knuckles of her hands gleamed white.

'He wasn't supposed to be here, was he? When your uncle entertains guests, Toby takes his meals in the kitchen.'

'Yes, with Meggie.' Eleanor raised her lovely eyes to mine. 'I don't know why he was in the parlour. He shouldn't have been.'

I did not press the matter. I could winkle the truth out of young Toby later. Meantime, I had a more important question for Eleanor Babcary, but one which I was loath to put to her in Isolda's presence. Fortunately, just at that moment, there was the sound of feet pounding up the stairs and, a second or two later, Toby himself put his head around the door. The sound of distant wailing reached our ears.

'You'd best come, Mistress,' he said to Isolda. 'Meg's dropped half a dozen eggs on the kitchen floor and is crying her eyes out. She won't be comforted by anyone but you.'

My hostess stifled what could have been an unladylike curse as, with a better grace than I think I could have mustered in the circumstances, had I been in her shoes, she rose and accompanied the apprentice downstairs. She did falter as she reached the parlour door, but, to her credit, her hesitation was only momentary. A second later, I heard the click of the latch.

I turned back to Eleanor to find her eyeing me askance. It was almost as if she knew what I was going to ask her.

'Mistress Babcary,' I said, 'what were your feelings for Gideon Bonifant?'

'My feelings for him?' Her eyes were warier still.

'Yes. Did you like him? Were you . . . Were you fond of him?'

I noticed with interest that at my reference to the murdered man, one of Eleanor's slender white hands had risen, almost unconsciously, to finger yet again the pendant on its thin gold chain. Her voice, when she answered, was somewhat constricted.

'He was Isolda's husband. Of course I liked him, for her sake.'

'Was that the only reason? Did you not like him for his own sake?'

'I don't know what you mean.' She sounded slightly breathless. 'I – I didn't think much about him. He was years older than I was. He was ten years older than Isolda. Gideon always seemed to me to be more of Uncle Miles's generation, although I suppose he wasn't really.' She blinked unhappily. 'Kit and I had only been here a year when he and Isolda were married and he came to live here, too. So . . . Well, I was used to him, you see. He was just another member of the household.'

I reflected for the second time that while this had probably once been true of Eleanor's attitude towards her cousin's husband, it was possible that her feelings for him might have undergone a change. I don't know what put this idea into my head, except that she refused to meet my eyes when speaking of Gideon, and continued, in the same restless, nervous way, to fiddle with her pendant. There was also the memory of her earlier tears.

I said, 'According to Mistress Bonifant, that jewel of yours was a birthday gift from all of them – herself, your uncle, your brother and Master Bonifant. Everyone had a hand in making it, is that not so?'

Eleanor looked bewildered by this change of subject, and for a second or two could do nothing more than nod her head. Finally, however, she answered, 'Yes. Uncle Miles was responsible for most of the work because he insisted that it must be done properly, that it had to be perfect for me. But they all had a hand somewhere in the fashioning of it.'

'And what was Master Bonifant's contribution, do you know?'

I heard the breath catch in her throat and her eyes suddenly widened with an emotion whose nature still eluded me.

'I – I was told he set the sapphires in the lover's knot.'

'And who told you that?' I queried gently.

'What?' She had been temporarily lost in some dream world of her own and I had to repeat my question. 'Oh,' she replied, once she understood, 'I can't remember. Uncle Miles, I expect. Or Kit perhaps. Or maybe even Isolda.'

'But not Master Bonifant himself?'

The door opened and Isolda returned to seat herself again in the chair opposite her cousin's.

'What a mess!' she exclaimed, torn between annoyance and laughter. 'Six eggs running everywhere among the rushes, and a bowl broken into the bargain. That's Meggie's second accident today. She cracked an earthenware cooking pot earlier on. Those are the sort of accidents that so infuriated Gideon.' Isolda grimaced and shrugged resignedly. 'Well, Master Chapman, and have you finished questioning Eleanor yet?' She cast one shrewd look at her cousin's face and continued, 'Nell, dearest, you look tired. I think you should lie down until suppertime. Come along!' She got up, holding out an imperious hand. 'I'll help you up to bed.'

Eleanor rose obediently and, I fancied, with relief. Isolda addressed me over her shoulder.

'I've told Toby to come up here to see you. He shouldn't be long; only a minute or two, or until he's finished whatever task it is that Father has set him.'

'And Master Christopher?' I murmured. 'I still haven't spoken to him.'

She heaved another sigh. 'Don't worry! I'll make certain that you do. You might as well finish your enquiries here all in one day.' She didn't add, 'And then you won't have to come back,' but I could hear the unspoken comment in her voice.

When the two women had gone upstairs, I waited several minutes before deciding to go in search of young Toby for myself. I wished to speak to Miles again, as well as to Christopher Babcary and the apprentice, and guessed that I should find them all together in the shop, which indeed I did.

The three men were busy and looked none too pleased at my uninvited appearance amongst them.

'Toby was just coming up to the parlour,' Miles said testily. He was bent over his workbench, putting the finishing touches to the coronet of gold and silver ivy leaves for Mistress Shore.

I ignored this remark and asked him why he had failed to mention the scene between his son-in-law and Meg Spendlove only some five weeks before the murder.

He answered sourly, 'Because I'd forgotten about it, that's why. I told you, I have too many calls upon my time to take much notice of such domestic squabbles. But yes, I do recall the occasion now that you jog my memory. Gideon indulged himself in a display of bad temper that was quite unnecessary in my opinion.'

'In everyone's opinion,' his nephew put in, looking up from the other end of the bench, where he was sorting and grading a bag of pearls.

'And you don't think that maybe Meg bore Master Bonifant a grudge for this unwarranted dressing-down?'

It was Toby's turn to abandon the tray of wax, in which he was drawing a pattern of leaves and flowers, and come forward to stand in front of me, his lower lip jutting aggressively.

'Meg wouldn't harm a fly,' he said. 'You let her alone.'

'That will do,' his master reproved him. 'Get back to your work.'

131

'No, no!' I said, putting a detaining hand on the apprentice's shoulder. 'I want to know, Toby, why you were in the parlour on the evening of the murder. I understand that when there are guests, you eat in the kitchen. So what were you doing upstairs? Both Mistress Bonifant and Master Babcary, here, have testified to your presence, as I'm sure Master Christopher could also do, if asked.'

'That's true enough,' Christopher confirmed. He glanced curiously at the apprentice. 'I hadn't really thought about it until now, but what *were* you doing skulking about in the parlour, when you should have been down in the kitchen with Meg?'

Toby glared defiantly at the three of us. 'I just went in to have a look at the table,' he said. 'At the goblets, really. They're so beautiful. I like to touch them. I like to feel the carving round the rims.'

Miles Babcary mellowed visibly in the face of this unlooked-for tribute. 'The boy has a natural eye for craftsmanship. I'll make a goldsmith of him yet.'

Toby simpered virtuously.

'And was that the only reason you went into the parlour?' I asked.

His eyes met mine for a fleeting moment before his glance slid sideways. 'Yes,' was the truculent reply.

'And did anyone else enter the room while you were there?'

This was an easier question to answer.

'Master came in with Mistress Perle and the other lady and gentleman, a few minutes after Master Bonifant and Kit and Nell. Mistress arrived last of all, and then I went downstairs.'

I noted that while Christopher and Eleanor were referred to with familiarity, Gideon had evidently remained on more distant terms with a lowly apprentice.

Toby, feeling that he had satisfied my curiosity, would, at this point, have squirmed free of my hand and returned to his task, had I not tightened my grip on his shoulder.

'Just a minute! According to Mistress Babcary, something else happened before you left the parlour. What was it that you were trying to tell her behind Mistress Napier's back? She says you were mouthing words at her and making signs.'

There was a tell-tale pause before Toby retorted defiantly, 'I was not!'

'She says you were, and I don't see why she should tell me a lie.'

'No, indeed,' Christopher cut in. 'My sister's a very truthful person.'

Toby went a guilty red. 'I'm not saying she lied,' he protested. 'I'm just saying she must have been mistaken.'

'How could she possibly be mistaken about such a thing?' I asked severely.

He then changed tack, claiming that his memory was at fault, and that he could remember nothing of the matter. But that, he conceded generously, didn't mean to say it wasn't true. And in spite of all my perserverance and the derision of uncle and nephew, we could not persuade him to alter his story. It was obvious, to me at least, that he was lying but there was nothing I could do against his obstinate persistence that he was unable to recollect the incident, and that, therefore, whatever it was that he had been trying to convey to Eleanor had been of no importance. Eventually, I gave up and released him, whereupon he retired again to his workbench with a heartfelt sigh of relief.

I turned my attention to Christopher.

'Master Babcary,' I said, 'perhaps you would tell me what you remember of that evening.'

He shrugged his broad shoulders and continued deftly sorting the pearls, assembling them into three different groups by size.

'I expect I'm only telling you what you have already heard,' he said, without looking up. 'We shut the shop early that evening and then went upstairs to change into our Sunday clothes, it being Mistress Perle's birthday feast.'

'Did you all leave the shop together?' I asked.

Christopher glanced at the older man, frowning. 'You went first, I think, Uncle Miles. If I remember rightly, you wanted to be sure that you were ready before Mistress Perle and her friends arrived.'

'That's true,' Master Babcary confirmed. 'And as well that

I did. I went straight to my room but, even so, I was barely dressed before I heard Barbara's knock.'

'And then?' I prompted. 'Who was the next to leave?'

Once again, Christopher shrugged and grimaced, implying that he was unable to remember. 'Is it of any importance?' he sneered.

'It might be,' I replied, trying to keep my temper. 'In any case, I should be interested to know the answer. Was it you or Master Bonifant or young Toby, here?'

'It was Master Bonifant,' Toby said, giving me a winning smile in order to make up for his former intransigence.

'Are you sure of that?' I asked.

'Of course I'm sure. He'd been applying some gilding to that silver chalice Master had made for Saint Pancras's church, and I remember him saying, "I've had enough of this! I'm off upstairs. I'll finish it in the morning." Only of course he never did. Master finished it himself a week or so later.'

There was an uneasy silence while Christopher, Miles Babcary and Toby avoided one another's eyes and I looked thoughtfully at the three of them. Finally, I enquired of Christopher, 'Is that your recollection, too? Was Master Bonifant the next to go upstairs?'

He nodded. 'Yes. Now I think back, I can recall Gideon using precisely those words. He'd been in a bad mood all day, more than usually grumpy and taciturn, although his temper seemed to have improved a bit by the time we were all assembled in the parlour.'

'And did you or Toby go upstairs next?'

Christopher glowered at me, irritated by my persistence. Once more, it was the apprentice who answered for him.

'I did. I knew Master would want me to look tidy, even if I wasn't eating with the family.'

'And how long after Master Bonifant's departure was that?'

Toby pulled a face and raised his eyebrows at Christopher. 'Ten minutes, would you say?' And when the other man did not answer, he went on, 'Yes, about ten minutes. Maybe a little longer.'

'Your bedchamber's on the top floor, so I've been told.'

Toby nodded. 'Next to Kit's.'

'You went straight up there from the shop?' Again he nodded. 'And did you see anyone else on the stairs?'

'No. Well,' he amended, 'I saw Master Bonifant when I reached the second landing. He was just going into his room. He said he'd been to the kitchen to have a word with Mistress Bonifant, which was why he'd been delayed.'

'And did you believe him?'

Toby blinked in surprise. 'Why shouldn't I believe him when he said so? Where else could he have been?'

For some reason that I was unable to explain to my own satisfaction, the delicate, flower-like features of Eleanor Babcary swam before my mind's eye. Had there been a brief, secret lovers' tryst between her and Gideon? Or was I, as ever, letting my imagination run ahead of common sense? I had no evidence – at least, not so far – to suppose that either was in love with the other. All the same, I would check with both Meg and Isolda to discover if this statement of Gideon's was true.

I turned back to the apprentice. 'And it was after you had made yourself fit to be seen in company that you sneaked down to the parlour?'

'Yes. I told you, I went to look at the goblets. I always do, when they're taken out for feast days and holidays.'

My host looked even more gratified than before.

'Master Babcary,' I asked abruptly, 'did you know that your son-in-law had been married previously? That your daughter was his second wife?'

He raised his eyes from Mistress Shore's coronet and looked both astonished and indignant that I could suppose him ignorant in this matter.

'Of course I knew. It's not the sort of circumstance a man would conceal.'

I bowed my head in agreement. 'So I should suppose. But I was curious as neither you nor Mistress Bonifant had mentioned the fact.'

He threw up his hands in exasperation. 'Why should we? It can have no bearing on his murder. The lady herself died many years ago, and can hardly have had anything to do with his death. Who told you about her?'

'Master Ford, the apothecary, Master Bonifant's old master.' I shifted my gaze to the nephew. 'Master Babcary, did you know, before Gideon's death, of the stories he was spreading concerning you and Mistress Bonifant?'

Christopher's fingers were suddenly stilled amongst the pearls that he had been so busily sorting. A tide of blood suffused his face. Miles Babcary nervously adjusted his spectacles.

'Of course I didn't,' the younger man answered with a menacing quietness. 'Had I done so, I should have made it my business to refute such an evil slander.'

I plucked up courage to ask, 'There was, then, not the slightest vestige of truth in the rumour?'

'None whatsoever!' His tone was venomous, and his eyes, now fixed on my face, dared me to pursue the subject.

I braved his wrath and said, as apologetically as I could, 'Master Bonifant also claimed to have overheard you boasting to your sister of being in love with an older woman, and of being almost certain that your love was requited. Was this true?'

Never, in my estimation, was guilt written more plainly on a man's face than it was at that moment on Christopher Babcary's but, having denied the charge in the past, and, presumably, having persuaded his sister to lie for him, he could do no other than refute it now, even though it was doubtful that he would wish to.

'Whatever Gideon thought he heard, he was mistaken.'

'I see. And do you know of any other man whose' – my tongue fumbled for a word – 'whose friendship with your cousin might have misled Master Bonifant into imagining that you were his betrayer? Or convinced him that he was indeed being betrayed?'

'I know of no one!' came the furious response.

'No one! No one!' echoed Miles Babcary, equally angry.

'But Master Bonifant must have got this idea from somewhere!' I cried despairingly. 'Something must have made him suspect that his wife was being unfaithful to him.'

Two mouths shut like traps; the looks from two pairs of eyes would have struck me down if they could. But I was there at the instigation of the King's mistress and of the Duke of Gloucester, and neither man dared to send me packing from the house, as I had not the smallest doubt he wished to do.

136

I swung round and faced the apprentice, who had given up all pretence of working and was staring at me, goggle-eyed.

'Do you know of anyone, Toby?'

Toby pulled himself together and gave my question his gravest consideration. But after some long, hard thought, he slowly shook his head.

'No,' he said, 'there's no one I can think of. Mistress was always a loyal wife as far as I could see. Besides,' he added with all the candour of youth, 'men just don't fancy her, do they? Not like Mistress Nell. But,' he added, his eyes suddenly sly, 'I did think, at one time, as how Master Kit was partial to Mistress Napier. I used to see the way he mooned at her whenever she visited the shop. And once, I caught him trying to kiss her.'

Fourteen

'And what happened then?' my wife enquired, her face alight with interest and curiosity. 'Did Christopher Babcary admit to the truth of Toby's accusation?'

I had returned to the Voyager just as dusk was falling, and was now cosily ensconced in our little room in front of a glowing fire, which Reynold Makepeace had insisted be lit for Adela's comfort, after what had proved to be a somewhat tiring day in the company of Jeanne Lamprey.

True to her promise, Jeanne, leaving Philip in charge of their shop, had taken my wife to see the wild animals in the Tower. But the walk from Cornhill, the cold, the noise, the crowds of people and the densely packed traffic of the streets, particularly around the Tower itself, had left Adela feeling, as she herself phrased it, 'like a wrung-out dishcloth.' She had arrived back at the inn sometime in the mid-afternoon, her exhausted appearance immediately exciting our host's ready sympathy. He had sent one of the pot-boys scurrying to set a lighted taper to the wood and coals freshly laid on our hearth, while the cook despatched two kitchen maids to our bedchamber with hot broth and rosewater jelly.

I was now drinking a bowlful of the same broth, together with a large slice of good wheaten bread and a couple of collops of bacon, all washed down with Reynold's best ale, glad to be free of the Babcarys' house and what I felt to be the family's growing hostility towards me. But Adela was anxious to know everything that had happened during the day, and so, between mouthfuls of food, I had regaled her with the facts. But when I reached the point of Toby's revelation concerning Christopher Babcary and Ginèvre Napier, I had been forced to go through to the taproom in search of more ale. I had, however, barely seated myself once again in my chair before my wife, stretched out on the bed, her aching back propped against the pillows, compelled me to continue my story by answering her question.

I laid down my spoon. 'Christopher denied it hotly at first, as you might imagine. But Toby was so persistent in declaring that what he had told us was correct, and Miles Babcary and I made it so obvious that we believed him – both of us having experience of the kind of woman preferred by Christopher – that, in the end, he grudgingly conceded it to be the truth. And finally, rather than allow me to question his sister again, he confessed that he had indeed boasted to Eleanor that he was in love with an older woman – although without naming her – and that he was certain that his love was returned. He had no idea at the time that his remark had been overheard by Gideon but when he learned how the other man had misinterpreted it, his one thought was to deny ever having said such a thing, and to persuade his sister to deny it, also.'

'So much,' Adela said, nodding sagely, 'for Miles Babcary's conviction that his niece was incapable of lying.'

I picked up my spoon again. 'I have no doubt at all,' I agreed, 'that she is as capable of telling untruths as anyone else, when it suits her to do so. I'm quite certain that she is concealing something concerning herself and Gideon Bonifant, but what that something is, I've as yet no real inkling. I can only guess that she was in love with him and won't own to it for her cousin's sake.'

'But do you think that Gideon was in love with her? Were they, in fact, lovers?'

I finished my broth and wiped my mouth on the back of my hand.

'I should think it well nigh impossible in a house with so many people in it,' I answered. 'Besides, as far as I can gather, he showed no interest in her except as his wife's cousin. The impression I've gleaned of Master Bonifant – although I admit it could be wrong – is of a cold, calculating man who probably married Isolda for no other reason than her dowry and the place in society that she could bring him. Had she not been so plain, she would most likely never have considered him as a husband, but he took advantage of her lack of suitors and her desire to be married to carve out for himself a comfortable niche in life. And I doubt that he would have jeopardised his position as Miles Babcary's son-in-law by betraying Isolda with Eleanor.'

I could see that Adela was not wholly convinced. She said something about people like Gideon having hidden fire in their souls, a remark I instantly derided as far too fanciful and romantic to have been uttered by anyone as sensible as herself, and put it down to her condition (which, as all men know, makes women a little unbalanced).

Adela gave me one of her quizzical looks, accompanied by a small, secret smile that somehow made me feel like a foolish schoolboy. But all she said was, 'What will you do next?'

'Next, I must talk to Mistress Perle and the Napiers,' I answered, adding guiltily, 'Will you go to the Lampreys' again tomorrow?'

My wife shook her head. 'They've very kindly asked me to do so, but I've refused. A day spent here, in the inn, will do me more good. Besides, I'm sure Jeanne and Philip need a rest from *my* company. I'll join them again the following day, if necessary.'

'I'm afraid it will be necessary,' I replied gloomily. 'As yet, I've no idea what really happened that December afternoon, only the conviction that nothing was as straightforward or as simple as it seemed.'

'You don't believe, then, that Mistress Bonifant murdered her husband?'

'Without proof that she really did have a lover, she appears to have had no motive for doing so.'

'And you've decided that, if she did, Christopher Babcary wasn't the man?'

I shrugged. 'He denies it, Isolda denies it, although that, of course, is only what I should expect them to do. But you saw for yourself the woman he was with yesterday, on the quayside – a woman as unlike Mistress Bonifant as it is possible to imagine. Miles Babcary also tells me that his nephew fancies himself in love with a different lady every few weeks. Why, then, would Gideon regard any flirtation between his wife and her cousin, supposing there was one, as seriously meant? No, I find it far easier to believe that Christopher was talking about Mistress Napier to his sister.'

Adela was silent for a few moments. 'That's probably true,' she said at last. 'But why, when Master Bonifant overheard that remark, did he instantly assume that Christopher Babcary was referring to his cousin?'

I pushed my chair back from the fire, which was now proving too hot for me.

'Because,' I answered slowly, reasoning things out as I spoke, 'he already believed Isolda to be unfaithful to him, and Christopher's confession to his sister simply confirmed his suspicions. Gideon jumped to the over-hasty conclusion that Christopher Babcary was the man.'

'But that still doesn't explain,' Adela argued, 'why Master Bonifant believed Isolda to be cuckolding him in the first place.'

'No,' I agreed, rubbing my forehead. 'I have already come to the conclusion that I shall have to go back and question Eleanor Babcary again, for if Isolda confided in anyone, I'm sure it would have been in her beloved Nell. But as it's already been proved that the young lady will lie to protect those she loves, I doubt I have much hope of finding out the truth.' I sighed. 'And where does young Toby Maybury fit into the events of that afternoon? What was he doing in the parlour? If it was just to look at the chasing on the goblets, as he claims, what was he trying to convey to Eleanor behind Ginèvre Napier's back?'

Adela turned on to her side. 'And the maid, Meg Spendlove, she had a grudge against Master Bonifant, you say?'

I finished my ale. 'She did. And I haven't really established whether or not she had an opportunity to return to the parlour on her own after helping Isolda to lay the table. Yes, I'm afraid I've no choice but to go back to Master Babcary's after I've visited Mistress Perle and the Napiers.'

'And when will that be?' asked Adela, sliding off the bed and coming to sit on my knees.

'First thing tomorrow morning,' I said, kissing her cheek.

But I had barely scraped the overnight stubble from my chin, and had only just returned from holding my head under the courtyard pump, when Reynold Makepeace came knocking urgently at our bedchamber door.

'A messenger's here from His Grace of Gloucester,' he

announced breathlessly when my wife had opened it in answer to his summons. 'He says he must speak with Master Chapman.'

'Then he must wait on me in here,' I called out testily. 'I've not yet finished dressing.'

A few moments later, the same young man who had shown me the way to Mistress Shore's house three days earlier was ushered in by a deferential Reynold Makepeace, whose only reward was a dismissive flick of the fingers.

'The Duke wishes to speak to you,' the young man announced, addressing me and ignoring Adela. 'You must accompany me immediately to Crosby Place.'

'His Grace will have to possess his soul in patience until I've had my breakfast,' I snapped, annoyed by this cavalier treatment of my wife.

'No,' the young man answered levelly. 'Now! My lord is in no mood to be kept waiting. You can eat in our kitchens afterwards, if you're so hungry.'

There was something in his tone, even though he had not raised his voice, that made me think twice about my gesture of defiance, and Adela also begged me to go.

'You must do as His Grace commands,' she urged.

I finished dressing as slowly as I dared with the young man's impatient eyes fixed upon me, then I kissed my wife, assuring her that I should be back within a very short space of time.

'I'll return here before I visit Paternoster Row,' I told her.

Two horses were tethered outside the inn, such, apparently, being the Duke's impatience to see me that he could not wait for us to make the journey to Bishop's Gate Street on foot. My guide swung himself into the saddle of one of the beasts and signed to me to mount the other.

'You can ride, I suppose?' he asked as an afterthought.

I assured him that I could, although it was not usually my lot to be mounted on such a spirited, thoroughbred animal.

We arrived at Crosby Place very speedily, a path through the teeming streets miraculously opening up for us at the sight of my companion's azure and murrey livery and his badges of the White Boar and the Red Bull. The mansion looked even more impressive by daylight than it had done at night: a large, strongly constructed house of stone and timber, built around a courtyard and surrounded by what would, in spring and summer, undoubtedly be a beautiful garden. I was again shown into the great hall with its oriel window, marble floor and arched roof decorated in red and gold.

'Wait here,' I was instructed. 'Someone will be with you very shortly.' And the young man disappeared through a door beneath the minstrels' gallery.

A number of servants and attendants passed through the hall, eyeing me with either curiosity or indifference, before the Duke's secretary came to escort me to his master. We found the Duke seated at a table, writing, in one of the smaller chambers, but he threw down his pen and swivelled round to greet me as soon as John Kendall had announced me and withdrawn.

'Roger! Thank you for coming so quickly.'

I felt ashamed of my former ill-humour and, at the same time, was shocked at Duke Richard's appearance. If he had seemed unwell four days earlier, I thought him positively haggard now. The dark circles under his eyes were almost black, the eyes themselves sunk deep into their sockets. His face was all bone and no flesh, while his furred gown hung so loosely about him that it was plain to see that he had lost more weight. The hand that he gave me to kiss was skeletal.

He motioned me to the window seat and sat down beside me; or, rather, he perched on the edge, getting up to walk restlessly around the room every few minutes or so.

'How are your investigations proceeding?' he asked, coming straight to the point. 'Have you been able to prove the innocence of Mistress Shore's cousin?'

'Not yet, my lord,' I answered, adding defensively, 'These matters take time. In any case, after a lapse of so many weeks, it may not be possible to uncover any proof that will solve the mystery one way or the other.'

He began to pace the floor, beating his clenched right fist into the open palm of his left hand.

'I must have something soon that will enable me to persuade Mistress Shore to use her influence with the King in favour of saving my brother's life.'

'If you'll forgive me for saying so, my lord,' I ventured, 'having met Mistress Shore since we last talked on this subject, I don't believe you need a bargaining counter in order to enlist her help. She strikes me as a tender-hearted lady who wishes no one any harm.'

The Duke rounded on me almost as though I had spoken blasphemy.

'Do you expect me to beg a *favour* of that woman?' He returned to sit beside me on the window seat, and I could see that he was trembling with anger. After a moment or two, however, he controlled his emotions and raised a faint smile. 'Forgive me, Roger! But for my own peace of mind I must have a bargaining counter, as you call it. Give me the truth about this murder, and I shall be able to enlist Mistress Shore's support without loss of face.'

'But what if Mistress Bonifant – Mistress Shore's kins-woman – is indeed guilty?' I queried.

My companion was once more on his feet, restlessly roaming from window to table, from table to door and back again. The agitation of his mind would not let him be still.

'In that case,' he answered, swinging round to face me, 'I shall use that fact as a threat to force her to do my will. I shall threaten to have her cousin arrested unless she does as I request.' The Duke gave a laugh that cracked in the middle. 'Oh, you needn't look so outraged and reproachful, Roger. Wouldn't you use any means in your power to try to save the life of someone you love?' He again sat down, seizing and gripping one of my wrists so hard that the marks of his fingers remained for hours afterwards. 'Don't put me on a pedestal, my friend. I can be as ruthless as any other man when it comes to something that is important to me.'

'Would His Highness really have his own brother put to death?' The words were jerked out of me before I had time to think.

I had hardly expected an answer to so impertinent a question, but Duke Richard was once more on his feet, banging with his fist against the wall until the knuckles were skinned and bleeding.

'Not left to himself, no! I feel sure of it! But with the Queen and all her family determined on George's death and constantly whispering in Edward's ear—' He broke off, suddenly aware of the impropriety of talking to me so openly, and stood, gnawing his underlip and nursing his injured hand. Then he went on harshly, 'My brother of Clarence was born in Dublin, did you know that? The Irish are wild men, untameable, and it's as though some of that wildness rubbed off on George. But they're charming, too, with the gift of the gab, and he also has both those attributes in abundance.' The Duke continued, talking now more to himself than to me, 'George has always been like a child, grabbing what he wanted with both hands and then relying on his silver tongue to get him out of trouble. But he looked after me when I was young, protected me, comforted me, during those terrible years of our childhood when we never knew what fresh disaster the next day would bring. I owe him more than I can ever repay.'

I said softly, fearing that I was intruding on private grief, but not knowing what else to say, 'It's small wonder that Your Grace is fond of him.'

Duke Richard turned to stare at me, blinking a little, as though he had been unconscious of my presence for the past few minutes, before sitting down again on the window seat.

'I'm fond of both my brothers, that's the difficulty, and to see them at odds like this—' He broke off, giving a shaky laugh. 'At odds, did I say? Now there's an understatement! They're both hell bent on one another's destruction.'

It was on the tip of my tongue to ask how George of Clarence could destroy the King, but I thought better of it. My companion had already confided in me more than he should have done, and I could tell by his suddenly wary expression that he thought so, too, and was probably beginning to regret his frankness.

I stood up. 'Your Highness may trust me. I hope you know that.'

He nodded, giving me his hand to kiss in farewell.

'Let me know as soon as you have resolved this mystery, Roger.' He added, half to himself, 'Even then, it may be too late.'

I wanted to say, 'Go to Mistress Shore, today, and ask her to intercede for the Duke of Clarence's life. She won't despise you for begging this favour.' But I knew that he would never do so. He was too proud. For reasons of his own, he disliked the King's leman too much to enlist her help without being able to offer her an inducement in return. So I merely bowed and promised to bring him word as soon as I had reached a conclusion regarding the death of Gideon Bonifant.

'I'm depending on you, Roger,' were his parting words.

Which was all very well, I reflected peevishly, as I made my way back to Bucklersbury and the Voyager, but if there was no proof to be had, all the dependence in the world couldn't produce any.

It was a bitterly cold day, with low-scudding clouds and a sleety rain that stung the face and hands, and I flung what alms I could spare to the blue-faced beggars, shivering in their scanty rags. I found Adela huddled over the fire in our bedchamber, her long, thin hands spread to the blaze, but otherwise contented and cheerful. She had been dozing, for pregnancy made her extremely sleepy, and was quite happy to doze again when I had gone. But first she wanted to hear all that had passed between the Duke and me.

When I had finished telling her, she grimaced. 'He's asking too much of you, Roger.'

Her assumption that I might fail Duke Richard irritated me and blew away my own pessimistic mood.

'Well, I shan't learn anything new by wasting my time here,' I answered briskly, and bent to kiss her. She laughed, but refused to tell me what it was that she found so amusing. Instead, she patted my cheek and instructed me to run along, just as though I had been Elizabeth or Nicholas. (I sometimes had the impression that she regarded me as another of her children.)

Having once again obtained her assurance that she could manage very well on her own for the next few hours, I promised that I should be back before nightfall.

'Send to Paternoster Row if you need me, to the house of either Mistress Barbara Perle or to that of Gregory and Ginèvre Napier,' I told her.

Paternoster Row, which, as I have already said, is where rosaries are chiefly made, is on the north side of Saint Paul's churchyard. But interspersed with the shops are several private dwellings, one of which I instantly recognised, four storeys high, the carved timbers of its gable picked out in scarlet, blue and gold. The upper windows were made of glass, three of them decorated with leaded trefoils and three with circles

146

within triangles, both signs of the Blessed Trinity. This was the Napiers' house, and I had last been inside it three years earlier, when I was investigating the disappearance of a brother and sister from their home in Devon. Circumstances, as I had told Master Babcary, had brought me to London to question Ginèvre Napier, who had been a friend of the children's mother.

Before renewing my acquaintance with Mistress Napier, however, I first wished to speak to her next door neighbour, Barbara Perle, but realised that I had no idea if her house were to the left or to the right of the Napiers'. I was still trying to decide which dwelling to approach first, standing well back in order to view them better, and unconsciously edging further out amongst the traffic, when the rattle of wheels and the sound of people shouting assailed my ears. The next moment, I was caught unceremoniously around the waist and dragged out of the path of a runaway horse and cart.

'That was a close run thing,' panted my rescuer, a stocky youth with a broken nose. 'You want to watch what you're doing, Master. You could've been killed.'

I acknowledged the fact and grasped his hand in gratitude; but it was not until after more passers-by had come to congratulate me on a narrow escape from death that a feeling of unease began to possess me. Despite my well-wishers' assurance that such accidents were commonplace in London owing to the general carelessness of the drivers, I was unable to rid myself of the suspicion that someone might deliberately have tried to kill me. No one seemed to have taken particular note of the carter's appearance, or be able to describe him, but considering the speed at which he had been travelling, this was hardly surprising.

I told myself that I was being foolish. Running me down would be a risky method of trying to dispose of me, and as far as I knew, the Babcarys owned neither horse nor cart. And yet, surely by now the murderer of Gideon Bonifant should have made some move to stop me enquiring further . . .

'Have you come to interrogate Mistress Perle?' a voice asked in my ear, and swinging round, I found Christopher Babcary standing at my elbow.

'Where have you sprung from?' I asked.

He looked at me, obviously surprised by my belligerent tone, and indicated the basket he was carrying.

'I've been delivering her coronet to Mistress Shore, in the Strand,' he answered, preparing to move on. 'If you want Barbara Perle's house, it's that one, there.' And he pointed to the one to the right of the Napiers'.

I thanked him mechanically, and stood staring after him as he turned away and continued walking along the street.

Fifteen

The skinny young maid who answered my knock informed me that the mistress had stepped out for a moment or two to visit a sick neighbour, but that she would return before long if I cared to come inside and wait. I accepted the offer, following the girl up a flight of stairs to a parlour on the first floor, a room similar in size and content to that of Master Babcary's house. On the face of it, there would seem to be little difference between his and Mistress Perle's respective fortunes.

The maid bade me be seated, but then, instead of leaving to continue with her household chores, she lingered, looking at me with suppressed excitement, plainly desirous of talking to someone.

'Do you know what today is, sir?' she asked shyly.

'The Feast of Saint Sebastian?' I hazarded.

'It's also the Eve of the Feast of Saint Agnes,' she said, her eyes sparkling with anticipation. 'They do say that on this night, if you do what you're told, you'll dream of your future husband.' She giggled nervously. 'I hope he's as handsome as you.'

'And what is it that you have to do?' I enquired, laughing.

'It's not a joke, sir,' she reproved me. 'Young girls like me do see things in dreams, you know. First of all, I have to fast throughout the day – though that'll not be easy – and I mustn't let anyone kiss me, not even a little child. Then tonight, before I go to bed, I have to take a hard-boiled egg, scoop out its yolk and fill the hollow with salt, then eat it, shell and all. After that, I've to put on a clean nightgown and walk backwards towards the bed – I can't turn round and look at it, or the spell will be broken – and I must say

149

this verse.' She screwed up her face and, with a great effort of memory, recited.

> 'Fair Saint Agnes play thy part,
> And send to me mine own sweetheart,
> Not in his best or worst array,
> But in the clothes of every day.'

The sound of the street door opening and closing recalled her to her duties.

'That'll be the mistress now,' she said hurriedly. 'You won't mention anything about what I've been telling you, will you sir? She'd say it's all nonsense and the waste of a good egg, but I say you never know! I'd like to see the man I'm going to marry, whoever he is.'

I promised faithfully that her secret was safe with me, and was still smiling and shaking my head, like some old greybeard, over the naivety of young girls, when the parlour door opened and Mistress Perle came in.

She was a good-looking, well-built woman with a broad, handsome face marred only by the fleshiness of her nose. It needed a second, possibly a third, glance to notice the network of fine wrinkles around the blue eyes, and to realise that she was not quite as young as she at first appeared. She was, I finally decided, in her middle fifties, just the right age for Master Babcary.

'You must be Master Chapman,' she said taking a seat at the table and motioning me to sit opposite her. 'Miles sent to warn me you might be arriving sometime or another, and here you are! What is it you want to know?' She evidently intended to waste no time on the usual courtesies.

I explained as briefly as I could the circumstances and reasons for my visit while she listened attentively, not revealing by so much as the flicker of an eyelid whether or not she was already in possession of these facts. Indeed, there was something unnatural about her general stillness, although I was conscious of the uneasy clasping and unclasping of her hands, as they rested on the table-top in front of her. But when she spoke, her voice was full and steady.

'I repeat, what is it you want to know?'

'Can you tell me what you remember about the afternoon of Master Bonifant's death?'

She was silent for a while, staring into space, but at last she shrugged and nodded her acquiescence.

Her account of the events leading up to the moment when Gideon died was in substance the same as that told by everyone else.

'When they had drunk my health,' she said, 'they all sat down. Oh, except Isolda, of course, who left the parlour in order to go down to the kitchen. That Meg of theirs can never be trusted to do anything properly by herself.' The small, full mouth was pursed in disapproval. 'Why Miles doesn't get rid of her I cannot understand. I've spoken to him often enough on the subject.'

'What happened next?' I interrupted, afraid that she was about to wander from the point.

'Oh, the men began talking – about the new tariffs on silver imported from Poitou, I think. They wouldn't be happy unless they'd something to grumble about. Ginèvre started telling Nell Babcary some rigmarole concerning a length of velvet she'd bought just that morning and which, when she got it home, she'd found to be flawed.'

Mistress Perle paused in order to clear her throat, so I took the opportunity to say, 'And Gideon Bonifant was talking to Christopher, or so Master Babcary informed me. Is that correct?'

My companion considered this. 'I don't recall that Gideon was actually *speaking* to Kit. It was more . . . more that he was staring fixedly at him. I remember thinking later that perhaps Master Bonifant had already begun to feel ill.'

'Was Christopher Babcary speaking to *him*?'

'He might have been,' she answered slowly. 'I do recollect that Kit was looking puzzled. Almost—'

'Almost?' I prompted.

'Almost as if something hadn't happened that he was expecting to happen.' She shrugged. 'But maybe I'm talking nonsense.'

I made no answer, but privately considered that if Mistress Perle were right, then it was possible that Christopher Babcary had put the monkshood in Gideon's cup, or known that Isolda

151

had done so, and had been anxiously watching his victim for the first signs of the poison taking effect.

'Pray continue,' I begged.

Mistress Perle shivered. 'You must know what happened next. Miles and Kit have surely told you. You don't need a description from me.'

'I should like to have one, all the same.' I added with a flattering smile, 'Women notice so much more than men.'

'Oh – very well. Gideon suddenly staggered to his feet, clutching his throat. He was plainly choking and, at first, I thought that some of his wine had gone down the wrong way. Then I saw that his face was turning blue. I could also see that he was trying to swallow, but couldn't. His throat appeared to be as stiff as a board. His lips, too, because when he tried to speak, he was unable to form the words.' She hesitated, frowning a little. 'And yet I thought at the time that I did hear something that sounded like "aconite".'

'So you think he realised immediately that he'd been poisoned?'

'Perhaps,' she conceded. 'He was desperately afraid, I could see that. But also—'

'But also?'

Mistress Perle put a hand to her forehead. 'Oh . . . I don't know! It's difficult to explain. There was an expression on his face that I can only describe as . . . as *outrage*. It was as if he couldn't really believe what was happening to him.'

'I should imagine death, particularly violent death, would make us all feel like that,' I replied gently. 'But please continue.'

'What? Oh . . . very well! Ginèvre told Gregory to run for the nearest apothecary. That would be Jeremiah Page in Gudrun Lane. In the doorway he almost collided with Isolda and the girl. They'd just come up from the kitchen with the food.'

'And what did they do?'

She snorted. 'Meg behaved exactly as you would expect her to – she screamed and dropped her tray, the stupid creature! Isolda simply stood and stared. Then Gideon – I swear I'll never forget it as long as I live – he raised his hand and pointed at her.' Mistress Perle gave an exaggerated shudder.

'It was obvious what he meant. He was accusing her of his murder.'

There was silence. My companion, lost in her own thoughts, continued to clasp and unclasp her hands, while I recollected Miles Babcary's words. 'Mistress Perle was almost fainting in horror, and I had to give her the better part of my attention.' It occurred to me that for someone in such a distraught condition, Barbara Perle's memory of events was remarkably detailed, and I wondered if her distress had been assumed for her lover's benefit, or if Master Babcary had been mistaken in the nature of her agitation. Stealing another look at her while she was still lost in her reverie, it struck me anew that she was ill at ease, and had been ever since the beginning of our conversation. I noticed that there was a film of sweat across her forehead, and the constant restlessness of her hands implied an unquiet mind. Did she have something to conceal?

I asked suddenly and loudly, 'Who do you think murdered Gideon Bonifant, Mistress?'

She jumped and glared at me for a moment as though I was some unknown intruder. Then she answered with an unnatural vehemence, 'Isolda of course! There's no doubt about it! Probably aided and abetted by that cousin of hers.'

'Do you mean Christopher Babcary?'

'Of course I mean Christopher Babcary! Who else? I'm not likely to be talking of Nell! Although come to think of it, she's the sort who could be persuaded into anything. She hasn't the brains of a goose. Hasn't Miles told you what Gideon said to him about Kit and Isolda a short time before he was murdered? Yes, he has: I can see the answer in your face. Only Miles has probably persuaded you that it's all a lot of nonsense. He won't listen to anything against his precious daughter. But of course she did it! Who else had such opportunity, both to obtain the monkshood and put it in the wine, as she did?'

There was a false, slightly hysterical note to Mistress Perle's anger, as though she were trying to convince herself, more than me, of Isolda's guilt. But I nodded as if in agreement and thanked her for her time.

'I have to call on your neighbours now,' I said, rising. 'Fortunately, Mistress Napier and I have met before, so we are not total strangers.'

153

My hostess gave me a look of startled enquiry, and I was forced, for politeness's sake, to repeat the story of my previous encounter with Ginèvre. It did nothing to reassure Mistress Perle, however, who appeared even more agitated than before, demanding to know if it were really necessary that I visit the Napiers. And it was not until I had made it perfectly plain that I was not to be dissuaded, that she reluctantly summoned her servant to conduct me to the door.

I followed the girl downstairs.

'Don't forget all you have to do tonight,' I whispered, and left her giggling on the doorstep.

Mistress Napier was, by great good fortune, at home, and, claiming to be an old acquaintance, I was shown by the same young woman into the same downstairs parlour that I remembered from three years earlier. The red and gold painted ceiling beams were slightly more smoke-blackened than they had been then, the tapestries covering the walls were a little dustier; but the three richly carved armchairs, the fine oaken table and the corner cupboard, with its display of bowls and cups and plates all crafted in gold or silver-gilt, were exactly as memory had preserved them. The filigree pendants of the candelabra, suspended over the table, still tinkled in every draught.

Ginèvre Napier, too, was true to my recollection of her, except that time had not dealt kindly with her. The lines around the grey-green eyes were more obvious, the brown spots on the backs of her hands more numerous. The plucked eyebrows and shaven forehead only emphasised her age, just as the many gold chains encircling her neck showed up the scrawniness of her throat.

She was seated near the window, busy with a piece of embroidery, but the heavy, almond-shaped eyelids were opened to their fullest extent as I entered the room, so that she could scrutinise me better.

'I know you,' she said in her husky voice. 'We've met before.'

'Some time ago,' I answered. 'You were so gracious as to answer some questions for me about Lady Skelton and her second husband, Eudo Colet. Her two children had been murdered.'

'Of course! Now I remember! And did you ever get at the truth of the matter? Sit down and tell me all about it.'

So, at her bidding, I pulled up one of the other armchairs and regaled her with a brief account of the events in Devon three years previously. Happily, she was not a woman given to exclamations of dismay or demands for repetition, merely remarking, when I had finished my tale, 'Rosamund always was a fool.' She added, looking me up and down, 'You've put on weight since last we met. You have the appearance of a contented man. You had a wife and little girl, as I recall.'

'I was in fact a widower at the time, but I've married again since then. I now have a stepson and another child of my own on the way.'

Ginèvre laid aside her embroidery and leant back in her chair. She regarded me from beneath the heavy, half-closed lids.

'I do hate people who are happily married,' she mocked. 'They're so horribly smug. But then, a big, virile fellow like you could keep any woman happy between the sheets, I'll be bound.' I felt myself beginning to blush and she laughed. 'All right, Master Chapman, I'll spare you further embarrassment. I know why you're here, although until you walked in, I'd no idea that you were the same chapman whom I'd met before. Barbara Perle heard from Miles Babcary that you were asking questions about the death of Gideon Bonifant, and warned me in her turn.' She frowned. 'These enquiries are on behalf of the Duke of Gloucester, as I understand it. Now why on earth should His Grace be interesting himself in the matter?'

I explained and Mistress Napier sniffed derisively.

'If you want my opinion,' she said, 'the man's deluding himself if he thinks that Mistress Shore or anyone else can influence his elder brother on this score. Clarence has been making a nuisance of himself for years, and I think King Edward will now grasp any opportunity to rid himself of Duke George once and for all. However, let us return to our sheep, as our French cousins so quaintly put it. What do you want to know about Gideon Bonifant's murder?'

'Anything that you can tell me,' I answered. 'Everything that you can recall.'

Savoury smells were beginning to emanate from the Napiers'

kitchen, reminding me not only that it was nearly dinnertime, but also that I had had no breakfast that morning. My empty stomach was starting to rumble.

'Are you hungry?' Ginèvre asked abruptly, and when I nodded, went on, 'Then you can eat with me.' She picked up a small silver handbell and rang it. 'Lay another place in the dining parlour,' she ordered when her maid answered the summons, and rose to her feet. 'Come along,' she said briskly. 'Gregory's at the shop and won't be home until this evening. I dislike eating alone.'

I followed her to a room at the back of the house and within easy reach of the kitchen, so that the food came hot to table, an arrangement many other households would do well to emulate.

'We can eat while we talk,' my hostess remarked, sitting down and indicating that I should do likewise. 'So! You want to know anything and everything about the afternoon that Gideon Bonifant died.'

A rich pottage of beef and vegetables was set before us and Ginèvre picked up her spoon. She did not, however, immediately fall to, but sat absent-mindedly stirring the contents round and round in the bowl, obviously immersed in her own thoughts. I waited in silence. Indeed, I was so busy cramming my mouth with lumps of bread soaked in this delicious broth that I doubt if I could have spoken even if I'd tried.

Arriving at a decision, Ginèvre suddenly raised her head and looked at me across the table. I was surprised to see an ugly, vindictive twist to the thin, heavily painted lips.

'Who have you talked to?' she asked, and when I named them, nodded. 'In that case, I don't suppose there's anything I could add about the events of that afternoon that you haven't been told already. But something I can tell you is that, even supposing Isolda did have a lover, as Gideon claimed, she wasn't the only one present at Barbara's birthday feast who had a reason for wanting to dispose of Master Bonifant.'

I paused in the act of conveying yet another hunk of bread to my gaping mouth, and stared at her. 'If you mean Christopher Babcary or Meg Spendlove,' I began thickly, but was allowed to get no further, being interrupted by a scornful laugh.

'Kit Babcary! And who's Meg Spendlove, pray?' My hostess didn't wait for a reply, but continued, 'No, I'm referring to my husband and the woman I foolishly, trustingly, thought was my bosom friend, Barbara Perle.'

My mind turned somersaults. 'Are you saying that . . . that Master Napier and . . . and Mistress Perle were . . . were—?'

'Oh, for heaven's sake don't be so mealy-mouthed,' Ginèvre snapped, slamming one hand down on the table so hard that her spoon jumped out of her bowl. 'Gregory and Barbara have been lovers this past year or more.' She yelled for her maid and, when the girl appeared, ordered her to remove the broth. 'Bring us something we can get our teeth into,' she said.

'Why are you telling me this?' I asked slowly. 'What does it have to do with the death of Master Bonifant?'

Ginèvre laughed. 'He found out about them. I don't know how, and I haven't bothered to enquire. But he had a long nose and a mean mind. He threatened to tell both Miles Babcary and me about their liaison. Liaison,' she repeated, smiling mirthlessly. 'What a splendid word that is. What respectability it bestows on something that is merely the adulterous humping around in a seamy, sweaty bed. However, let us once again return to our sheep. Gregory immediately told Gideon that he would confess to me himself.' Her lip curled. 'He knew he had little to fear. There had been too many other women in the past. They meant nothing to him, as Barbara Perle meant nothing. He'll never leave me, nor do I wish him to. He's a good provider. I bawled him out and called him all the names I could lay my tongue to, and that, as far as I was concerned, was the end of the matter.'

'But it was different for Mistress Perle?'

Venison steaks, stewed in red wine and peppercorns, were set before us, and then the maid slipped quietly from the room.

'Of course it was different for Barbara. Gideon Bonifant was threatening to tell Miles, and that would have meant the end of all her hopes to become the second Mistress Babcary.'

'What did Gideon want? Money?' I asked, before filling my mouth with the deliciously tender meat.

157

'No. He wanted Barbara's promise to refuse Miles's offer of marriage, should he make one.'

I could see that such a demand made sense to a man wishing to protect his wife's inheritance and his own place in the Babcary household. His father-in-law's proposal to buy the house in Paternoster Row and give it to him and Isolda, generous as it was, had no appeal for Gideon. He wanted no outsider, in the shape of Barbara Perle, influencing any of Miles's future decisions. For who could tell what he might or might not be persuaded to do if neither his daughter nor his son-in-law was present to restrain him?

'So what course of action did Mistress Perle decide on?' I wanted to know, as soon as I had emptied my mouth.

Ginèvre lifted her thin shoulders in a disdainful shrug. 'She didn't. All she could think of doing was to come bleating like a frightened sheep to Gregory. Oh yes, he told me. Once the affair was out in the open, he saw no need to keep anything a secret from me.'

'And what was Master Napier's solution?'

'Oh, he could think of nothing but to offer Gideon money – a very large sum of money – to keep him quiet.' My hostess looked as if she were about to spit. 'I soon put a stop to that, I can assure you. I didn't mince my words. I told Gregory that if he parted with so much as a single groat to Gideon Bonifant, I should make Miles free of the whole sordid affair.'

I thoughtfully chewed another slice of venison. 'And that's how matters stood last December, on Mistress Perle's birthday?'

I understood now Mistress Perle's vehement assertion that Isolda had murdered her husband and her apparent unease throughout our talk together. My new-found knowledge also explained her attempt to dissuade me from speaking to Ginèvre. She had rightly been afraid that her friend, in a moment of pique and spite, would reveal to me the truth about herself and Gregory Napier.

'So you see' – my hostess was speaking again – 'Barbara had quite as good a reason as either Kit Babcary or Isolda to wish for Gideon's death.'

'And so had you,' I thought, but did not say so aloud.

Nevertheless, there was a possibility that Ginèvre might

have come to the conclusion that Gideon was better dead than alive. Perhaps Gregory had, after all, decided to defy her and made up his mind that he would try to buy the blackmailer's silence. She was astute enough to realise that if Gideon agreed, it could result in far more than a single payment, and I guessed that she was too proud a woman to put an end to such a situation by blabbing all to Miles Babcary. Furthermore, it was extremely likely that her husband had already confided to her Gideon's accusation against his wife and Christopher; an accusation that would immediately point the finger of suspicion at Isolda, leaving everyone else as seemingly innocent bystanders.

But if Gregory or Ginèvre Napier or Barbara Perle was the murderer, where had they obtained the monkshood? But of course the answer to that was simple. From the same source as Miles Babcary: a liniment for aches and pains procured from Jeremiah Page of Gudrun Lane.

Sixteen

I glanced up to see my hostess eyeing me narrowly. Before she could say anything, however, I asked quickly, 'Do any of your friends and acquaintances in these parts own a horse and cart, Mistress?'

She was obviously startled by this unlooked-for change of subject, and stammered a little over her reply.

'No . . . Yes . . . What I mean is that Hugo Perle used to keep both horse and cart in the stables just around the corner, in Old Dean's Lane. But I believe Barbara sold them after his death. Why do want to know?'

'Do you have any idea who bought them?' I went on, ignoring her question and posing another of my own.

'No. No, I don't. I'm not absolutely certain that Barbara did decide to sell.' Ginèvre had recovered her poise and was growing irritable. 'Although . . . Wait a moment! Now I think about it, I seem to recollect her mentioning that Miles Babcary was the purchaser. Or am I mistaken?' she added to herself.

'Have the two families, the Perles and the Babcarys, always been friends?'

Ginèvre swallowed a mouthful of venison, frowning at this continuing diversion.

'Of course. Barbara is a Lambert by birth and a cousin of the late Mistress Babcary.'

It was my turn to frown. This fact had not previously been revealed by either Isolda or her father. To be fair, it had probably seemed irrelevant to them, but it could account for some of Gideon's hostility towards the marriage between his father-in-law and Mistress Perle. His late wife's kinswoman might well exert a stronger influence over Miles than a perfect stranger, who knew nothing of the family's affairs, would do.

160

'Why did you wish to know about the horse and cart?' my hostess asked, pushing her plate aside with a slice of venison still uneaten. I averted my greedy gaze and explained that I had almost been run over outside her house, but she made little of this. 'If you were standing in the middle of the thoroughfare, as you say you were, then I'm hardly surprised. People drive recklessly in London, with scant regard for life and limb. I doubt very much if it was a deliberate attempt on your life, if that's what you're thinking.'

I had to admit that she was right. I told her of the other two occasions on which I had felt, if not exactly in danger, then threatened by some unseen presence.

'Yet it seems you were wrong both times,' she said. 'On your own admission, there is no evidence of harmful intent towards you on anyone's part.'

'No, but there ought to be,' I blurted out.

Ginèvre smiled shrewdly at me, raising her plucked eyebrows, her thin lips lifting slightly at the corners. 'You mean that Master Bonifant's murderer should be trying to prevent you asking any more questions?' I nodded and she gave her low, throaty chuckle. 'I take your point. There might, of course, be an explanation, but I must admit that I can't see . . .' Her voice tailed away and she stared at me unblinkingly for a moment before shaking her head decisively. 'No! Impossible!'

'What's impossible?'

But she refused to say another word on the subject, resisting all my pleas for her to tell me what was in her mind on the score that she had to be wrong, and that what she was thinking made no sense. And with that I had to be content.

I finished my dinner and took my leave of her, no nearer a solution to the murder of Gideon Bonifant than I had been yesterday or the day before that. I walked as far as the stables in Old Dean's Lane and questioned a couple of the ostlers there. They both confirmed that Master Babcary had indeed bought the horse and cart belonging to Hugo Perle after the latter's death, but also assured me that neither had left the premises so far that day. And they pointed to a placid cob, looking over the door of a stall in one corner of the yard, and to a cart lined up with three others against the northern wall. When I told them the reason for my curiosity, both men were unanimous in agreeing that the horse and cart that had so nearly run me down probably belonged to a brewer living in Knightrider Street, who had driven abroad that morning and whose recklessness was a byword in the area.

Once again, my fears had proved groundless. Gideon's murderer, whether Isolda or another, seemed to feel sufficiently secure to allow me to pursue my investigations unhindered. All the same, I wondered, as I walked slowly back along Paternoster Row, if I were not being lulled into a false sense of security. And what was that impossible something that had occurred to Ginèvre Napier that had not yet occurred to me?

This thought reminded me that I had not so far spoken to Gregory Napier, but I doubted if he were at his goldsmith's shop in West Cheap or he would surely have returned home for dinner. And if I were truthful with myself, I had to admit that I was in no mood, just at that moment, to listen to a further account of the events leading up to Gideon Bonifant's death. I needed somewhere to sit and think quietly about what I already knew, and to try to make sense of it all.

I directed my steps towards Bucklersbury. I did, however, make one more call before returning to the Voyager. As I had to pass the entrance to Gudrun Lane in my journey along West Cheap, I decided that I might as well pay a visit to Jeremiah Page and enquire if either of the Napiers or Mistress Perle had bought any monkshood liniment from him lately. A question and a groat to a legless beggar, squatting on his little trolley at the corner of the lane, quickly ascertained the exact whereabouts of the apothecary's shop, and a few minutes later, I was standing in its dim interior.

Master Page was a small man with a luxuriant auburn beard and a pair of sharp, beady eyes that regarded me suspiciously the second I mentioned the names of Perle and Napier.

'If it's to do with the murder of Master Babcary's son-in-law,' he snapped, 'I've said all that I have to say on that subject. I told the Sheriff's officer what I knew – which wasn't much – at the time. I'm not being dragged into it any further.'

'I'm making enquiries on behalf of His Grace, the Duke of Gloucester,' I said importantly.

'And I'm the great Cham of Tartary,' was the scathing response.

It took me a few minutes to convince Master Page that I was serious, but in the end I managed it. His manner became a little more unbending, although not by much, and in reply to my original question, he said that nearly everyone in the area who was over a certain age bought his monkshood liniment.

'And when you're as old as they are, my young master, you'll know the reason why. Joints get stiff and painful with the passing years, and my embrocation is the best.'

'I'm sure it is,' I answered soothingly. 'Does that mean Master and Mistress Napier and Mistress Perle also buy it?'

'They might,' he admitted cautiously. 'I'm not saying they don't. But why do you want to know? None of them were implicated in Master Bonifant's killing. It was that wife of his, or her cousin, or both. I'd lay any money on that, especially after what Gideon confided to me about the pair of them.'

'Ah! So he told *you* that story as well, did he?' I asked.

The beard jutted angrily. 'No story, was it, in view of what happened subsequently? Lucky for Mistress Bonifant that she has a kinswoman who's leman to the King. At least, that's *my* opinion for what it's worth.'

I ignored this remark. 'When you reached Master Babcary's shop that afternoon, was Gideon Bonifant dead?'

This time the beard waggled up and down in affirmation. 'But only just. The body was still warm. However, there was nothing I could do to revive him, so I sent for the physician, who, in turn, called in the Sheriff's officer. It was too late to make Master Bonifant sick – although that remedy can often do more harm than good because, of course, the throat's so stiff, it's well-nigh impossible to make the victim swallow an emetic.'

'What were the Babcarys and their guests doing when you entered the parlour?'

Jeremiah Page hunched his shoulders. 'That girl of theirs – Meg I think they call her – was having hysterics, and Miles Babcary was flapping about like a demented hen. The rest were looking as though someone had taken a poleaxe to them.'

'Even Mistress Bonifant?'

'Even her,' the apothecary admitted grudgingly. He stroked his beard thoughtfully. 'Oddly enough . . .'

'Go on,' I urged. 'Oddly enough . . . ?'

'Well . . . It's just that you've made me think; made me picture the scene again in my mind. Most of them, as I said, were staring at Master Bonifant, who was slumped face downwards across the table, as if they couldn't believe their eyes. But then the younger woman, Master Babcary's niece, suddenly smiled. I don't think anyone saw her but me; they were all, as I've said, looking elsewhere.'

'What sort of a smile?' I asked, intrigued.

The beard twitched from side to side as its owner considered the question.

'It was very fleeting, you understand. It had vanished in less time than it takes to tell. But I'd say it was a smile of . . . of relief. Yes, that's it! It was definitely a smile of relief.'

'You mean . . . as though she were glad that Master Bonifant was dead?'

'I'd say so, yes.'

'You might have been mistaken, of course.'

'I might have been. But somehow I don't think I was.'

He remained adamant, and I walked the rest of the way back to the Voyager lost in thought. Why would Eleanor Babcary be relieved that Gideon was dead? If she had been in love with him, she should have been deeply upset. But was the apothecary's interpretation of what he had seen correct? According to him, the girl's expression had been fleeting, barely long enough for it to have registered as a smile.

My head was beginning to ache by the time I reached the inn. The bitter cold and intermittent showers of sleet were partly responsible, but I was also concerned by my lack of progress. I had accepted the Duke of Gloucester's request to investigate the death of Gideon Bonifant four days ago, and every passing hour brought the sentencing of George of Clarence that much closer. If only Duke Richard would beg Mistress Shore to intercede for his brother without feeling that he had to offer her an inducement, all might yet be well. But he wouldn't: that was one thing of which I could be certain.

To add to my worries, there were now only two more days, the second being the day of the tournament at Westminster, before Adela and I were due to meet Jack Nym at Leadenhall market to begin our journey home to Bristol. As things stood, Adela would have to go alone, and while I trusted Jack to take every care of her, the prospect was not one I relished. Moreover, I could well imagine the tongue-lashing I would receive from my quondam mother-in-law when I finally arrived home – particularly if I had not managed to solve the mystery and it had all been for nothing.

The Voyager was quiet when I entered, most of its customers being gripped by a post-prandial lethargy. I made my way to our chamber and found that my wife, too, was lying supine upon the bed and gently snoring. Without more ado, I kicked off my boots and stretched out beside her. Less than two minutes later, I was sound asleep.

It was dark when, with a snort and a violent twitch, I awoke to find Adela sitting beside the fire, watching me in some concern. A tray with the remains of her supper and all of mine, now gone cold, reposed on the floor at her feet.

'God's teeth!' I exclaimed, swinging my legs off the bed. 'What time is it?'

'The church bells are ringing for Vespers,' she said. 'You must have been asleep for hours.'

I cursed softly. 'I meant to return to the Babcarys' shop this afternoon. There are still some questions I want to put to the family.'

'You're going nowhere,' Adela retorted in a very wifely spirit, pushing me back on to the bed. 'You're worn out and, Duke of Gloucester or no Duke of Gloucester, you're remaining here for the rest of the evening.'

I knew that there was no arguing with her in this mood. Not that I was prepared to put up much of a resistance anyway: I did indeed feel worn out. Furthermore, I needed to think or, preferably, to talk things over, so I settled myself once more against the pillows and, when I had filled myself up with bread and cheese and other cold viands from the tray and drunk the ale, patted the empty space beside me invitingly. Adela was only too happy to cuddle up, and understanding enough to accept that I was, at present, in no mood for lovemaking.

'Tell me what's troubling you,' she commanded.

My first and most pressing worry, that she would, in all likelihood, be forced to travel back to Bristol without me, she dismissed as a mere nothing.

'I shall be perfectly safe with Jack Nym. And even if it weren't for the children and taking them off Margaret's hands – for I'm sure she must have had a surfeit of their company by now – I still wouldn't accept the Duke's offer for me to remain in London until this matter is satisfactorily concluded. I think you'll feel far less trammelled on your own.'

I couldn't argue with her, at least, not convincingly, so I simply gave her a hug. In reply, she sent me one of those half-mocking glances that never fail to remind me of my late mother.

'Will you listen while I talk?' I asked.

'Of course,' she answered readily. 'Tell me everything.'

So I recounted all I knew about the Babcary, Perle and Napier households, what I had gleaned from Masters Ford and Page, and all the details, insofar as I knew them, of the afternoon that Gideon Bonifant died. When I'd finished, we sat in silence for a while, watching the flames of the fire flicker and curtsey on the hearth, spurting now blue, now red and yellow.

'That means,' Adela murmured at last, 'that apart from Isolda, there were at least two other people present that afternoon who would have been happy to see Gideon Bonifant dead: Mistress Perle and Gregory Napier.'

'There may have been more than just those two,' I pointed out. 'If Isolda had been cuckolding her husband with her cousin, as Gideon claimed, then Christopher Babcary must be a suspect, also. Then there's Meg Spendlove, who had been so upset after Gideon had verbally chastised her for mixing up the family goblets at Eleanor's birthday feast. She may well have borne him a grudge that grew in her mind until it was out of all proportion to his offence. And what about Miles Babcary? I don't say that there's a strong case to be made against him, but it's obvious to me that he didn't much care for his son-in-law, and if he had entertained any inkling that Gideon disapproved of his proposed marriage to Barbara Perle and was trying to prevent it, I don't think we could rule him out.'

Adela nodded in agreement. 'And, from what you've told

166

me of her, perhaps it might also be unsafe to discount Mistress Napier. She sounds a formidable woman. And if she were afraid that her husband was about to defy her and offer Gideon a large sum of money to hold his tongue, she might have decided to take matters into her own two hands and end the blackmailer's life. And if I understood you correctly, Apothecary Page intimated that his monkshood liniment has been bought by both the Napiers and Mistress Perle, so the means would have been there, handy.'

I frowned. 'But not easy to administer. After their arrival, the three guests were conducted upstairs by Miles Babcary to the parlour, where the table was already laid. But at that point only Isolda knew where each person was sitting. It was she who later directed them to their various places.'

'Couldn't the guilty person have worked out which was Gideon's seat by the initials on his cup?'

I shook my head emphatically. 'Impossible! The carving around the rims is so ornate that only a close inspection can reveal to whom each one belongs. From even a short distance, they all look the same. Moreover, there were already four people in the room when Miles Babcary and his guests entered the parlour: Christopher and Eleanor, Gideon and the apprentice, Toby Maybury. Isolda arrived a few moments later. Neither Gregory nor Ginèvre Napier nor Barbara Perle could have found the opportunity to drop poison into any of the cups.'

I sighed despondently. 'It looks as though it *has* to be one of the Babcarys, and Isolda seems the most likely suspect.'

'What about the other cousin, the girl, Eleanor?' Adela asked.

'I can't find any reason why she should have wanted to murder Gideon Bonifant. If I'm right, she was in love with, or at least very fond, of him.'

'But if the apothecary's right, then she was relieved that he was dead.'

'Mmmm . . . But did Master Page see what he thought he saw?' I muttered doubtfully.

Adela nestled her head against my shoulder. 'We haven't mentioned the apprentice yet. What was it, do you think, that he was trying to tell Eleanor behind Ginèvre Napier's back?'

I grimaced. 'I don't know. And Toby isn't going to tell me.

So unless I can work it out for myself . . .' I shrugged and let the sentence go.

There was silence while my wife and I each pursued our own thoughts. Then Adela asked suddenly, 'You don't think that Toby could have been in league with either Mistress Perle or one of the Napiers? That *he* put the poison in Gideon's cup, then got frightened and was trying to warn Eleanor of what he'd done?'

'No, I don't.' I bent my head and kissed her. 'My darling, I think you're grasping at straws. I don't want the murderer to be a member of the Babcary household, because I like them all, but I must remember that my emotions have misled me before. The fact that the Napiers and Mistress Perle had very strong reasons for wanting Gideon dead mustn't blind me to the fact that they had no opportunity for poisoning his wine.'

'Could Gregory Napier have managed to do it while Mistress Perle was being presented with her birthday gift?' my wife suggested after a pause. 'All eyes would surely have been on her and this jewelled girdle that Master Babcary had ornamented for her.'

I considered the idea, but it would have involved an extraordinary sleight of hand, and I reluctantly shook my head.

'No, I don't think so. The sad fact is that it was Isolda who laid the table, deciding where everyone should sit. It was Isolda who poured the wine into the goblets. It was Isolda who had the time and opportunity to enter her father's bedchamber, next door, and who knew where the bottle of liniment was kept. The only thing I can't be sure about is that she had a good reason for killing her husband. Was Gideon telling the truth when he accused her and Christopher of cuckolding him?'

'Why would he lie?' Adela wanted to know, echoing my own thoughts and the thoughts of so many others. 'He may have been a far more despicable character than you realised at first, but no man is deliberately wishful of making himself look a fool without good reason.' She added after a pause, 'Apart from the three immediately involved, does anyone but you know of the liaison between Mistress Perle and Gregory Napier?'

'I shouldn't think so. If as much as a hint of it had reached

Miles Babcary's ears, I doubt he would still be so anxious to marry Dame Barbara.'

'Why do you suppose that Ginèvre Napier confided in you?'

'I've been asking myself that question, and I can only think that she suddenly felt the need to tell someone. She's bottled up the secret for all these months and today, at last, she could bear to do so no longer.'

'I wonder she wasn't afraid that you'd inform the Babcarys or the Duke or the Sheriff's men, and so implicate her and Gregory in Gideon's murder.'

'I don't believe that, at that particular moment, she cared. She just wanted to share the knowledge of her friend's and her husband's perfidy with another person, and to do them a mischief. But I feel sure that when she's had time to think things over, I shall hear from her again, begging for my discretion.'

'She hasn't yet sworn you to secrecy,' my wife pointed out, 'nor even extracted a promise that you'll keep her confession to yourself. Don't you think, therefore, that you should inform the Sheriff's officers of what you know?'

I again shook my head. 'Not until I'm absolutely sure that one of them is the murderer. At the moment, I cannot see how any of them could have administered the poison, and until enlightenment dawns – if it ever does – it would be wrong of me to entangle three possibly innocent people in the coils of the law. If Isolda stood in imminent peril of being arrested and tried for her husband's murder, that would be a different matter.' I leant back against the pillows. 'I wish I could rid myself of this feeling that the quarrel between Gideon Bonifant and Meg Spendlove has a significance that I have somehow overlooked.'

Adela made no answer and her head was growing heavy on my shoulder. When I glanced down, I saw that her eyelids were beginning to droop and that her lower jaw was slack. I roused her gently.

'Time to get undressed and ready for bed.'

She made a feeble attempt to resume our conversation, but it was very half-hearted and by the time I had carried our supper tray back to the kitchen – explaining to the cook why my bowlful of broth was untouched – and returned to our bedchamber, my wife was between the sheets and sound asleep. I stripped off my boots and outer clothing and thankfully rolled in beside her.

Seventeen

I was dreaming.

As always, I knew that I was dreaming, but, at the same time, everything that happened seemed very vivid and very real.

I was in the Babcary house, walking upstairs from the shop, Toby Maybury hard on my heels.

'He was just going into his room,' Toby kept saying. 'He was just going into his room.'

As we reached the top of the first flight of stairs and emerged on to the landing, Isolda came out of the parlour, and although she looked straight at us, she appeared to see neither myself nor the apprentice. She simply turned to her right and mounted the second flight of stairs to her bedchamber. I glanced over my shoulder to speak to Toby, but he had disappeared and when I pushed open the parlour door and went inside, he was already there, standing beside the table.

'We mustn't let Meg be blamed,' he said – then was abruptly transformed into Mistress Perle's maid.

The girl had on a clean nightgown and was holding a hard-boiled egg, one half in each hand. The yolk had been scooped out and replaced with salt and, as she began to walk backwards, away from me, I noticed that she was wearing Eleanor Babcary's pendant around her neck.

I moved towards the table, which was ready laid for a meal, stretching out my hand for one of the gold-rimmed goblets that stood beside each place.

'Don't!' a voice exclaimed behind me. 'I've just poisoned the wine in that cup.'

I spun round with a great cry – only to find myself sitting up in bed, sweating profusely, and Adela shaking my arm.

'Roger! What is it? Have you been having one of your

171

dreams?' She smoothed back the damp hair from my forehead.

I nodded mutely, then became aware that someone was tapping gently on our bedchamber door.

'Master Chapman, is everything all right?' whispered Reynold Makepeace. 'Is Mistress Chapman well?'

I got out of bed and opened the door a crack. 'I was riding the nightmare, that's all, I'm sorry if I disturbed you.'

Reassured, the landlord crept away and I went back to Adela, slithering down beside her and, by now, shivering with cold. She held me in her arms and soothed me, but I had no sooner fallen asleep again than I was back in the Babcarys' house, and this time Isolda was standing beside me, outside the closed parlour door.

'Have you seen Gideon?' she asked me, adding with a frown, 'He wanders about the house at nights, you know. He says he's unable to sleep.'

She vanished, and now I was inside the room, gripped by fear, convinced that someone who wished me dead was waiting outside on the landing; someone who would kill me, given half a chance. In a sudden access of bravado, I wrenched the door open, only to find myself face to face with Ginèvre Napier, who was convulsed with merriment.

'There's no one here except me,' she laughed. 'No one wants to harm you.'

'But someone *ought* to want to harm me,' I argued. 'Someone should be trying to prevent me asking any more questions.'

She looked both knowing and amused and to the sound of her throaty chuckling, I woke to find the first grey shreds of daylight rimming the shutters of our room.

Adela was asleep beside me, her face, framed by the pillow, calm and peaceful in its repose. I sat up in bed and looked down at her, thanking God, as I did each morning, for sending her to me, and for bringing me to my senses before I let her slip through my fingers and marry another man. After a while, as though suddenly becoming conscious of my gaze, she opened her eyes and smiled.

'You had a restless night,' she said, wriggling into a sitting position and kissing my unshaven cheek. 'Did your dreams bring you any enlightenment?'

'Not yet,' I admitted, returning her kiss, 'But give them time and they might become clearer. What will you do today?'

'I've promised to visit the Lampreys. It will be my last chance, because tomorrow, we are going to watch the tournament at Westminster, and the day after that, I, at least, must start for home.' She tilted her head to one side and looked sidelong at me. 'What are your plans?'

I sighed. 'I must go back to West Cheap and talk to the Babcarys yet again. To Eleanor especially. There's something that I haven't yet discovered concerning her relationship with Gideon, but which I feel in my bones holds a vital key to this mystery. And tomorrow,' I added defiantly, 'I shall accompany you to the tourney ground. The King is hardly likely to decide Clarence's fate on such a day, and I refuse to be parted from you during your final hours in London.' I was suddenly racked with guilt, and took her in my arms. 'Sweetheart, I'm afraid this visit, which you looked forward to so keenly, has been spoilt by this business of Gideon Bonifant's death.'

'It's not your fault,' she murmured consolingly. 'As you said, if your Duke could only bring himself, like a sensible man, to appeal directly to Mistress Shore for her intervention on behalf of his brother, you need never have been involved in this murder. You mustn't blame yourself.'

But that was just what I was determined to do. 'I should have refused,' I said.

'No, no!' On that point, Adela was adamant. 'It never does to offend those in authority, particularly anyone so highly placed as the Duke of Gloucester. We're poor people, Roger, of no account except unto God. And one day in the future, who knows but that we may be glad of Duke Richard's protection? It was certainly fortunate for Isolda Bonifant that her kinswoman is leman to the King.'

But still my sense of guilt would not be assuaged.

'I haven't even bought you a keepsake to remind you of your visit to London,' I moaned.

Adela clapped a hand to her mouth, the childish gesture making her look, all at once, absurdly young.

'What is it?' I asked, bewildered.

For answer, she freed herself from my embrace, got out of

bed, shivering with the sudden cold, and padded over to our travelling chest, where it stood in a corner of the room. She opened the lid and took something from inside.

'I forgot to tell you. I bought this from a stall in the Leadenhall market, on Monday. Jeanne Lamprey and I went there before she took me to see the animals in the Tower.'

Adela climbed back into bed and snuggled up to me, warming her now icy feet on mine and ignoring my yelp of protest. She was holding a small leather bag which, having released its drawstring, she upended on to the white linen quilt. Some sort of necklace fell out which, when my wife held it up, resolved itself into a chain and pendant.

'The man I bought them from swore they were silver,' Adela laughed, 'but I don't think they can be. They were much too cheap.'

I took them from her and was about to examine the metal from which they were made more closely, when I paused, my attention arrested by the design of the pendant: a true lover's knot enclosed within a circle.

'What's the matter?' asked my wife, studying my face. 'Are you angry with me for buying them? As I said, they didn't cost a lot.'

'No, of course not,' I answered. 'It's just that this is a replica of Eleanor Babcary's pendant, only hers is fashioned in gold and studded with tiny sapphires.'

Adela was intrigued. 'The man who sold it to me said that it's a very old design, and one that's imbued with magical powers. If a woman wears it in bed, she'll see the man she's going to marry.'

'I thought that was only on Saint Agnes's Eve,' I protested. 'And something to do with a hard-boiled egg—' I broke off, demanding indignantly, 'Why would you want such information? You're already married!'

Adela burst out laughing. 'Do you think I've forgotten that fact? I just think it's pretty. The pendant, I mean. And anyway, I'm far too old and sensible to believe in such nonsense.' She sighed wistfully, 'I was old at sixteen. I grew up early.'

'But that doesn't happen to all women,' I said reflectively. 'Some women are protected and cosseted and retain their innocence to a much greater age.'

'Are you speaking of Eleanor Babcary?'

'Yes.' I handed the pendant and chain back to Adela. 'Wear it today and to the tournament tomorrow.' I kissed her again. 'And don't dream of any man but me.'

'I haven't since the moment I met you.' She must have seen the self-satisfied smirk on my face, for she gave one of her sudden laughs. 'Don't let that admission go to your head, my love. There's plenty of time for me to change my mind and plenty more fish in the sea.' But the kiss she planted on my cheek, before getting out of bed, drew the sting from her words.

Half an hour later, just as we were finishing breakfast in the taproom, I asked, 'Are either Philip or Jeanne Lamprey coming to fetch you this morning?'

My wife shook her had. 'No, I forbade it. It's not far, and by now, I'm sufficiently familiar with the streets around here to be able to find my own way to their shop.'

'Good,' I said. And in answer to her enquiring lift of the eyebrows, went on, 'Will you come with me first to the Leadenhall and point out the stallholder who sold you the pendant?'

She looked mystified, but asked no questions and willingly agreed. Consequently, fortified by Reynold Makepeace's hot, spiced wine and wrapped warmly in our cloaks, the hoods pulled well up around our ears, we set out as the church bells were beginning to ring for Tierce. The street cleaners were already hard at work, shovelling yesterday's evil-smelling refuse into their carts, their hands blue with cold beneath the grime. But, in general, they were a cheerful bunch of men, calling and waving a greeting as we passed.

The Leadenhall was a hive of activity, as always on those days when 'foreigners' from outside the city limits were allowed in to set up their stalls. That day, too, a load of wool had arrived from the Cotswolds to be weighed on the King's Beam and sealed by the customs men before being carted down to the wharves. To add to the crowds and general confusion, a fine but icy rain had begun to fall as we were turning out of Bucklersbury into the Stock's Market, and many people had pushed their way into the Leadenhall for shelter. By the time we entered, the place was packed to the doors, and Adela doubted that she would be able to locate the man we were seeking.

In the event, however, she found him with surprising speed, a tall, lanky fellow selling cheap jewellery made from base metals, which, with barefaced effrontery, he declared to be silver and gold. I pushed my way to the front of the little crowd gathered around his stall, and indicated the lover's knot pendants, hanging by their chains from one of the horizontal poles that held up the canopy.

'Are those of your own making, friend?'

'They are.' He smiled, displaying a gap between his two front teeth. 'But the design is magical, and was shown to me by an ancient who had brought it back, at great risk to his own life, from the lands of Prester John.'

I forbore, with difficulty, from remarking that it looked like a perfectly ordinary English love knot to me, and asked what magical property the pendants possessed.

'If a maid wears one in bed, she'll see the face and form of the man she's going to marry,' was the prompt response.

'And do you tell this tale to every woman who buys a pendant from you?' I sneered.

'Ay, and also to those who just come here to waste my time. Like you, I fancy,' the man added, his expression turning sour.

'My wife has already bought one,' I said, urging Adela forward. She obligingly opened her cloak to show the stallholder the pendant clasped around her neck.

The man was mollified but, when asked, denied all knowledge of anyone by the name of Babcary or Bonifant.

'I'm from Paddington village, a fair way west of here. I know no one personally hereabouts.'

'But you set up your stall in the Leadenhall every week?'

'I do, and have done for the past year or more.'

I thanked him and, taking Adela's arm, moved away. My wife regarded me curiously.

'So, what have you learned?' she asked, as we stood in the shelter of the porch, looking out at the lancing spears of rain.

I put my arm around her. 'I've learned that any member of the Babcary household could have heard our friend's story about the magical properties of his pendants any time during

176

the past twelve months. So which of them suggested a pendant of the same design when it came to deciding on Eleanor's birthday gift?'

'Is it important?'

'I'm not sure,' I answered slowly, 'but I think it might well be, especially if that person was aware that Eleanor herself had visited the jeweller's stall in Leadenhall market and believed what she had been told by the owner.' I nodded to myself. 'Which she probably would, being the innocent that she is.'

Adela hugged me. 'Then you'd better be off to West Cheap immediately to find out what you can. Don't worry about me. The Lampreys' shop isn't very far.'

The goldsmith's shop was empty except for Toby Maybury, busy about the necessary but monotonous task of stoking up the furnace with the bellows. He glanced over his shoulder as I entered and scowled when he saw who it was.

'Oh, you're back again, are you? What do you want this time? Why don't you leave us alone?'

I remained determinedly friendly, ignoring his hostile manner.

'Toby, my boy, I need your help. You've proved yourself to have a good memory; to be a bright, observant lad. So tell me, who suggested the design of the pendant that was made for Mistress Eleanor's birthday?'

Won over by my flattery, the apprentice put down the bellows and strolled across to talk to me, his young face puckered in a thoughtful frown.

'I believe it was Gideon,' he said after a moment or two's reflection. 'Yes, the more I think about it, the surer I am that it was Master Bonifant. Wait!' There was a pause, then he went on triumphantly, 'I definitely remember now! It was one afternoon towards the middle of last October. The master called the other two over to the main counter here, and asked what they thought he should make Mistress Nell for her seventeenth birthday. Master Kit didn't have any suggestions to offer. Well, he wouldn't, would he? He's like all brothers. Not much interested in the likes and dislikes of a sister. But Master Bonifant, he knew at once. "She bought a cheap pendant off some stall in Leadenhall market," he says, "that seems to have taken her fancy. Let's refashion it for her in gold." And then he went on about it being a simple design of a lover's knot in a circle, easy to do. In fact, the master thought it was too simple and decided that the centre of the pendant – the knot itself – should be studded with sapphires.'

'Master Bonifant didn't mention anything about such a design possessing magical powers?' I enquired.

Toby regarded me pityingly. 'Of course not! Why should he? Lovers' knots are as common a design in jewellery as they are in embroidery.'

I apologised profusely, admitted that I had been scatterbrained since childhood, and deferred to his superior knowledge.

'Pray continue,' I begged.

Toby shrugged my foolishness aside. 'That's nearly all there is to tell. Mistress Bonifant, urged on by her husband, went to look for the original pendant in Mistress Nell's room, when she was absent from the house one day, but couldn't find it. But Master Bonifant's description was good enough for the master. The gold replica was easily made.'

'And was Mistress Babcary pleased with her gift?'

Toby thrust out his bottom lip. 'Funny you should ask that,' he said after a few seconds' musing. 'Now that I come to think of it, she wasn't as pleased as I should have expected her to be. But at the time, I put it down to the fact that we were all upset by Master Bonifant's outburst against Meg for getting the goblets mixed up. No one was in very good spirits after that.'

'But did Mistress Babcary wear the pendant very often?' I persisted.

Toby considered the question. 'She's worn it a lot lately,' he said.

'Since Master Bonifant's death?'

'Well . . . Yes, I suppose so. But she might have worn it just as much before. I don't recollect.'

Miles Babcary, followed by his nephew, came into the shop. The former beamed for a moment until he realised that it was not a customer who was claiming the attention of his apprentice, but the same nosy chapman whose constant poking and prying and questioning was becoming so unwelcome. Afraid to vent his ill-humour on me – the emissary of the Duke of

Gloucester and the King's favourite leman – he shouted at Toby instead.

'If you've let the fire go out, you stupid boy, I'll have the skin off your back! Get back to that furnace and those bellows immediately.' He turned to me. 'And what do you want this time, Master Chapman?'

'That's exactly what I asked him,' Toby proclaimed, not noticeably cowed by his master's displeasure. But all the same, he scuttled off to the furnace and worked the bellows with renewed vigour.

'I just want another word or two with Mistress Eleanor,' I answered humbly, 'if I may.'

I think that Miles Babcary, prodded in the back by Christopher, would have refused his permission had not Isolda, just at that moment, entered the shop from the back of the house. She was hot and flushed, wearing a big linen apron and holding a ladle in one hand. She was obviously in the middle of preparing dinner, the wholesome smell of cooking hanging about her, and lovelier by far to my nostrils than any exotic perfumes of the East.

'What's going on here?' she demanded, and I repeated my request before either her father or her cousin could reply. 'Oh, very well,' she agreed. 'You'll find Nell upstairs in the parlour, busy at her embroidery.' Her menfolk started to protest, but she cut them short. 'The sooner Master Chapman finds out what he wants to know, the sooner he'll leave us in peace,' she said, and vanished again in the direction of the kitchen.

Her common sense prevailed and I was given grudging permission by Miles to proceed upstairs to speak to his niece.

Eleanor was seated in front of her embroidery frame, which had been set up close to the fire, two large working candles, in silver candlesticks, on the table beside her. She looked round as I opened the parlour door and remained, needle poised above the canvas, staring at me.

'Master Chapman,' she murmured warily, 'why are you here?'

'I've come to speak to you,' I answered, drawing up a stool and sitting down beside her.

'I've told you all I know about Gideon's death.' Her voice

179

had acquired a shrill note and I noticed that her hands were trembling.

'Not quite all,' I demurred. 'Sometime or another, you bought a pendant in Leadenhall market, and the man who sold it to you told you that it had magical properties. If you wore it to bed, you would see the face and form of the man you would one day marry. Isn't that true?' She nodded, looking at me with round, frightened eyes. 'And you confided this secret to Gideon Bonifant?'

'Yes,' she whispered.

'So let me guess,' I went on. 'It was after you began wearing the pendant to bed that you started seeing him in your room each time you woke up. Am I right?'

Eleanor gave a shudder. 'I'd be asleep, and then something, a touch on my cheek or forehead, would rouse me just in time to see his likeness gliding out of my room. Of course, I realised that this was a hallucination of the Devil. How could Gideon possibly be my future husband when he was already married to Isolda? I didn't know what to do.'

'And you couldn't confide in her, as you would have done about anything else that was troubling you, because she was the person most nearly concerned. Did you think of saying anything to Gideon himself?'

The colour flooded her cheeks. 'No, I couldn't. That would have been worse than telling Isolda. It might have looked as though . . . as though . . .' Her voice tailed away into silence.

'As though you might have been making it up as a way of offering yourself to him,' I suggested.

Eleanor covered her face with her hands and nodded.

'So you said nothing to anyone?'

She raised her head again. 'No, but I didn't wear the pendant in bed any more. And when that didn't stop the visitations, I threw it away.'

I wondered how Gideon had found out about this, but I was convinced that somehow he had done so.

'And then your uncle and cousins gave you a pendant made to the selfsame pattern for your birthday. But this was made of gold, studded with sapphires. You couldn't possibly throw this one away.'

'No.' She was trembling so much that I put an arm about her shoulders for comfort. 'And then, of course, I started seeing Gideon's likeness in my room again each night.'

I asked as gently as I could, 'And did it never occur to you that it could be Gideon himself whom you were seeing? That it was a flesh and blood man and not some hallucination, as you call it, of the Devil?'

Eleanor turned her head slowly to stare at me. 'You mean . . . ? You mean that Gideon was coming to my room every night *in person*? That it was a trick to frighten me? But why on earth would he want to do that? No, no! He would never have been so unkind.'

'I don't think it was meant as unkindness,' I answered. 'Quite the opposite. I believe he was hoping to make you fall in love with him by planting the idea in your mind that you and he would one day be married.'

Eighteen

'But how could we ever have been married?' Eleanor asked. She pushed aside her embroidery frame with shaking hands. She repeated, 'He was married to Isolda.'

I shrugged. 'But who knew what the future held? Fatal illness, accidents, both these things are everyday occurrences, which, by his reckoning, could have happened to your cousin at any time. He wished to accustom you to the idea that, one day, you and he could possibly be man and wife. But Gideon was like all of us: while he could quite easily envisage the death of somebody else, he regarded himself as immortal.'

Eleanor considered this idea for a second or two, then emphatically shook her head. 'No! You're wrong! Isolda and Gideon were happily married.'

It was my turn to demur. 'Maybe Mistress Bonifant was happy, but I wouldn't be certain about her husband. My guess is that he'd fallen in love with you. You were only a child when they were first married but, over the years, you'd grown into a beautiful woman. I suspect that he suddenly – perhaps to his own surprise – found himself attracted to you. Maybe, to begin with, it was against his will. Let us give him the benefit of the doubt and say that he struggled to suppress his feelings for a while, but that, eventually, they proved too strong for him. That was when he started to spread rumours about Isolda and your brother.'

Eleanor lifted her lovely eyes to mine. 'You mean that he was lying?'

'Have you never considered the possibility that he might have been?'

My companion drew a deep breath. 'I thought Gideon was mistaken about the man being Kit, who has never been enamoured of . . . of . . . well, ugly women.' Eleanor pressed her hands to her cheeks and hung her head. 'That's a horrible thing for me to say about Isolda, but . . . but . . .'

'Why be ashamed of stating the truth?' I soothed her. 'I know very little of your brother, but judging by the woman who was hanging on his arm last Sunday, I would be prepared to wager good money on Master Christopher feeling nothing for Mistress Bonifant beyond normal, cousinly affection. But please go on. You were implying that while you thought Gideon to be wrong about the identity of Isolda's lover, you nevertheless believed that there might, in fact, have been one.'

Eleanor raised one hand to her forehead. 'Did I imply that? Yes, I suppose, to be truthful, I did.'

'You thought Isolda was in love with someone other than her husband? What made you think so?'

My companion, however, seemed to have no clear idea why she had entertained such an idea and, as far as I could make out, it rested on nothing more than the belief, already expressed to me by my wife, that no man would claim to be a cuckold without good reason.

'But who could your cousin's lover possibly have been? Were there any men that you knew of with whom she was particularly friendly?'

It seemed there was no one to whom Eleanor could immediately put a name, and she was too anxious to return to the subject of Gideon and his nocturnal prowlings to give the idea any positive thought.

'Are you serious in your suggestion, Master Chapman, that what I imagined was a . . . a spirit haunting my room, was really Gideon himself, in the flesh?'

'I'm convinced of it,' I answered gently. 'Mistress Bonifant herself told me that, over the past months, Gideon had risen from his bed on many occasions and gone wandering about the house at night. This sleeplessness was one of the reasons why she had begun to fear for his health. In reality, of course, he was not ill, merely lovesick. And he had seen a way to turn your confidence about the magical properties of the original pendant – the one you bought in Leadenhall market – to his advantage. He would enter your chamber which, I believe, is next to his and Mistress Bonifant's, touch you lightly on your cheek or forehead in order to rouse you and, then, before you were properly awake, remain just long enough for you to recognise him before slipping from the room and hurrying back next door.'

'But – but the visitations stopped after I threw the pendant away.'

'Not for long, I should guess. Only until you received the new one for your birthday. Am I not right?' And when she nodded, I continued, 'According to Toby Maybury, it was Gideon who not only proposed a pendant as the family gift, but who also suggested the design for it. Did you know that?' This time she shook her head, an expression of increasing horror on her face. I asked softly, 'Were you fond of Gideon Bonifant?'

'No!' Eleanor shivered, wrapping her arms around her body for comfort. 'No, I wasn't. I didn't dislike him, not for years, and he was always kind to me, although he could be sharp-tongued with other people. But I was never fond of him. There was always something about him that, deep down, I didn't really care for. That's why I was so distressed when . . . when these nightly visitations started. I wouldn't have wanted him for my husband even if he'd been free, but I thought that fate had . . . had decreed that I should marry him one day.' She gave a little laugh that faltered in the middle. 'I was worried for Isolda's life, not his. I was afraid, as you said just now, that she was the one who was going to die. Every time she left the house or complained of a headache I was worried. And then, after all, it was Gideon who died, who was poisoned.'

'Tell me honestly,' I said, 'do you believe your cousin discovered that Gideon was in love with you and murdered him as a consequence?'

'Yes, tell Master Chapman honestly, Nell, my dear, what you really think.' Isolda Bonifant's voice sounded behind us, although there was no rancour in her tone.

Neither of us had heard her enter the parlour and we both started with surprise. Eleanor gave a muffled cry, jumped up, pushing past her cousin, and fled from the room. Isolda made no attempt to detain her.

'How long have you been there, Mistress?' I asked, when I had recovered my breath.

'I've been listening outside the door, which you failed to close properly, for quite some time,' she admitted unashamedly. 'Long enough to understand what Gideon was up to.' She moved towards the fire, sitting down in her cousin's vacated chair and idly playing with the needle that Eleanor had left jabbed into the canvas of the embroidery frame.

'And did you ever suspect that your husband was in love with Mistress Babcary?' I asked bluntly.

She made no answer for a moment or two, then suddenly shrugged and looked me full in the face.

'I had my suspicions, but I didn't want to believe it was true. He was twenty-two years older than she was, and I'd managed to convince myself that what he felt for her was no more than the affection of, say, an uncle for his niece.' She laughed and looked away again. 'What a self-deluding fool I was! But as for his attempt to persuade her into thinking of herself as his future wife in the manner you've just explained to Nell, of that I had no idea.'

'Had you known, what would you have done?' I asked.

She regarded me straitly. 'I should have done my utmost to put a stop to such nonsense – but not by murdering Gideon.'

And suddenly, I found myself believing her without any of my former reservations. There was something about Isolda Bonifant that commanded my respect. She might be considered ugly by many men's standards of beauty – although not by mine – but her mind was like her face, strong and honest. And there had been too many others, that night of Barbara Perle's birthday feast, either around the table in the parlour or downstairs in the kitchen, who benefited from Gideon Bonifant's death. For Miles Babcary it removed a son-in-law uninterested in the goldsmith's trade, and who would quite possibly have sold the shop the moment it became the property of his wife. It rid Meg Spendlove of one whom she saw as a tyrannical master, and prised a thorn from Toby Maybury's side. Eleanor Babcary was freed from a continuing nightmare, while her brother was no longer the target of Gideon's false accusations. The Napiers ceased to suffer from the threat of exposure, he as a philandering husband, she as a cuckolded wife (surely something not to be borne by a woman as proud and as vain as Ginèvre). Most important of all, however,

Barbara Perle's future as the second Mistress Babcary still lay before her whenever she chose to accept Miles's proposal of marriage. She would neither be forced to give up her pretensions to being his wife nor revealed as an adulteress. Of all of those around that supper table, she, perhaps, had more to gain than anyone else.

I suddenly realised that if I went to the Duke of Gloucester with as much knowledge as I now possessed, he could lay enough evidence before Mistress Shore to convince her that her kinswoman was far from being the only possible murderer of Gideon Bonifant, and demand his favour in return. On the other hand, if these facts became common property, they would not only throw suspicion on the innocent as well as the guilty, they would also destroy at least two lives, Miles Babcary's and Barbara Perle's. It was therefore my duty, if I could, to unmask the real murderer, even if it meant giving up a chance to return home with Adela the day after tomorrow.

'You're looking pensive, Master Chapman.' Isolda's voice broke through my thoughts, making me jump. 'Have you come to the conclusion that I'm speaking the truth?'

'I might have,' I answered cautiously. I longed to tell her the whole story, but there were secrets that had to be preserved, at least until the truth was exposed. And perhaps – who could tell? – even after that revelation. I leaned forward, resting my elbows on my knees. 'Mistress Bonifant,' I asked abruptly, 'why do you think no one has tried to kill me?'

'Why has no one tried to kill you?' she repeated blankly.

'Yes. Oh, several times I've thought my life was in danger, but on each occasion so far, it seems to have been a false alarm, arising out of a natural expectation on my part that the murderer of Master Bonifant would try to prevent me discovering his – or her – identity. After all, a person who has killed already has less reason to fear killing again. However many your victims, you can only be hanged once.'

'Master Chapman!' Isolda rose to her feet. Her face was white and strained, like someone who was holding her emotions on a very short rein. 'This has been a trying morning. I have found out things about my husband I would far rather never have known – or at least not known for certain – so I have no wish to be further burdened by talk of hanging. It's almost ten o'clock and dinner will soon be ready. Will you stay and eat with us?'

I declined her invitation, wanting to get back to the Voyager to spend as much time with Adela as I could before her departure the day after next.

'But there is one more question I should like to ask you,' I murmured apologetically. Taking Isolda's resigned expression as permission to proceed, I said, 'On the evening of the murder, did Master Bonifant visit you in the kitchen before going upstairs to change into his Sunday clothes?'

She frowned. 'I don't recollect his doing so, but I may have forgotten the incident if it was of no significance. Who claims that he did?'

'Toby Maybury. He says that he saw your husband going into your bedchamber some while after he had left the shop. According to Toby, Master Bonifant explained away his tardiness by saying that he had been to the kitchen to have a word with you.'

Isolda gave a crack of laughter. 'If I were you, Master Chapman,' she advised, 'I wouldn't believe a word that Tobias Maybury says.' She spun on her heel and made for the parlour door, where she paused, her hand on the latch. 'That boy is a menace and always has been. Well, I doubt if we shall run into one another tomorrow at the tournament. The crowds will be far too dense. But in case we do, promise me that, just for once, we won't talk about my husband's murder.' She passed a hand wearily across her forehead. 'And now I must go to Nell and reassure her that what I overheard this morning will not affect my fondness for her. None of it was her fault. And I have been used to hearing myself described as ugly throughout my life.'

Isolda's prediction that the tourney ground at Westminster would be crowded proved to be correct.

It was a bright, clear day, warmer than of late, but still with a sharp wind blowing off the river; a day necessitating woollen cloaks, stout boots and pattens for the women, but one also that encouraged people to be out of doors rather than languishing at home.

The Duke and Duchess of Gloucester were notable only

by their absence, and the Duke of Clarence mouldered in the Tower, still uncertain of his fate. But the lack of the King's family was amply compensated for by Mistress Shore, wearing her ivy-leaf coronet, and by the multitude of Woodvilles, their courtiers and sycophants, who surrounded him and the infant Duke and Duchess of York, not only in the loges, but also in the arena. Leading the Party Without were the Queen's brother, Anthony, Earl Rivers, and her elder son from her first marriage, Thomas Grey, Marquess of Dorset, while the ranks of the Party Within were swollen by others of her numerous relatives, including Sir Richard Haute, who was to win one of the principal prizes.

In accordance with the rules laid down by the first Edward, two centuries earlier, no contestant could be accompanied by more than three armed knights or squires, and the carrying of knives, clubs and daggers was strictly forbidden. Heralds and spectators had to be weaponless, and a fallen participant was allowed time to rise. Even so, some ugly injuries were sustained, and the sight of these, together with the noise, dust and incessant clash of arms, were enough to test the strongest nerves. I was not surprised, therefore, when Adela apologised to the Lampreys, who had accompanied us, and insisted that she and I leave the tourney ground and go in search of quieter pleasures. In her condition, peace and rest were becoming daily more essential.

As usual at these affairs, the vendors of drinks and hot pies were doing a roaring trade but, although I bought two meat pasties, one for each of us, Adela said that all she wanted was to quench her thirst, so I was obliged, with very little persuasion, to eat them both. We discovered a man selling cups not only of ale but also of primrose wine, and having purchased one of the former for myself and one of wine for Adela, we retired to some tables and benches that had been placed near Westminster Gate under a makeshift awning. At that distance, the sounds of the jousting were muted.

'Ah, that's better,' Adela sighed, some of the colour coming back into her cheeks. She took another sip of her wine, then leant across the table, proffering me her cup. 'Try this, Roger. It's very good. You'd like it.'

I gave a decided shake of my head. 'No, I shouldn't. I hate primrose wine. You know I do.'

'But this is different. I don't know what's in it, but it has a more pungent smell to it and a stronger flavour than any other primrose wine I've ever drunk. I'm sure you'd agree with me if only you'd taste it.'

Once again, I shook my head vehemently, setting down my beaker of ale on the table between us, while I finished off the second of the two pasties.

'Primrose wine is primrose wine,' I observed thickly, through a mouthful of pastry.

Adela never argued with me when I was in one of my unreasonable moods. She had other methods of dealing with my obstinacy.

My attention was momentarily distracted by a brawl between a couple of drunkards which was taking place some twenty paces distant, the distraught wives hanging on to their husbands' jackets and vainly trying to separate them. Not that there was likely to be much physical damage done: it was mostly hot words and posturing. Grinning to myself, and keeping my eyes on the contestants, I put out my hand, picked up my cup and raised it slowly to my lips . . . The flavour burst, like a golden bubble, inside my mouth. There was a delicate hint of sage, of rosemary, of wild arum, like nothing I had ever previously tasted. It was like drinking the essence of spring.

'Delicious, isn't it?' demanded my wife.

'I . . . What? That isn't my ale.' I stared indignantly from the table to Adela, who was smiling at me and looking ineffably smug.

'I switched the cups while you were watching those two men. Be honest, Roger! Admit it! That primrose wine is like no other you've had before.'

'It's better than Margaret's or Goody Watkins's, I'll give you that,' I answered grudgingly, unwilling to concede her the victory. Our eyes met and she held my gaze. After a moment or two, I burst out laughing. 'All right! You win! It does indeed have the most wonderful flavour, and just to prove to you that I'm sincere, I'll buy myself a cup.'

I swung my legs over the bench and went in search of the wine-seller. I found him eventually, his tray slung around his neck by its leather strap, but its contents diminishing fast. In response to my request for the recipe for the primrose wine, he shook his head lugubriously.

'I don't know what's in it, friend. I'm not allowed to know. My goody makes it, and the secret's been in her family for generations, handed down from mother to daughter. But it sells well, which is the most important thing as far as I'm concerned.'

I was elbowed aside by other customers returning for second cupfuls, and I made my way back to Adela, who had now been joined by the Lampreys.

'We've come to say goodbye,' Jeanne said, stooping to kiss my wife's cheek. 'We must get back to the shop and I've had enough of men playing at being warlords. Adela, my dear, we shan't see you again as you're off home tomorrow. I hope you have a safe journey with only this Jack Nym, or whatever his name is, for company.' She raised her head and stared at me accusingly. 'I suppose we might see you, Roger, as you're remaining in London on the Duke of Gloucester's business.'

It was only later that I pieced together what she had been saying because, at the time, I was like a man in a dream. For no apparent reason, I had just recalled a remark made earlier by Adela, and this had inspired a train of thought concerning Gideon Bonifant's murder that had absorbed my whole attention. All at once, it was as though a candle had been lit in a darkened room: suddenly, I could begin to see my way forward.

Philip, ever sensitive to an atmosphere of female disapproval, pressed my hand in sympathy as we took our farewells, but it was a gesture whose significance was lost on me at that particular moment.

'You're very quiet,' Adela remarked, as we made our way back to the Voyager. 'Do you regret not going home with me tomorrow?'

Most ungallantly, I shook my head. 'No, I trust Jack Nym.' I was scarcely conscious of what I was saying. 'My love,' I went on, putting an arm about her shoulders as we pushed against a strengthening wind, 'I must leave you at the inn and go on to Crosby Place. I need to borrow a horse from His Grace's stables.'

'A horse?' Adela stopped in the middle of the Strand, forcing me to do likewise. She knew that I was a poor rider and was puzzled. 'Why do you want to borrow a horse?'

'I have to go to Southampton,' I answered, urging her forward. 'If I walk, it will take me over a week to get there and the same amount of time to return. On horseback, each journey can be accomplished in two or three days.'

'But why do you have to go to Southampton at all?' my wife demanded, none too pleased by this unexpected development in my plans.

I couldn't explain until I was more certain of my ground.

'It's where Gideon came from,' I said feebly. 'He lived there before he moved to London, after his first wife died.'

Adela glanced doubtfully at me, but she was wise enough not to ask any more questions. I guessed that her anxiety stemmed from her concern that something might happen to me during my travels, and I hastened to reassure her.

'Don't worry, sweetheart. I'm in no danger. I know that now.'

She made no further comment, but her sleep that night was broken, and I suspected that my words had been of little comfort to her. With the coming of daylight, she was no less preoccupied, and said almost nothing as we made for the Leadenhall, our box loaded on to a handcart pushed by one of Reynold Makepeace's cellarmen. (I had extracted my few belongings from the box earlier and stuffed them into a canvas sack lent to me by our ever-accommodating host.)

Jack Nym was before us, and, at first, viewed my intention to remain behind with even greater disapproval than that shown by Jeanne Lamprey. But once he understood my reasons, and that no less a person than the King's brother was involved in my decision, he changed his tune, assuring me that he would take every care of Adela, and that not the smallest risk would be taken that might endanger her health.

'Trust me, Roger!' he exclaimed, clapping me on the shoulder. 'Trust me!'

I told him that I did, embraced Adela passionately, helped her mount to sit beside Jack, and watched the cart until it was out of sight, lost among the noonday crowds as it crawled towards the New Gate, the village of Holborn and the open countryside beyond. Then I went back to the Voyager, where I paid our shot, saddled the horse lent to me from the Crosby Place stables the previous day, settled the canvas sack containing my belongings on my back, where it felt instantly at home, and set out, crossing to Southwark by London Bridge before turning the roan's head in a south-westerly direction.

Nineteen

M y late start on Friday, coupled with the fact that I rested myself and the horse for the whole of Sunday at a wayside inn somewhere between Farnham and Winchester, meant that I did not reach Southampton until Monday afternoon.

I entered through the squalid suburbs of Orchard Lane, and, inside the walls, the perilous state of the streets had not altered since I was last in the town three years previously. My mount stumbled frequently over the broken paving stones and potholes in the road. There was the usual number of foreign sailors wandering aimlessly about (the babel of different tongues making me suddenly homesick for the Bristol Backs), while the shopkeepers and stallholders vied for their custom.

From East Street, I turned south, carefully studying the gabled ends of the houses that faced on to High Street, the small courtyards to the side and rear of each dwelling forming narrow alleyways between them. When I saw the public latrine, I knew I was nearing my journey's end, although my nose had warned me of the fact sometime earlier. The scents of newly baked pies and pasties, boiled ham, braised beef and roast fowl had been assailing my nostrils for several minutes past. I directed my tired horse along the little passageway that separated the latrine from the neighbouring building, to where, some twenty paces in, and set at right angles to the other houses, stood John Gentle's butcher's shop.

Master Gentle himself, in spite of the coldness of the day, had set out his wares on a large trestle table in front of his booth, and was directing the purchase of a leg of mutton by a respectable dame who, I guessed, was housekeeper to one of the local gentry. Time somersaulted backwards and it was once again the summer of the English invasion of France, that invasion which ended in the humiliation of our troops and a fat annual French pension in King Edward's pocket.

I had no idea if Master Gentle would remember me but, as soon as he glanced up, the round, weather-beaten face split into a welcoming grin and the hazel eyes twinkled.

'Well, well! Roger Chapman, as I live and breathe.' He eyed my horse and grimaced. 'You've come up in the world since last I saw you. It used to be Shank's mare for you.' He turned his head, yelling for his wife. 'Alice! Come and see who's here!'

Mistress Gentle, as small as her husband was large, appeared round the side of the booth from the cottage at the rear, her mild brown eyes blinking in puzzlement.

'What is it, John? What's the matter?' Then her glance alighted on me and her delicate features were instantly creased with pleasure. 'Master Chapman, come in! Come in!'

I had to excuse myself for a time while I located the nearest livery stable and made sure that the Duke's horse would be looked after for the night, or for as long as it was necessary for me to remain in Southampton. Then I returned to the Gentles' shop. The customer had gone and no other had as yet arrived to demand the butcher's attention, so he and his wife were both waiting for me in the cottage kitchen, where a bright fire burned and a pan of stew was warming amongst the flames.

We spent the next hour catching up on one another's news, Master Gentle having routed out a neighbour's son, who, for a consideration, was willing to watch over the stall and booth and shout for John whenever he was needed. So it was they learned that I had married again, had a stepson as well as a daughter, with a third child on the way. They also learned that I was at present on an errand for the Duke of Gloucester, which intrigued them, but without eliciting a torrent of prying questions. They were a discreet couple, content with such snippets of information as came their way.

In return, I heard that their only child, Amice, with whom I had once fancied myself just a little in love, was still a seamstress in the household of the King's mother, the Dowager Duchess of York, and that she was happy with the young groom of the stables whom she had eventually married. After which,

I was invited to share their meal and the three of us sat down to an early supper of beef stew and herb dumplings, a good strong cheese and slices of wheaten bread. The Gentles lived well, if simply.

'And now,' asked the butcher when we were all replete and the empty dishes pushed to one side, 'what do you *really* want with us?' He added with a self-mocking grin, 'Apart, that is, from the pleasure of our company?'

I grinned back at him. 'It's a very great pleasure to renew our acquaintance, Master Gentle,' I said. 'But, of course, you're right. There is another purpose to my visit. Do you by any chance remember – or do you know of anyone who might possibly remember – a man, an apothecary's assistant, by the name of Gideon Bonifant, who once lived in this town? He left here some seven years ago, after the death of his wife.'

John Gentle furrowed his brow in thought, but his wife knew immediately of whom I was speaking. Women are invaluable in matters of gossip, even after such a lapse of time.

'I know who you mean!' she exclaimed, clapping her hands together in triumph. 'You recollect him, John, surely! He worked for Apothecary Bridges, who has a shop in All Saints' Ward.' She turned back to me. 'The shop's on this side of High Street, but above All Saints' Church, towards the Bar Gate.'

Her husband shook his head. 'I know Apothecary Bridges, of course. Who doesn't in S'ampton? But he's had so many assistants, and seven years is a long time to remember them all. I don't recall this Gideon Bonifant.'

Alice Gentle grew impatient.

'Yes you do, John,' she insisted. 'Long-faced, pious fellow with very cold, staring, grey eyes. I never much liked being served by him whenever I had need to go into the shop, which was more frequently than I cared for. I preferred Apothecary Godspeed in French Street, except that he was too often drunk to serve me. He was always saying that he'd give up the ale, but—'

'Do you remember Gideon Bonifant's wife?' I interrupted, afraid that my hostess was about to digress and treat me to a dissertation on the failings of the unknown Master Godspeed.

'Oh yes,' was the ready response. 'She was from All Saints' Ward as well, but from the poorer part, outside the walls.

A buxom enough girl, all the same, when Gideon Bonifant married her, but after a year or so she became ill and just wasted away. A sad sight, she was, by the time she died.'

'And Master Bonifant, so I understand, couldn't bear to remain in Southampton any longer, once she was in her grave.'

Alice Gentle raised her eyebrows. 'And who told you that, pray?'

'Apothecary Ford of Bucklersbury, in London. He employed Gideon as his assistant when Master Bonifant arrived in the city looking for work.'

My informant frowned. 'That's not quite how I remember it,' she protested. 'My recollection is there was more to it than that. I rather fancy Master Bonifant left Southampton because there was a good deal of whispering and gossip about him – but I can't recall exactly what at this distance of time.'

'Glory be!' exclaimed John Gentle, laughing. 'Wonders will never cease! I've never known your memory to fail before, girl, in such matters.'

His wife joined in the laughter. 'No, that's true enough. There must have been something else occupying my mind at the time of his departure. Seven years ago, you said, Master Chapman, since he left here?'

I nodded. 'The year of the battle at Tewkesbury and the subsequent death of King Henry.'

'That would be it then. That was the summer that Amice fell sick of a fever and nearly died.' She sighed. 'I'm sorry, Master Chapman, but if you want more information, you'll have to find someone else.'

'Can you advise me as to who might know the whole story?'

It was the butcher who answered.

'Apothecary Bridges's dame is the person you need. She's an even bigger gossip than my Alice, here.' He squeezed his wife's arm affectionately, robbing the words of any sting of criticism. 'She'd certainly have known what was going on in the life of her husband's assistant. I'm willing to bet my own on it.'

Once again, Mistress Gentle nodded. 'And that's no lie! You'd best go to see her now, lad. They'll be shutting up shop soon. The evenings are drawing out a little, but not by much. By the way, where are you staying tonight? You're welcome to sleep here, in Amice's old bed, if you wish. We've only the one bedchamber, but neither John nor myself snores, so far as I know.'

I accepted her generous offer with the proviso that it was only for a single night. If I had to stay longer in the town, I would find myself accommodation elsewhere. But somehow, I did not think that much of a possibility: I felt I was already in possession of the facts and all that was needed now was confirmation of my suspicions. I would set out for Apothecary Bridges's shop immediately.

I set off up High Street, past All Saints' Church, towards the Bar Gate, and, following Alice Gentle's carefully detailed instructions, found Apothecary Bridges's shop without much difficulty. One mention of Mistress Gentle's name and I was welcomed effusively by the good lady of the house, who was minding the counter while her husband, so she instantly informed me, was in the back room making a brew of wild basil and calamint for a customer with a bad chest infection – a certain Master Simmons of Blue Anchor Lane.

Such a willingness to impart information augured well. And, indeed, as soon as I made known to her the reason for my visit she was only too eager to reveal all she knew concerning Gideon Bonifant.

'It's a long time ago now, as you say, since Gideon was assistant to my dear husband, but I remember him very clearly – and that poor wife of his.'

'What did she die of?' I interrupted.

Mistress Bridges pursed her lips. 'You may well ask. But you'll be fortunate if you can find anyone to give you an answer. Marion Sybyle was a fine-looking girl when Gideon married her, and they were happily wed for five years or more, although they weren't blessed with any children, more's the pity.'

Here she was forced to break off in order to serve a customer, complaining of an upset stomach, with a packet of powdered limestone and chalk.

'Mix it with a little goat's milk, my dear,' she instructed the woman, 'and swallow it straight down. It'll do the trick all right.' She turned back to me. 'Where was I?'

I jogged her memory, adding, 'Why did you say "more's the pity" when referring to Gideon Bonifant's and his first wife's lack of children?'

'Because it might have prevented him having an eye for other women,' was the censorious reply. 'Oh, things were fine between them, as I said, for five years or so, before Marion began to get a bit scrawny and lose her looks. She'd been a very pretty young woman – she had three or four lads after her at one time, as I remember – but as she got older, her features started to coarsen. It might not have mattered so much if Geraldine Proudfoot hadn't come on the scene.'

Another customer arrived for some feverfew tablets and to gossip about a neighbour, leaving me once again to contain my impatience as best I could. Eventually, however, she departed and I was able to resume my conversation with Mistress Bridges.

'Who was Geraldine Proudfoot?'

'She moved here with her parents from over Winchester way. Beautiful she was, too good for an apothecary's assistant, even supposing Gideon had been free to marry her, and so I told him. "Her father's a lawyer. She's not for the likes of you," I said. Of course he denied having any interest in her, but I knew better, and so did anyone else who had an eye in her head. And I understood Master Gideon well enough by that time to know that Geraldine's superior status was more than half her attraction for him. That man always thought himself worthy of a better fate than the one that God had planned for him.'

A third customer, a man this time, bought some water parsnip seeds, but, thankfully, proved disinclined to talk and left the shop within a very few minutes.

'Water parsnip seeds, taken in a little wine, are an excellent relief for hernia,' Mistress Bridges whispered confidentially, leaning towards me across the counter. 'If you happen to have one, let me recommend—'

'No, I don't,' I assured her hurriedly. 'Pray continue telling me about Master Bonifant.'

'Well, I suppose there really isn't much more to tell. I couldn't honestly say – nor could any of my friends – that I ever saw Gideon and Geraldine Proudfoot together, except in the way of business. The elder Mistress Proudfoot was a sickly creature and Geraldine used to come into the shop to buy medicines for her mother. I don't think she was aware of Gideon but as the person who most often served her, my husband, you understand, being kept busy in the back, making up the potions and pills. But she and Gideon did chat together, and I saw the way he eyed her up and down when he thought she wasn't looking. As I told you just now, I did my best to warn him off, but he'd simply stare right through me as though I hadn't spoken.' Mistress Bridges chuckled. 'Oh, he'd have liked to tell me to mind my own business, interfering old gossip that I am, but he didn't dare for fear of losing his job.'

There was a further diversion while she sold a young girl a poultice of rue and borage for a swelling on the knee, but finally, having enquired after the health of every single member of the girl's innumerable family, she was free to give me her attention once more.

'Mistress Gentle told me that Gideon's first wife just seemed to waste away,' I said.

'That's true.' Mistress Bridges nodded her head emphatically. 'She was a fine, buxom wench when he married her, but as I remarked a while back, Marion did lose a bit of weight as she got older. Nothing in that: her mother was like a rasher of wind. But then it got worse – much, much worse. Before she died, Marion was a walking skeleton, and in constant pain. Of course, there was gossip. I told one or two of my greatest friends what I'd observed concerning Gideon and Geraldine Proudfoot, but naturally I swore them to secrecy. My husband had dared me to repeat my suspicions. And I have to admit that the way Gideon nursed his wife silenced a lot of the whispering.'

'But you still suspect that he might have poisoned her?'

Yet again, Mistress Bridges nodded, but this time she glanced uneasily over her shoulder towards the room behind the shop, and put a finger to her lips.

'Well, it wouldn't surprise me to learn that he had,' she answered, lowering her voice. 'Most people thought him no more than a rather humourless and taciturn young man, but I knew him better than that. There was a ruthless streak in Gideon Bonifant. There was a stray dog that used to hang around the shop. I encouraged him, I have to confess, by putting out scraps. But then he started to make a nuisance of himself, coming into the shop and barking if he didn't get his food on time, until, one day, in a fit of bad temper, my husband said he wished that someone would get rid of the animal. That dinnertime, Gideon offered to prepare the dog's meal in order, he said, to save me the trouble. He'd never suggested doing so before, and I should have been suspicious, but I was very busy that morning. By mid-afternoon, the dog was dead, stretched out stiff and cold beside his half-empty plate. When I accused Gideon of deliberately poisoning the poor creature, he just laughed.'

'What happened after the death of his wife?' I asked. 'I know he went to London, but I was told that it was because he was so grief-stricken, he was unable to remain in Southampton any longer.'

Mistress Bridges laughed shortly. 'If he was grief-stricken, it was on account of Geraldine Proudfoot's marriage to young Oliver Braine, a highly suitable young man of her parents' choosing. Not that she was averse to their choice, and a very happy, blushing bride she made. It was after her wedding that Gideon announced he was off to London to try his fortune there.' She eyed me shrewdly. 'What's this all about? Has he been accused of poisoning someone else?'

'No-o,' I answered slowly, and stood for a moment, lost in thought. Then I added, 'Didn't I say? It was Gideon himself who was poisoned.'

'Gracious Mother of God!' gasped Mistress Bridges. 'There's divine justice for you!'

I smiled. 'You really are convinced that he murdered his first wife, aren't you?'

'I am.'

She would have said more, but the sudden appearance of her husband effectually put an end to our conversation. Apothecary Bridges peered at me short-sightedly over the top of his spectacles and asked if I were being attended to.

'Not that you look to be ailing from anything much,' he added drily. 'I've rarely seen a healthier specimen of young manhood.'

'I – I've got what I came for, thank you,' I answered hastily, opening my cloak and patting the pouch at my waist as though there were something in it. 'Goodbye, then, Mistress, and my gratitude for all your help.'

I quit the shop swiftly and in a very cowardly fashion, leaving Mistress Bridges to think up the answer to her husband's inevitable question of what was wrong with me. But I was indeed genuinely grateful to her. As I walked back to John Gentle's butcher's shop, pushing my way through crowds making last-minute purchases, or heading for an evening's convivial drinking in the local taverns, I reflected that I could start for London first thing the following morning. I had learned more about Gideon Bonifant than I had dared to hope for when I had set out from the capital the preceding Friday.

I was sure now that I had the answer to who had murdered him. I might never be able to prove it to the total satisfaction of a lawyer or a Sheriff's officer, but my reasoning must surely be sufficient to raise doubts as to Isolda Bonifant's guilt in the most prejudiced of legal minds. And as soon as I had imparted my knowledge first to the Babcarys and secondly to the Duke, I should be free to set out for Bristol. I would be home by the middle of February.

I began to whistle tunelessly to myself.

It was again late afternoon when, on Thursday, I crossed London Bridge and made my way once more to Bucklersbury, to beg a room from Reynold Makepeace.

Having heard my request, he took a deep considering breath. 'We're very full, Roger, and I've had to let the chamber you shared with Mistress Chapman to someone else. Will it be for long?'

'Two nights only. Tomorrow should see my business in London completed. I'll be on the road at daybreak on Saturday.'

'In that case, you can share my bedchamber for two nights, if you've no objections to sleeping in the same bed as me.'

I assured him that I hadn't. 'And I've another favour to ask you,' I added. 'Can you spare one of your pot-boys to take a message to Master Babcary in West Cheap? I'm too tired, or I'd go myself.'

Reynold, somewhat reluctantly, agreed and, when the lad at last appeared, he also muttered under his breath about the inconvenience of being dragged from his work. But when he understood that my request entailed a journey for which I was prepared to recompense him, he cheered up considerably.

'Tell Master Babcary,' I said, 'that I shall be with him first thing tomorrow morning, and ask him to ensure that he and all his household are present. Tell him that I believe I have the answer. He'll understand.'

The boy sped away, reporting back to me an hour or so later with Miles Babcary's reply.

'He says he'll do as you ask, Master, and he'll keep the shop closed until after your visit. But he hopes as how it'll be worth it, because he doesn't like losing money.'

I spent a restless night, trying not to disturb my host too much with my tossing and turning. Fortunately, Reynold was so tired from his day's exertions that he slept like a child, barely moving on his side of the goosefeather mattress. Was I correct in the assumptions I was making? Much would depend on the testimony of Toby Maybury. If he confirmed my suspicions, all would be well. And on this thought I finally fell into an uneasy doze.

I rose with Reynold at the crack of dawn and breakfasted on dried herrings and oatmeal, standing up at one of the tables in the Voyager's kitchen, too anxious even to sit down, as the harassed kitchen maids begged me to do, forced as they were to work around me. But eventually, I was off, making my way through the already crowded streets to West Cheap.

I need not have worried that I might be too early. Master Babcary and every member of his household were awaiting my arrival. They all laid claim to a disturbed night on account of my message, and Isolda, especially, looked pale and strained.

'Come up to the parlour,' Miles said without preamble, seizing me by the arm the moment I entered the shop and forcing me towards the stairs.

He had no time for the niceties of formal greetings, and the others closed in at my back to make sure that I did as I was told. In the parlour, a fire was already burning on the hearth, for it was a cold morning and there was a touch of frost in the air. I was very glad to stoop and warm my hands.

'Now then, Chapman,' Master Babcary said, closing the

door behind him and coming forward, 'no beating about the bush, if you please. Tell us straight out which one of us you suspect of murdering my son-in-law.'

A definite atmosphere of menace pervaded the room, and I wondered fleetingly what might have been my fate had my answer been any other than it was. But I had no need to worry. I straightened my back and turned to face them all.

'Gideon Bonifant poisoned himself,' I said.

Twenty

For several seconds there was total silence, then Miles gave an incredulous laugh, echoed nervously by Isolda. But it was Christopher who first found his voice.

'Are you trying to tell us that Gideon committed suicide?' he asked in a tone of cautious relief; cautious because he could not yet permit himself to believe that I was serious.

'Oh, no,' I answered. 'It was an accident. The person he intended to kill was you.'

Christopher looked dazed. 'Me? Why me?' he demanded. 'Are you sure this isn't just a farrago of nonsense, Chapman?'

'I can't prove anything,' I said, 'I can only guess at what happened from the facts at my disposal. But I think what I'm about to tell you would raise considerable doubt concerning Mistress Bonifant's guilt in the minds of any lawyer or Sheriff's officer. Indeed, I hope that it would convince them of her innocence. And when I leave here, I shall go straight to the Duke of Gloucester and lay my conclusions before him, which he can then pass on to Mistress Shore, thus setting him free to ask his favour of her.'

'Oh, never mind the Duke or Cousin Shore,' Miles Babcary interrupted impatiently. 'For goodness sake, sit down, Roger, lad – everyone sit down! – and explain matters to us.'

I noted that within a very brief space of time I had progressed from 'Master Chapman' to 'Roger, lad', and suppressed a smile. I was no longer a potential enemy, but their possible saviour.

Obeying Miles's instructions, we all, with the exception of Meg Spendlove, seated ourselves around the table, Meg preferring to crouch over the fire to make the most of this unaccustomed source of warmth. I glanced at the circle of

204

eager, and now friendly, faces, reflecting that I had been right not to ask for the presence of Mistress Perle or the Napiers at this gathering. Neither Miles nor any member of his household had the least suspicion that any one, let alone all, of those three had a motive for murdering Gideon, and it was kinder to let sleeping dogs lie. It was not my place to reveal the affair between Gregory Napier and Barbara Perle, and if the latter did ever become the second Mistress Babcary, the subsequent domestic upheaval was for Miles and his daughter to sort out between them.

'Well, Roger? Well?'

Miles was growing red in the face and looked as though he might swell up and burst if he were starved of the facts for a moment longer. I cleared my throat and began.

'Since last Friday, I've been in Southampton – returning late yesterday afternoon – and first I must tell you what I discovered.' I repeated all that Mistress Bridges had told me about Gideon, his first wife and the girl called Geraldine Proudfoot. 'So you see,' I concluded, 'although there is no definite proof that Gideon poisoned Marion Sybyle, I believe it to be the truth in view of what happened here last November.'

Isolda shook her head. 'No, no! You're wrong, Master Chapman. You must be. I lived with Gideon for over five years. He wasn't, I freely admit, the most loving of husbands, but, then, he didn't marry me because he loved me, I'm quite aware of that. But I can't and won't think that he would ever commit murder. Besides, you said his intended victim was Kit. It doesn't make sense.'

'It does if *you* were accused of the murder,' I answered. 'It was, I believe, a very subtle plan. But we're going too fast. We must return to when Gideon first arrived in London.

'He came here a disappointed man. The woman he had hoped to wed, with a view to raising himself in the world, had married someone else: he had killed his wife for nothing. But then, a year later, he met you, who – who fell in love with him.'

Isolda put her elbows on the table and cupped her chin in her hands, sending me a fierce, almost contemptuous glance.

'We might as well be honest about it, Roger. There was no love on either side. I'm a plain woman whom men have

205

never fancied and I was desperate to be married. Gideon knew that, just as I knew that he wanted me for the position I could bestow and the inheritance that I should one day bring him as my husband. It was a marriage of convenience for us both, but that doesn't mean to say that we were unhappy.'

There was a pause before I continued, my voice rough with pity, 'Your husband, I suspect, was content only until he fell in love with Mistress Eleanor. When you married, she was only a mere child of twelve, but then she grew up into . . . into—'

'A beautiful young woman,' Isolda supplied drily, ignoring her cousin's murmur of distress.

'Exactly,' I hurried on. 'But there was a difficulty. Gideon also wanted Master Babcary's money, and the only way he could achieve that was to ensure that Mistress Eleanor became her uncle's sole heir. So not only you, but also Master Christopher had to be removed. What better way was there than to have you arrested, tried and executed for *his* murder?'

'But would anyone believe that I wanted to do away with Kit?' Isolda demanded to a general murmur of agreement.

'Of course not. Gideon meant to make it seem that you had intended to poison *him*, but had accidentally killed your cousin instead. Before that happened, however, he had to persuade Mistress Eleanor that fate had decreed that they were eventually to be man and wife. As you and she already know, he saw a way to do that after she bought a pendant in Leadenhall market and confided to him her belief in its magical powers.' And for the sake of Miles Babcary, his nephew and apprentice who, by the blank expression on their faces, were totally bewildered, I repeated the story of the two pendants.

'Gideon did *what*?' thundered Miles, springing to his feet. 'He dared to enter my niece's bedchamber, while she was sleeping! Isolda, did you know about this?'

'No, certainly not, Father. I knew Gideon was restless and had taken to wandering around the house at night, but I thought he was ill. I had no idea that he was playing such a trick on Nell, and I'm hurt and angry that you could think otherwise.'

Miles had the grace to apologise, and resumed his seat looking shamefaced. 'Pray continue,' he muttered, glancing at me.

I inclined my head. 'Gideon's next step was to put about

the story that Isolda was cuckolding him with her cousin. He told you, Master Babcary, he told his former master, Apothecary Ford, and he told Gregory Napier. There may have been others, also, to whom he talked in confidence, tavern acquaintances and the like. And as people have pointed out to me, a man doesn't willingly admit to being a cuckold unless he is both sure of his ground and deeply shocked and hurt by his wife's conduct. Gideon counted on this fact to command his listeners' belief in the tale. Everyone knew that Mistress Bonifant was not really the sort of woman preferred by Master Kit' – Christopher shifted uncomfortably on his stool – 'but, with the exception of you, sir,' I nodded at Miles, 'they all accepted the truth of the story.'

I paused to clear my throat again, and a chorus of impatient voices urged me to continue. I was only too willing to oblige.

'Having prepared the ground,' I went on, 'fate then played into Gideon's hands when, at Mistress Eleanor's birthday feast, last October, Meg mixed up the two goblets belonging to him and Master Christopher. As Mistress Bonifant once pointed out to me, the initials G.B. and C.B. look very much alike amid all that elaborate carving around the rims.'

Meg Spendlove rose like an avenging fury from where she was crouching in front of the fire.

'I did not mix them up!' she screamed, seizing my arm and shaking it violently.

'Meg, behave yourself!' Isolda exclaimed wrathfully. 'Release Master Chapman this minute! As he has so kindly reminded us, it's very easy to confuse those two sets of initials.'

'But I didn't!'

'Wait,' I said, removing Meg's hand from my sleeve and holding it soothingly between both of mine. 'She could be telling the truth, you know. Why shouldn't Gideon have switched the goblets himself? Yes, yes! The more I think of it, the more I wonder that I didn't consider the possibility earlier. It established in your minds a precedent for such a mistake being made.' I heard the girl's sharp intake of breath as she prepared to make further protest, and squeezed her hand reassuringly. 'No, Meg, no one's blaming you. Master Gideon switched the cups himself, I feel almost certain of it. Go and sit down by the fire again.' When, somewhat sullenly, she had complied, I leant forward excitedly. 'You all said that Gideon's explosion of anger was unusual, that, normally, he didn't indulge himself with such displays of rage. But on the occasion of Mistress Eleanor's birthday feast, it was necessary for him to do so in order to impress upon you all what had happened, and to ensure that you wouldn't be surprised if the same error was repeated.'

Miles Babcary nodded, a grim expression on his face. 'I'm beginning to understand what you're getting at, Roger, lad.' He sucked in his breath. 'To think that all those years we were harbouring a cold-blooded killer in our midst and didn't know it – a killer with such an evil, devious mind.'

'Well, I don't understand,' Isolda protested defiantly. 'You'll have to explain matters more clearly for me, Master Chapman.'

I answered as gently as I could, 'It's as I said just now, Mistress. Your husband planned to poison your cousin and lay the blame on you, admitting to the Sheriff's officer – with the greatest reluctance, I'm sure – that you must really have intended to murder him. I can only guess, but I feel as certain as it's possible to do in the circumstances, that he would have claimed *you* put the poison in his cup, but that Meg had somehow muddled it up with Master Kit's when she was helping to set the table.'

'When, in fact,' Christopher interrupted, also beginning to see the light, 'it was Gideon himself who put the poison in his own goblet and then switched it with mine. That's what he was doing after he left the shop and why he took so long to reach his bedchamber.'

'Exactly,' I said. 'Something delayed him.'

'Wait a minute!' Miles exclaimed peremptorily, holding up a hand. 'Aren't you forgetting that it was *Gideon* who was poisoned? If he'd switched his own goblet with Kit's, someone must have switched them back again.'

I nodded and looked across the table at the apprentice, whose cheeks had suddenly flamed with colour.

'I think it's time you owned up, Toby. Don't be frightened. There's nothing to be ashamed of in what you did. You simply thought that you were helping a friend, isn't that so?'

All eyes swivelled in his direction. He had now grown very pale, and I repeated my assurance that he had done nothing wrong. Eventually he seemed to accept my word.

'I came up to take a look at the table, like I told you. I know I'm not supposed to be in here when there's company coming, but those goblets are so beautiful, real craftsman's work, and I don't get the chance to see them very often.' I could guess that Miles was ready to forgive the boy anything after that paeon of praise, even if Toby admitted to murdering Gideon himself – which, in a way, he had. The apprentice went on, 'While I was admiring everything, I remembered the awful fuss Master Bonifant had made at Mistress Nell's birthday feast, just because Meg had mixed up the cups.'

'And what did you do, Toby?' I asked hurriedly, before Meg could proclaim her innocence afresh.

'I examined the rims of all the goblets carefully, and, sure enough, I discovered that Meg had made the same mistake again. She'd given Christopher Master Bonifant's cup and Master Bonifant Christopher's. So I changed the two over. It was difficult to do without spilling the wine, but I managed it – and only just in time. Next moment, Master Bonifant appeared. Then the master came in with Mistress Perle and Master and Mistress Napier, followed by Christopher and Mistress Nell.'

I glanced anxiously at Meg to see how she had taken Toby's assumption that it was her carelessness that had caused the mix-up, but she was staring at him open-mouthed, an expression of adoration on her small, pointed face. For a moment, I was at a loss to interpret it, but then I understood. Toby had cared enough for her welfare to risk getting into trouble himself, for if he had spilled the wine and ruined all Isolda's careful table arrangements, he would probably have received a thrashing. But he had been willing to take that chance for her sake. From now on, he would be a hero in her eyes.

I turned my attention back to Toby, now basking in the approval of both Miles Babcary and Meg Spendlove, and said, more as a statement of fact than a question, 'And that is what you were trying to tell Mistress Eleanor while she was talking to Ginèvre Napier, that you had averted another unpleasant scene between Meg and Master Bonifant.'

'Yes.' Toby's tone was unusually subdued for one in such

high favour. 'I killed Master Bonifant, didn't I?' he asked unhappily.

'He killed himself,' Christopher answered warmly. 'You saved my life, Toby, and I shan't forget it. Next time I'm tempted to berate you for some stupidity or other, I must try to curb my tongue.'

Eleanor rose from her place and went round the table to kiss the apprentice's cheek.

'You have my undying gratitude, too, Toby. What would I do if I lost Kit?'

Isolda caught my eye and sighed. 'Holy Mother preserve us,' she muttered. 'At this rate, the boy will soon be too big for his breeches. Roger, tell us what made you first suspect that Gideon might have accidentally poisoned himself.'

I scratched my head. 'The idea grew on me very slowly, and it's not easy to pinpoint one particular thing. Odd as it may seem, I found it strangely worrying that no one was trying to kill me or do me harm. I did suffer two or three false alarms, but that was all they turned out to be. It was logical to assume that if one of you was Gideon's murderer, that person would be eager to prevent me discovering the truth. Even if you, Mistress, were the culprit, you wouldn't want people's suspicions confirmed. Yet nothing happened.

'Then there was something that Mistress Perle told me. She said that after everyone had drunk her health, and while you were waiting for Mistress Bonifant to return from the kitchen with the food, Gideon was staring fixedly at Master Christopher, as though he were expecting something to happen – which, of course, he was.'

'That's right!' Christopher Babcary exclaimed. 'I remember now. His look puzzled me. Later on, however, it slipped my mind.'

I nodded and went on, 'Mistress Perle also commented on the expression on Gideon's face after the poison had begun to work. She said he looked outraged, as if he couldn't really believe what was happening to him. She also thought, probably correctly as matters have turned out, that she heard him mutter the word "aconite", but of course his lips were so stiff by that time that she couldn't be sure. Furthermore, Mistress Perle was not the only person to mention Master Bonifant's expression of horror – understandable, you may think, in the circumstances – but it suggested to me that he knew at once what had happened. He knew that somehow or other he had drunk from his own cup and that he would be dead within a very few moments. No one mentioned an expression of surprise or bewilderment. A small thing, perhaps, and of no significance on its own, but it added to the sum of knowledge that was slowly coming my way.

'There was also Mistress Bonifant's alleged infidelity with her cousin. The source of this rumour was Gideon, and only Gideon. I could find no evidence for his claim, and nothing, either, to support the idea that he might simply have hit upon the wrong man. No one could suggest anyone with whom she might have been cuckolding her husband.'

I saw Isolda wince, although I doubt if the others noticed. They were too busy pondering on all that I had just told them.

'What made you think that the goblets might have been switched over?' Miles Babcary asked me.

'It was something that happened while my wife and I were at the Westminster tournament,' I explained. 'She changed my cup for hers while we were eating our dinner, for reasons that are too uninteresting to burden you with. Suffice it to say that the incident suddenly opened my eyes to what might really have happened on the evening of Master Bonifant's murder. From what Mistress Eleanor had confided in me about the pendants, and Master Bonifant's behaviour, I guessed that he had fallen in love with her and determined to make her his wife. That, in its turn, made me wonder if something similar could have happened before, with his first wife, and was the reason I decided to visit Southampton. I was well rewarded.

'And now,' I added, rising to my feet, 'I must take my leave of you and go to beg an audience of Duke Richard at Crosby Place.'

They were loath to let me go and profuse in their thanks for solving the mystery, for the Babcarys, like myself, were convinced that they now held the answer.

The Duke, having listened intently to my story, was of the same opinion.

'Well done, Roger,' he said quietly, offering me his hand

to kiss. 'I shall make sure that Mistress Shore is in possesion of the facts before nightfall, after which—'

He broke off, declining to say more, unwilling, possibly, to raise his hopes too high. I don't think he entertained any doubt that Jane Shore would intercede with the King on behalf of his brother George, especially in view of the favour he, Richard, would just have done her, but I do think he was beginning to have misgivings concerning Edward's eventual clemency. There was a bitterness in his tone when he spoke of the King that I had never heard before, and deep worry lines had carved themselves into his face from nose to chin. The Richard Plantagenet I had known until then always had a lurking twinkle in his eyes, as though he could see the ridiculous side of life even while coping with its grim, and often dangerous, reality.

But the man who prowled around the great hall of Crosby Place, listening to my story, was a different creature; an animal at bay, surrounded by enemies all snapping and snarling at his heels, not knowing what the next moment would bring. I reasoned that if the King pardoned the Duke of Clarence yet again, Duke Richard would return to his normal self; the gay and gallant young man who had survived an uncertain childhood, plagued by ill health, to become the chief stay and prop of his elder brother's throne. But if the Queen and her family persuaded the King to sign Clarence's death warrant, then I feared for Duke Richard's future, not so much at the Woodvilles' hands, but as a victim of his own embittered nature.

Then, suddenly, he was smiling his usual sweet smile, and I dismissed my bleak thoughts as fancies.

'You must forgive me, Roger, for spoiling your wife's visit to London. How will you return to Bristol?' he added. 'Do you wish to retain the horse?'

I shook my head vigorously. 'My lord, I'm happier on my own two feet. Horses and I have never seen eye to eye, and I find them uncertain beasts at the best of times. With good weather, good luck and some friendly carters, I should be home by the middle of next month.'

He laughed and again held out his hand. But this time, when I would have knelt to kiss it, he stopped me, saying, 'Shake the hand of your friend, Roger, for you are one of the few people I count on for unquestioning loyalty. Tell me I'm not wrong.'

'You're not wrong, my lord,' I promised. 'Whatever happens, now or in the future, you may rely on my friendship.'

The weather, luck and the whole fraternity of carters were with me on that journey back to Bristol. I was home by the second week in February.

I was greeted with joy by my children, with warm and loving affection by my wife and was soundly scolded by my quondam mother-in-law. But Margaret's original indignation and anger at my allowing Adela to return home without me had long since cooled, and her remonstrations were only half-hearted. Secretly, she was proud of my involvement with those in high places, and I had to describe over and over again my visit to Mistress Shore's house. Adela was far more interested in the outcome of the mystery, and, once she was in possession of the facts, agreed that my conclusion was probably the correct one.

'I've no doubt at all that you're right, my love. You're a very clever man. Now! We need fresh kindling chopped, water fetched from the well and then it's time you were out on the road once more. We are short of money.'

So life had settled back into its normal pattern by the end of the month, when the knowledge of what had happened in London first burst upon us. As so often, information reached the castle before the town, and it was Adela's former admirer, the Sheriff's officer, Richard Manifold, who brought us the news.

'Well,' he said, seating himself at our table and accepting a mazer of ale, 'it's done then. The Duke of Clarence is dead; executed, presumably, but no one as yet knows how. Rumour talks of drowning in a butt of malmsey wine, but I don't know that one can put much store by such a tale.'

I sat down slowly on the stool opposite him. 'King Edward signed his brother's death warrant?' I asked incredulously.

'Must have done.' Richard Manifold wiped his mouth on the back of his hand. 'As far as I can gather from the messenger who brought the news, the sequence of events was as follows. On the seventh day of this month, the Duke of Buckingham, as

213

Lord High Steward, passed sentence of death upon Clarence. But even at that late stage, the King hesitated for so long about signing the warrant that, on the eighteenth, the Speaker of the Commons requested that whatever was to be done, be done quickly. And on the very same day, the Duke was executed in the Tower, having first offered up his Mass penny and been shriven. After that, all's secrecy and mystery. They say that even his mother, the old Duchess of York, doesn't know for certain how he died. But he is dead, that's for certain. But as for details, we'll have to contain our souls in patience for a while longer.'

So it was done, I thought to myself. The Woodvilles had triumphed. Those three brothers who had been through so much together were now only two, and I wondered what Duke Richard was feeling. Did he fear that the Queen's rapacious family would one day turn on him?

I grieved silently for him. He faced a lonely and very dangerous future.